J. FitzGerald McCurdy

The Fire Demons

The Mole Wars, Book One

 HarperCollins*PublishersLtd*

Library and Archives Canada Cataloguing in
Publication

McCurdy, J. FitzGerald (Joan FitzGerald),
1943–

The fire demons / J. FitzGerald McCurdy. –
2nd ed.

(The mole wars trilogy ; bk. 1)
ISBN-13: 978-0-00-639332-0
ISBN-10: 0-00-639332-2

I. Title. II. Series: McCurdy, J. FitzGerald
(Joan FitzGerald), 1943– . Mole wars trilogy ;
bk. 1.

PS8575.C87F57 2005   jC813'.6
C2005-901928-X

HC 9 8 7 6 5 4 3 2 1

Printed and bound in the United States
Set in Sabon

The Invasion

They came like death—swift and cold-blooded. They came out of hyperspace in vast swarms like locusts. They were destroyers from an uncharted galaxy—alien terrorists driven to destroy for the sake of destruction.

We had no warning. Our star disappeared and the morning sky turned as black as night. And then they were upon us—terrible creatures with ripping claws and fanged muzzles, shielded by bony carapaces front and back. They came to kill. They came to ravage our planet until it had been wiped clean of all living things.

—Excerpt from *The Wardens' Logs*,
translated from the original
by Master Memphis,
Mage, seventh plane

Chapter One

The Bully

Gripping the handle of his guitar case, Steele Miller ran along the deserted sidewalk, keeping close to the buildings where the street lights didn't penetrate the shadows. It was only four-thirty, but already growing dark—a typical November day in Toronto. Four nights earlier, on the last Sunday in October, he and his father had turned the household clocks back one hour, marking the start of winter and shorter days.

As a rule, Steele preferred summer. He liked the long evenings when he could play outdoors until nine, or walk around Taddle Pond with his father and watch the setting sun stain the western sky purple, red, and orange, and bathe the CN Tower in an eerie golden glow.

But today he was thankful for the darkening streets. He didn't think they had spotted him, but he had glimpsed the familiar, dreaded figures of Dirk and his gang of bullies just as he was leaving his guitar teacher's studio in a high-rise residential building on Davenport Road, just west of Christie Street. The gang was hanging around the corner of Davenport and Christie, spitting on the sidewalk at old people shuffling past, and jumping out from doorways to scare little kids half to death. Steele's stomach ached. He knew they were waiting for him. Somehow they had found out about the guitar lessons.

He wondered for a moment if his life would ever change. Would he ever be able to walk out his front door without fear clawing at his heart, without seeing Dirk lurking behind every parked car on the street or in every dark alley? Somehow, the bully even managed to get into his dreams, ruining the best ones, like the one of him and his father at a Blue Jays game at SkyDome, and the Jays are ahead 4–nothing, and then, suddenly, the ball would turn into Dirk's head; or the one where they're fishing for tuna off North Rustico on Prince Edward Island, where they went for two weeks every summer, and out of nowhere an enormous Great White Dirk shark would start circling the boat, its cold, unblinking eyes fixed on Steele.

Steele wished that he could go back in time and change the past. If he could, he'd go back exactly two years and change the day the school bully saw him leaving the bank where he had gone with his father to open his very own account. Bursting with pride, and clutching his new ATM card and passbook tightly in his hand, he had glanced at the group of boys hogging the sidewalk in front of the bank. He had recognized Dirk, a tough kid in grade five, and some of the others, but because they weren't part of his immediate circle of friends and because all he could think about was his new bank account, he promptly dismissed them.

But on his way home from school the next day, Steele walked straight into an ambush. Two boys jumped out at him from a gap in a tall, wooden fence and dragged him through the opening, away from the busy street and the watchful eyes of parents collecting their kids from school. Dirk was waiting behind the fence.

Steele's face burned now as he remembered his first run-in

with the bullies. They held his arms while Dirk rifled through his jacket pockets, found the bank card and passbook, and discovered the $500 he had deposited into his new account the previous afternoon.

The $500 was long gone. Dirk had taken it, and more, over the past two years. Worried that Steele's father might get the bank statements and grow suspicious if he saw large withdrawals, Dirk had demanded small amounts at first, five or ten dollars, but when Steele accidentally let it slip that his father had stopped monitoring his account, Dirk's greed mushroomed and his demands escalated until he wanted $20 and even $40 at a time.

At first Steele laughed in Dirk's face when the bully demanded money. But his laughter had turned to fear when Dirk threatened to scare his grandmother so badly she'd have a heart attack, and perhaps die. And when the bully said he'd go after Mac and Riley, Steele's best friends, and hurt them, too, Steele had finally caved.

Now, as he ran along the sidewalk, he wondered how Dirk and the Jerks had found out about the guitar lessons.

The guitar and money for lessons were a birthday gift from his father and grandmother. Steele had been attending lessons every Thursday afternoon for two months and had managed to keep the bully from finding out about them. Every week since school began in September, he had handed Dirk the allowance money his father gave him. The bully had seemed satisfied—at least he hadn't demanded Steele's passbook or made him produce a printout of his bank balance.

Steele wished that he could tell his father about Dirk and the money—not that he hadn't tried. But when it came to the topic of bullies, his father couldn't understand why his son—

the son of a police officer—allowed himself to be victimized. *As if I had a choice,* thought Steele bitterly. He remembered trying to tell his father how afraid he was of the bigger boy. But afterwards, he was ashamed, as if the bullying were his fault, as if he had asked for it. He couldn't understand why, if he was the victim, he felt so bad.

"You've got to stand up to him, son," his father had said with such finality that there was little Steele could say without sounding like a wimp.

But Steele knew it wasn't that simple. Maybe adult bullies listened when another adult, like his father for instance, confronted them. But not Dirk! He and his gang would bust your face to pulp if you so much as looked at them without asking. Steele knew because he'd done it once—the day after his father had said standing up to Dirk was the only way to stop the bullying. His ribs still ached whenever he remembered how they had hurt him when they finally got him alone.

As soon as he spotted Dirk and the others, he had ducked back into the lobby and pressed Mrs. Fret's bell, hopping nervously from foot to foot as he waited for the answering buzzer to unlock the door. As soon as he heard the buzz, he raced through the foyer and out the service entrance at the side of the building. Without pausing, he cut across the above-ground parking lot and ran through Hillcrest Park, heading north until he reached Tyrrel Avenue. Stopping to catch his breath, he argued with himself over the best route to his house.

It was awfully tempting to chance it and take the shortest way but, in the end, Steele decided to go an extra block north just to be on the safe side. At Benson Avenue he turned right, dashed across Christie Street, and didn't stop running until he reached Wychwood Avenue.

Gasping for air, Steele stopped and slipped behind a huge tree, dried fallen leaves crackling under his feet. After running such a long distance, it was like trying to breathe with an elephant standing on his chest. He set his guitar case on the ground and peered south along Wychwood, his heart racing as if it hadn't yet realized he had stopped running. Because he had never encountered the bullies in his park before, Steele reasoned that if anything bad was going to happen to him, it was going to happen here, before he reached Wychwood Park. He remained as still as the giant tree and watched, but nothing moved on the street. No Dirk! No grovelling on the ground, begging the bully not to hurt him.

The feeling of relief that washed over him was so intense his legs buckled, and he almost collapsed. Instead, he took a deep breath, crossed Wychwood Avenue, and hurried south, his guitar case slapping awkwardly against his right leg. Slipping through the open gate, he followed the pedestrian pathway into Wychwood Park, pausing to check things out before making a run for his house on the opposite side of the pond.

It was always quiet and spooky in the park after dark, but today it seemed quieter and spookier than usual. There were no bright streetlights. The dim lighting on the winding, circular road came from small round lamps mounted halfway up the power poles. The white glass in the lamps was coated with decades of grime, and the light that managed to escape cast only faint patches on the pavement.

Steele scanned the dark places in the park that he knew as intimately as the nooks and recesses of his house. He stared into the shadows of a stand of birch and other trees that stood like sentinels guarding the west side of the pond. But nothing moved in the blackness there. Next, he focused on a copse of fat bushes near the tennis court by the side of the road just ahead. Nothing.

Finally, he shifted his eyes to Taddle Pond in the middle of the park at the bottom of the ravine. It was always the last place he checked out before crossing the park. His eyes followed the silvery water to the fountain occupying the north end of the pond. The fountain was a figure of a woman sitting on a stone bench in the middle of a round, shallow basin. The woman fascinated Steele. He couldn't remember ever passing through the park without stopping and staring at her.

She was sculpted from green-black marble or some other stone, and she was cold and beautiful. Her blank eyes seemed fixed on something in the sky, farther away than Steele's eyes could see. Coiled about her ankles were six green snakes. In her hands she held a seventh, and her arms were lifted and outstretched to show the snake's full length, the tail coiled about her arm almost to her elbow. Steele imagined that she was holding the snake up to show it to someone looking down at her from the sky. The water had been shut off for the winter, but in the summer it trickled from the serpent's open mouth and washed over the woman's arms, filling the basin and spilling into Taddle Pond.

Steele didn't know the woman's name or anything about her, but he had a feeling she preferred snakes to people. Everyone in the neighbourhood called her the Wytch.

She certainly looked like a witch now. The darkness hid her perfect chiselled features and turned her into a menacing black-shrouded presence. He blinked repeatedly to stop her from coalescing into a scary, writhing shape and reaching out to snatch him and drag him into the black place with her.

"She's not real, so get a grip," Steele said to himself out loud as he did whenever darkness settled over the park. He forced a devil-may-care chuckle from his throat to show any creatures that might be lurking about that he wasn't afraid. Then he tightened his hold on the handle of the guitar case and moved purposefully down the side of the ravine, following the worn footpath that ran along the south bank of the pond.

He reached the pond and had taken only half a dozen steps when he heard a harsh, muffled voice.

He froze, his heart pounding like running footsteps. The voice was coming from just ahead, near the fountain. Steele gulped. The Wytch had come alive!

Afraid to breathe, he peered at the black shape, listening intently, until his vision blurred and his ears popped in protest. Everything looked the same as before. Still, he could have sworn he had heard a voice.

Go back through the gate, he urged himself. *Go around the block.*

Steele hated movies where the hero hears a noise in the basement and, instead of calling 9-1-1, creeps down the stairs to investigate. He couldn't stop squirming or tear his eyes away. "Are you crazy? Don't go down there!" he'd shout at the television. Now, as he ignored his own advice and took a slow step toward the fountain, he wondered, if this were a movie, would all of the viewers be screaming at their TVs, "Go back! Don't do it!"

He inched closer to the fountain, his eyes locked on the Wytch. He was almost close enough to step off the path into the basin when he heard the voice again—much closer this time.

"Aiii!" Instinctively, he jumped back, as if the Wytch had

suddenly leaped from her perch on the bench and sprung at him—a living darkness.

"Who's there?" he gasped, wishing he could see into the shadows behind the Wytch. She was certainly large enough for five or six people to hide behind, and the basin that in summer collected the water from the serpent's mouth was empty at this time of year.

Slowly, Steele walked forward, moving closer to the Wytch, his ears straining to pinpoint the location of the voice.

I am Darkness! Come to me! I'm waiting!

The hair on Steele's neck stood on end. The voice was coming from under his feet. He stumbled backwards, eyes dropping to fix on the spot where he had been standing. Something was down there, in the ground. For one horrifying second he expected to see a fleshless clawed hand push through the frozen earth. When nothing happened, he dared himself to kneel on the hard surface and press his ear against the flattened reeds and grass where the basin of the fountain almost touched the bank.

I'm scared, man! I'm not going in there!

Shut up. It's too late for that, so quit your snivelling!

He's the Devil! You know what they call him—the Prince of Darkness!

I'm warning you! Shut up!

Do what you want. Not me! I'm out of here!

Come back, you piece of vomit!

There was no doubt about it, there *were* voices coming from down there. For a moment Steele forgot his fear. "Hey!" he said, using his hand as a megaphone and speaking through it into the earth.

Sudden silence.

"Hey!" he repeated, pushing himself to his heels, ready to run for his life if something suddenly erupted from the ground.

"Hey! Look, guys! It's Steele the Squeal. Who are you talking to, creep?"

Dirk stepped out from among the trees beside the pond, a square bulldog shape blocking the path, his baseball bat making sharp slapping sounds as he smacked it against his palm. Like five rats following the scent of mouldy cheese, the Jerks fanned out from behind him.

Dirk and the Jerks were in Wychwood Park!

Steele swallowed the rancid taste of fear and stood up, forcing himself to look into the bully's mean, narrowed eyes.

"I heard voices . . . down there," he said, pointing.

As soon as the words left his mouth, he desperately wished he could take them back. He should have lied to them, told them it was the Wytch.

Dirk rolled his eyes and turned to the Jerks. "Hear that? Squeal says there are little men trapped in the ground."

Steele's face burned at the jeers that burst from the Jerks' throats. They held their sides or stamped their feet as if in the throes of dying of their own laughter.

"That's not what I said," protested Steele.

"Wh-who's th-there?" called Dirk, kneeling down and pressing his mouth against the ground, his backside sticking up at Steele.

The Jerks dropped to their knees. "Come out, little aliens," they sneered, grabbing sticks to smash the life out of whatever might wriggle up, just in case.

Steele wanted to kick Dirk's fat butt. "I did hear something—"

"Shut up, liar!" snapped Dirk, pushing himself to his feet.

"Yeah, liar! Shut up!" aped the Jerks.

Steele's jaws snapped shut. He wished he were magic—wished with all of his heart that he could make himself grow big and strong right before their eyes. How he'd love to see the looks on their faces then.

"Bash his face in, man," snarled one of them.

The others snickered and whacked their palms with their sticks.

Steele reached for his guitar case, but Dirk put his foot against it and pushed it away. The case slid toward the Jerks.

"Where do you think *you're* going?"

Steele opened his mouth but he couldn't find his voice.

"Hey! I'm talking to you, creep!" Dirk rammed the head of the bat into Steele's stomach.

"Yeah! He's talking to you, creep!" chorused the rest of the gang.

Steele doubled over, his eyes stinging. "Nowhere. Home," he gasped.

"I think you've been holding out on us," said Dirk.

"I haven't!" protested Steele. "I've given you my allowances."

The bully strode over to the guitar case and tapped it with the toe of his boot. "What's in the case, Squeal? Your batty old grandmother?" He turned to the Jerks and rolled his eyes. They laughed on cue.

"My guitar."

Dirk grinned knowingly at his gang. "Guitar lessons cost money, don't they?"

"Duh! Yeah!" said the Jerks.

Dirk turned back to Steele. "So, where's the money for the

lessons coming from?" he demanded, butting the ground
with the bat.

Steele fought the rage that was building inside him, rage
that could make him do something stupid. "My father. He
pays the teacher. I haven't got any more money," he fibbed.

"You're lying." Dirk kicked the guitar case onto its side
and raised his bat.

"Wait!" cried Steele, dropping to the ground and shielding
the guitar with his body. "Don't smash it. Please. I'll get some
money for you."

"Please don't smash my little *pwecious*," taunted Dirk.

He reached down, grabbed Steele by the back of his jacket,
and yanked him to his feet. "Here's the deal, Squeal." He
tapped the bat against Steele's chest for emphasis. "Bring
your bank card to school tomorrow and I'll spare your *pwecious*, and maybe your *gwanny* and your little *fwiends*. Forget it, and you can say goodbye to them."

If hearts could break, Steele's broke at that moment. He
swallowed, his shoulders slumping in despair. He wished that
Dirk would die.

"Did you hear me, creep?"

Steele nodded.

"Say it," barked Dirk, jabbing the bat into his stomach
again.

"I heard you," gasped Steele, feeling like he might throw
up.

"Now take off!" ordered Dirk. "Go on! Beat it!" And he
raised the bat threateningly and lunged at him.

Steele didn't wait to be told twice. He grabbed the handle
of his guitar case and took off.

"Hey, Squeal!"

Steele skidded to a stop and looked over his shoulder.

Framed in the weak light, Dirk's face was ugly and distorted with malice. Steele glanced up the ravine toward his house, gauging the distance to his front door. Could he make it before they caught him? Quickly he looked back at Dirk.

Drop dead! "Go on, say it," he whispered to himself. "Just this once, say it and run." But he knew he wouldn't. He swallowed the biting retort and waited.

"Say one word to your old man and . . ." Dirk moved his hand across his throat in a slicing motion. Then he turned and walked away, back up the ravine toward Wychwood Avenue, the Jerks trotting obediently after him.

Steele groaned and scrambled up the ravine, his eyes locked on the light outside his house as if it were a lifeline. Only when he reached the front door of number six Wychwood Park and had his hand firmly on the doorknob did he dare turn around.

The park was as still as a graveyard. Dirk and the others were nowhere to be seen, gone as suddenly as they had appeared.

The Killing

Until the destroyers came, Arjellans were peaceful beings. We had lived in harmony with the other intelligent life forms that inhabited our planet for twelve billion years. When the destroyers exploded onto Arjella and the killing began, our elected governors sent emissaries to reason with them. The gentle emissaries were tortured and broken. They suffered horribly before they died. Other emissaries went to negotiate terms for an end to the killing. They too died. We tried everything, we offered everything, and still we died.

Until the destroyers came, we did not know about evil—our language had no word for it.

But as the killing continued, we learned to hate.

—Excerpt from *The Wardens' Logs*

Chapter Two

GM

Steele's hands shook as he unlocked the front door. But instead of entering the house, he dropped onto a wrought-iron bench against the outside wall, between the large main door and the smaller service entrance. He stayed there until he stopped trembling and the ache in his chest went away.

As he sat there feeling alone and powerless, his mind desperately searched for a way to stop Dirk from getting his hands on the money in his bank account. Counting the money his father had deposited this morning for this month's guitar lessons, and what he had earned walking Chester, the black Labrador retriever that lived at number three Wychwood Park, he had exactly $272.23.

During the summer he had even tried to open another account at a different bank, but when the girl at the counter asked for the names of his parents, he had panicked and hurried away.

"It's not fair," he whispered. "I don't care what happens! He's not getting my money." But his mind seemed to be on a treadmill, running flat out and going nowhere. After a few minutes, having failed to come up with a plan to outfox the bully, he sighed heavily and went inside.

Steele lived with his father and grandmother. His mother

had died when he was three years old. She went to a movie with his father and caught a cold. The cold turned into pneumonia and three weeks later she was dead. Riley, one of his two best friends, was always asking him if he missed her, and when he said he didn't know, Riley usually started to cry. For Riley, not having a mother was the saddest thing in the world. In his heart Steele knew that he didn't miss *his* mother—after all, he could barely remember her—but he missed . . . something. He missed having *a* mother. After his mother died, his maternal grandmother—he called her GM—insisted Steele and his father come to live with her in the rambling three-storey house at number six Wychwood Park.

They had just settled in when something really weird happened to his grandmother. According to his father, she changed. First, she ordered a roomful of yarn and some knitting needles, and then she stopped speaking and started knitting. Steele's dad tried everything to draw her back from wherever she had gone. He coaxed and begged, but nothing worked. He gave her little surprises. Once, it was a miniature gold box filled with chocolate-covered blackberries. Another time, it was a blue enamelled locket with a picture of Steele's mother inside, in a delicate painted frame. He bought goofy board games that he and Steele played to entice GM out of her silent world. Finally, he brought doctors and psychiatrists to look at her. Nothing worked. She ignored them, or didn't see them. She smiled and knitted as if she were the sole inhabitant of the planet.

Eight years had passed since Steele and his dad moved into the old house. Not once over the years had Steele heard his grandmother utter a single word. The scarf, or whatever she was busy knitting, was now so gigantic it dominated the living room. Once a week, Steele rolled the completed knitting into the huge bale of wool that brushed the ceiling. While his father fretted over GM's odd behaviour, Steele worried more about the knitting. Soon it would be too big for the room. What were they going to do then?

He set his guitar case on the floor in the hall, hung his jacket in the front closet, and went into the kitchen to make tea.

"Tsit! Tsit!" The excited sound came from a large wire-mesh cage hanging from a hook on a stand in a corner near the back door, by the aqua-coloured curtains with creamy fleurs-de-lis.

Steele reached up and unlatched the sliding wire gate, talking softly. "Hi, Pyrus. Are you hungry?"

A piece of the curtain tore off and dropped onto the back of Steele's hand. An aqua-and-cream blur ran up his arm, launched itself at his head, and then clung on tightly, the colours wavering and changing to dark brown as the salamander camouflaged itself to match Steele's hair.

Steele picked up the kettle with one hand and tried to catch the small amphibian with the other, but he wasn't fast enough. In a flash, it slithered down the back of his shirt and raced about his back and chest like an animated lump under his skin.

"Cut it out!" he laughed as the salamander's claws tickled his ribs. He wriggled so much he almost dropped the kettle into the sink.

For as long as Steele could remember, Pyrus had been his pet. According to his father, it had belonged to Steele's mother, who gave it to Steele on his first birthday. His friends couldn't believe that it was still alive.

When tea was ready, Steele put everything on a large tray, including a bowl of Halloween chocolate from the stash he had collected last evening, carried it into the darkened living room, and placed it on the coffee table. From a small radio on the window seat came the voice of a man talking about two girls who had disappeared last night in Lake County, Illinois, from a place called Libertyville. Steele listened with half an ear as he switched on a table lamp and smiled at the diminutive woman rocking gently back and forth in a rocking chair near the window, her knitting needles making a soft clicking sound as they tapped together.

Lara Mahoney and Kathy Lee O'Shea were last seen leaving a neighbour's house while trick-or-treating on Appley Street with one of the girls' fathers. Mr. Mahoney told Libertyville Police that he was waiting on the sidewalk and happened to glance up at the train on the overpass, and when he looked back toward the house there was no sign of the youngsters. An early morning search of nearby Lake Minear has turned up nothing. Both girls are eleven years old. Volunteers are . . .

As the voice droned on, Steele thought the news story sounded familiar, as if he knew what the announcer was going to say before he said it. Then he realized that he'd heard news like this before. Lately, it seemed that whenever he watched TV or listened to the radio, there was some mention of missing kids. He hadn't paid much attention, though, because it didn't affect him. Kids didn't disappear in his world, which was relatively safe—except for run-ins with bullies like Dirk the Jerk.

"Hi, GM!" he said, after he had turned down the radio. He poured heated milk into the bottom of the cups, filled them with tea, and sweetened each cup with six sugar cubes. He didn't know if his grandmother liked sweet tea because he had never asked her, but he wasn't going to meddle with success; she never complained and the cup always ended up mysteriously empty. Besides, that's how he took his tea, and it was just right. After placing GM's cup and saucer on a small, delicate wooden table next to her chair, he dragged a footstool across the carpet and sat down beside her.

His grandmother wore her habitual secret smile. She acknowledged neither him nor the teacup. But then, she never did. Her kind blue eyes remained fixed on a place that only she could see. She looked especially tiny and frail today. Lately, that worried Steele even more than the knitting. He was afraid that as the scarf grew bigger and bigger, his grandmother was getting smaller and smaller, as if she were knitting herself into the scarf.

Still shaken and sore from his ordeal with Dirk the Jerk, Steele wrapped himself in silence and listened to the gentle *click! clack!* of his grandmother's knitting needles, his thoughts as tangled as a ball of yarn after Pyrus had finished with it. Were the voices he had heard coming from the ground in the park real, or had he imagined them? Who was the Prince of Darkness? And who or what was it waiting for? Was there really a Devil?

Suddenly a groan burst from his lips as an image of Dirk filled his mind. He had almost forgotten about the bully and the money. He glanced at his grandmother, noticing that her cup was, as usual, suddenly empty.

"Something bad happened on my way home," he began softly. He grabbed a handful of his T-shirt that included Pyrus's tail, then reached under the shirt and tried to pull the animal out, but four sets of claws clung so tightly to the fabric that holes were forming. Finally, he managed to separate salamander claws from T-shirt and pluck the creature free. Pyrus wriggled out of his hands, leaped to the carpet, and streaked under the gilt settee, flashing into gold as it merged with the wooden legs.

"Dirk was waiting in the park—him and the Jerks, hiding in the woods near the Wytch," he continued. "He wants more money. That's all the money I've got, GM. If I give it to him I won't be able to take guitar lessons." He thought for a second. "But if I don't, he'll hurt my friends and smash my guitar." He had purposefully left out the part about Dirk threatening to scare her to death. "It's not just the money. You know I'd gladly give it to him if he'd leave Mac and Riley alone. It's Dad. He'll kill me if he ever finds out. . . . What am I going to do?"

The Great War

We named the destroyers Tsilihin, because they cared nothing for life, not even their own. Flawed by evolution, they had not developed intellect to guide them and curb their crazed impulses. They were empty husks, driven solely by instinct. And their killing instinct consumed them, and threatened to annihilate us. Our hatred grew, and we learned to fight.

The Great Arjellan War raged for eight hundred years. We fought with fire, but for every hundred Tsilihin we destroyed, a thousand more took their places. And then, near the end of the eighth century of war, when all seemed lost, the Mages broke the spells that warded the resting place of an ancient black globe. They placed their hands upon the orb's opaque surface and evoked an ancient magic.

—Excerpt from *The Wardens' Logs*

Chapter Three

Caught

On November fifth, a boy named Ryan Massey disappeared in Toronto's Riverdale area.

According to Steele's father, and confirmed by the media in the city, Ryan had taken Milton, the Massey's golden retriever, for a walk around the block. His mother glanced out the window and saw the boy coming back, Milton heeling obediently. As they crossed the street and approached the house, Mrs. Massey looked away for a second. Then she heard Milton barking at the front door. When she opened the door, the dog was alone, its leash trailing behind it on the sidewalk. There was no sign of Ryan.

Steele had never heard of Ryan Massey until the boy's disappearance hit the news. As he walked to school the next morning, he was so preoccupied with thoughts of the missing boy that he didn't notice his two best friends waiting impatiently outside the school until he was practically on top of them.

"Isn't it awful about Ryan Massey?" said Mac, a frown replacing his usual good-natured grin.

Steele blinked from the glare of the sun on Mac Moran's dazzling white hair. "It's scary," he said, troubled by a feeling that something evil was loose in Toronto and coming closer. "And it's strange the way he disappeared right outside his house."

"Yeah," agreed Mac, nodding vigorously. "But don't you think it's even stranger that his mother didn't see anything?"

"And what about the dog?" said Riley Puddle, Steele's oldest friend. "It didn't bark."

"Everything about the case is weird," said Steele. "My dad is so frustrated because it's like Ryan just disappeared into thin air."

"My parents won't let me walk to school anymore," said Riley. "But you know, I don't really mind. In fact, it's sort of a relief."

Steele slung his arm about Riley's shoulder as they continued toward the school. She was almost as tall as Steele, and at least five inches taller than Mac. Her eyes were the soft clear blue of a robin's egg and, depending upon the colour of her clothes, sometimes appeared green. Steele's eyes were a darker, deeper blue, while Mac's were such a pale shade of gray, they were almost indistinguishable from the whites.

Steele had known Riley exactly a half hour longer than he had known Mac. She and Steele were absolutely devoted to one another and, for the most part, inseparable. Her relationship with Mac, however, was turbulent at the best of times. Sometimes Steele thought that Riley tolerated Mac only because of him. The pair argued incessantly, about everything and nothing. If Mac said salt was white, Riley would argue that it was black. If Riley liked something, Mac hated it. Even though their spats sometimes escalated almost to blows, Steele suspected that they enjoyed arguing.

But today, they weren't arguing. The news about Ryan Massey seemed to have fostered a truce between them.

Throughout that day, and for the next week, Steele and his friends and classmates talked of nothing else. They shared news stories, and speculated about whether the missing boy would ever be found, and if so, whether he would still be alive. As the days passed, Steele noticed that Ryan Massey's unexplained disappearance had changed his school, perhaps forever. New rules were added to old ones, posted in the corridors and classrooms, and read over the intercom every morning immediately following the national anthem. Students were forbidden to leave the school unless accompanied by an identifiable parent or guardian. They were encouraged to work and play in groups, and to report suspicious strangers hanging about outside.

But the change that Steele noticed wasn't something tangible like posted lists of rules. It was something that couldn't be seen at all, although it was as real as his classroom and his desk. It was fear—stark and ugly and sweaty.

One evening toward the end of November, Steele had finished his homework and was watching the news on TV with his father. He was so engrossed in the program, he didn't hear the phone ringing or notice his father leaving the room. A few minutes later, the television screen went black.

Steele groped among the cushions for the remote, then saw his father framed by the doorway, the gadget in his hand.

"That was Mrs. Fret."

Steele was conscious of his heart fluttering wildly. Pyrus chose that moment to claw a comfortable spot on his stomach. Steele squeezed the salamander.

His father continued. "She wanted to know why you haven't shown up for guitar lessons the past three weeks."

Steele squeezed Pyrus tighter. "She wanted to know how you were managing with your broken wrist, and when she could expect you to return to your lessons."

Steele couldn't make himself meet his father's eyes. When he had invented the broken wrist to explain why he couldn't attend guitar lessons, he hadn't once considered the possibility that Mrs. Fret would actually call his house to check up on him. Now, he couldn't believe he'd been so stupid.

"She said you've missed three lessons this month. What's going on, Steele?"

Steele didn't know what to say. He stared at his feet. "Nothing."

"That's not an answer. Why haven't you been going to your lessons?"

"I couldn't, Dad." Pyrus was struggling desperately to escape Steele's viselike grasp.

"Why not?"

"I can't tell you."

"What do you mean, you can't tell me?"

"I can't tell you."

"If you weren't at your lessons, where were you? You know I worry about you—with that boy Ryan still missing."

"Here. Home. Honest." He grimaced as Pyrus's sharp teeth sank into his thumb. He snatched his hand away; Pyrus streaked under the sofa cushions. Steele could tell from the quietness in his father's voice that his dad was controlling his anger with difficulty.

"Do you still have the money I gave you for the lessons?"

Steele nodded slowly. "Yes," he lied.

Hearing his father's deep sigh, he ached to blurt out all of the things he had bottled up inside for so many months. He wanted to say, *The money's gone. Dirk made me go to the bank machine and take it out and give it to him because he said he'd scare GM and hurt my friends and bust my guitar if I didn't and he said he'd kill me if I told anybody.*" But he said nothing, forcing himself not to squirm under his father's blistering stare.

"I want to see your bank statements since September."

Steele's world was rapidly spinning out of control. The minute his father saw the latest statement, he'd know that Steele was a liar. It wouldn't take a financial wizard to figure out that most of the money was gone. In fact, as of this moment, the balance in his account was $12.

He knows I'm lying! I've got to stop him from finding out!

In the heavy silence that fell on the room, Steele could hear his father's watch ticking faintly, halfway across the room. He tried to think of something to say to erase the look he pictured on his father's face, but he knew if he opened his mouth he'd only make things worse, or end up telling more lies.

"Did you hear me? I want those bank statements . . . and kindly look at me when I'm speaking to you."

"I heard you," he said finally, briefly meeting his father's gaze. "November's hasn't come yet." More lies.

His father sighed again. "Son, are you in some kind of trouble?"

Steele was staring at his feet so hard he wouldn't have been surprised if holes suddenly appeared in the toes of his socks. *Yes!* his mind screamed. He shook his head.

"You'd tell me if you were?"

Steele nodded. "But I'm not."

He felt as if he had just punched his father in the face. When he looked up a few seconds later, the doorway was empty. He listened intently, relaxing only when he heard his father slowly climbing the stairs. Since Ryan Massey's disappearance, Steele's father had been working practically day and night, catching a few hours' sleep whenever he could. Steele was glad his dad was going to bed early tonight.

Feeling wretched, he went in search of his grandmother, who, thankfully, was easy to find since she was always in her rocking chair by the window in the living room. Catching hold of the arms of the old woman's chair, he pulled it about until she was facing the middle of the room. Then he closed the drapes and dropped heavily onto the gilt settee.

In a rush, he blurted out what had happened. "I'm in really bad trouble, GM. I just lied to Dad. I don't think he believed me. Even *I* wouldn't believe me." He laughed bitterly. "He wants to see my bank statements. The last two are OK, because I didn't deposit my allowances. But when he sees that I took out over $250 on November second, he'll never trust me again."

The old woman smiled sweetly, rocking steadily back and forth, not giving any sign that she had heard Steele's story. Her delicate fingers danced on the long knitting needles as if they were acting independently. But—was it Steele's imagination or had the knitting needles clicked faster for a second? As if his grandmother were trying to send him a message. And now that he thought about it, he was sure that when he had quietly entered the room he hadn't heard the familiar incessant clicking of the needles. He shook his head as if to organize his thoughts, and caught sight of Pyrus making a beeline for the giant baled scarf.

"Remember how I used to hate it when Dad went through

my bank statements?" he said. "He always said, 'You should have your own account, but I'll monitor it.' I hate to admit it—maybe if he was still monitoring it, I wouldn't be in this mess."

The knitting needles tapped softly. Steele wished that he could share his troubles with his father. Perhaps then they wouldn't seem so insurmountable. But he was also determined to make his father proud of him by solving his problems on his own.

"Dad's wrong about Dirk," he said, so softly he might have been thinking out loud. "I did what he said. I stood up to him once. You know what happened. It just made things worse."

He looked at his grandmother, waiting for a sign that she understood. She seemed so small—five of her could have fit into the rocking chair. She continued to knit and stare blankly into space.

Steele stayed with her until bedtime. Then he kissed her cheek, untangled Pyrus from the scarf, and climbed two flights of stairs to his third-floor room.

Steele closed the door and dropped Pyrus onto the bed, then pulled the drapes across the windows and walked over to his desk. Kneeling on the floor, he opened the bottom drawer and retrieved the top three envelopes with the name of his bank in the upper left-hand corner. He was reaching for the doorknob when he hesitated. Quickly, almost furtively, he slipped the latest statement from the others and shoved it under his mattress. Then he placed the other two envelopes on the floor outside his father's bedroom on the second floor.

That night he couldn't sleep. He tossed and turned, the flat envelope hidden between his mattress and box spring seemed to dig into his sides like a sharp rock. When he wasn't grinding his teeth, he was arguing with himself over what he could have or should have said to his father. It was pitch black when he kicked the duvet to the foot of the bed and got up. Morning was still several hours away. Steele pulled on his clothes and crept down the stairs to the second-floor study, with its large leaded-glass windows. He parted the lace curtains, pressed his nose against the frosty window, and peered down into Wychwood Park.

Number six Wychwood Park stood on the crest of a hill overlooking the ravine and Taddle Pond. The house was built in the mid-1870s by Marmaduke Matthews, a landscape painter from Oxfordshire, England, whose head was bursting with dreams of establishing an artists' colony in the park-like setting.

Wychwood Park sat at the headwaters of Taddle Creek, a historic creek that used to flow above-ground through the heart of the city and through the University of Toronto campus. Although the creek now ran underground as part of Toronto's sewer system, it still flowed through Wychwood Park before entering a storm sewer on Davenport Road.

As he stared out the window, Steele couldn't see the Wytch. He had been avoiding the fountain in the park ever since the afternoon that he heard voices coming from the ground—the same afternoon Dirk and the Jerks had ambushed him. Instead, he had stuck to the road, skirting the pond and taking the long way home. But tonight the park looked peaceful and inviting. It seemed to beckon him.

Dropping the curtains back in place, Steele moved slowly down the stairs, carefully avoiding the five creaking steps halfway down and stepping over Pyrus in the act of blending with the bottom step. He moved silently to the hall closet.

Then he pulled on his jacket, picked up his guitar case, opened the service door, and slipped quietly outside.

Crouching to make himself less visible, Steele darted across the open street. When he reached the tennis court, he stood up straight and glanced over his shoulder, half expecting to see lights go on in his big rambling house, warning him that his father had discovered that he wasn't in bed. But the big house was a looming black giant whose shadow darkened the street and flowed toward him like a rising tide.

A ghostly stillness had settled over the neighbourhood. Steele had never been outside alone in the early hours of the morning before. The eerie pre-dawn silence and the luminous stillness amazed him. Even the wind was still. The dry air caught in his throat and he coughed involuntarily, tensing as the sound shattered the silence like a car backfiring.

Steele walked through the crisp leaves toward the nearer of the two wooden benches that faced the ravine. He sat on the slatted seat, and although the cold seeped through his jeans and numbed his backside, it wasn't bad enough to drive him back to the warmth of his bed. The silence and the stillness here seemed deeper than outside Wychwood Park. From the bench, he could see the pond at the bottom of the ravine. The still water shone silvery white in the moonlight. The Wytch was a dark, motionless blob below him, her shadow creating a long, dark stain on the empty basin of the fountain.

Steele remembered the blood-chilling voice he had heard, or imagined he had heard, the last time he was here—the voice that called itself Darkness. And there were those other voices too, only they had sounded more scared than evil. He debated going down into the ravine and listening for the voices, but it seemed darker down there, away from the weak lamp light. He strained his ears but he heard nothing. Then he shook his hands out of his gloves and opened the guitar case.

Steele spent a few minutes tuning the guitar. He strummed the strings softly, almost tentatively at first, and then he began to play a haunting classical melody, his fingers finding and plucking the strings effortlessly. The notes sounded pure and sweet on the night air.

As he played he felt the tension and weariness ease from his body. He forgot about the voices. He forgot about Dirk and the Jerks, and the money gone from his bank account. He forgot about being scared most of the time. The horrible guilt he felt because of lying to his father left him and in its place came an enormous sense of peace. For a fleeting moment he wondered if this was how his grandmother felt. If so, he could understand why she refused to come back from her silent world.

If the earth had abruptly opened at his feet, he probably wouldn't have noticed. He certainly didn't hear the clanking of metal wheels on the asphalt and the faster rattle of a twisted wheel that wobbled crazily. He didn't notice the old man shuffling along Wychwood Park behind the rickety shopping cart heaped to overflowing with empty bottles and cans, and plastic supermarket bags stuffed with treasures acquired from Dumpsters and recycling bins. He wasn't aware of the old man pausing in his seemingly aimless journey to stare with wild, red-rimmed eyes at him. If he had, he might have dropped the guitar and fled from the park faster than if the Prince of Darkness had tired of waiting and come out of the ground to snatch him up and away.

He didn't notice anything until much later, when he sensed

a presence on the wooden bench beside him. He stopped playing and looked at his father, dressed for work in a sports jacket and dark grey trousers.

"I'm sorry about skipping guitar, Dad," he said.

His father gave him a worried look, but he said nothing.

"I'll tell you about it. I promise. I just need to work it out myself first."

His father nodded and stood. "Come on, son. I don't want you out here alone."

As they crossed the park in silence, Steele felt sad and empty. Something had changed in the close relationship he had always enjoyed with his father. Something good was gone, lost, and it could never be recaptured. When they reached the house, his father placed his hand gently on Steele's shoulder.

"Get dressed for school," he said. "Unless we get a lead in the Ryan Massey case, I'll be home for dinner. I'll pick up a pizza." Then he turned and walked along Wychwood Park toward the nearest subway stop, at St. Clair and Bathurst.

Steele watched until his father disappeared, promising himself that he'd win back his father's trust, no matter what.

A Hollow Victory

We defeated the Tsilihin in an historic battle on the plains of Elva Longa. The Mages unleashed their magic and nothing could stand against it. It slammed into the front lines of the alien terrorists and turned them to ashes. Those that were absent from the front lines were taken prisoner. The Great War was finally over.

But Arjella was a graveyard—a place of death. Three billion Arjellans had died defending their homeland. From mountaintop perches, we looked out over the land and despaired. Our great cities now lay in shambles. Mighty virgin forests had been stripped and burned. Agricultural fields and flatlands had been ravaged and poisoned so that nothing would grow for millennia. Our rivers and oceans were fouled and contaminated with the bloated bodies of land and sea creatures.

We met with the Mages to determine the fate of the enemy prisoners.

—Excerpt from *The Wardens' Logs*

Chapter Four

The New Girl

"Pssst!"

Steele pretended to ignore the muffled voice coming from the giant maple tree on Bathurst Street, near the cul-de-sac that he used as a shortcut from his house to Hillcrest Community School.

"Help! I'm trapped. Get me out of here."

Without warning, Steele lunged at the tree, disappearing behind its girth and reappearing almost immediately with his hands locked firmly about Mac's neck.

"Ack!" squawked Mac, grinning despite Steele's hands squeezing his windpipe.

Steele released his stranglehold on Mac's throat, and the other boy slumped to his knees onto the ground.

"Come on! Admit it," giggled Mac, rubbing his neck. "You thought it was the tree."

"Not! I knew it was you. I saw you sneaking about back there," said Steele, grabbing Mac's arm and pulling him to his feet.

Mac mumbled something that Steele couldn't hear as he brushed at the knees of his trousers. Then he brightened. "Do you want to hear my latest brilliant idea?"

"Well?" Steele lifted his eyebrows questioningly.

"Last night, I was lying in bed and it just came to me all of a sudden," explained Mac. "Like that!" He snapped his fingers.

Steele waited. Every week for as long as he could remember, Mac had shared one of his brilliant ideas. At least Mac *thought* they were brilliant. Steele was more inclined to keep his opinion to himself.

"You're taking guitar lessons, but I've heard you play and you're good. Right?"

Steele shrugged.

"Well, I can sing."

Steele burst out laughing. "Since when?"

"Since I saw this kid on TV. He's only eleven and already a millionaire."

"Listen, Mac. I've heard you sing. OK? Forget it."

"OK, OK! So I can't sing, yet. But for a million bucks, I could learn to fly. Hey, for that kind of money I'd do anything."

"Anything?" asked Steele.

"Except a sex change," said Mac. "The last thing I'd want to be is a girl."

"I don't know," said Steele, trying to keep a straight face. "I think you'd be cute as a girl." He winked mischievously at Riley, who had dropped into step beside him, her backpack slipping off her shoulder.

"Mac's considering a sex change," Steele explained. "What do you think, Riley?"

"A change to what?" she asked, playing along.

"A girl! Don't you think he'd look cool as a girl?"

Riley paused and gave Mac one of her penetrating looks. "Nah!" she said finally. "Definitely not a sex change. Maybe a species change."

"Ha! Ha! Very funny!" said Mac.

"Hey listen, guys," said Steele, suddenly becoming serious. "I need to tell you something before we get to school."

The good-natured squabbling stopped as quickly as it had begun. Mac and Riley turned to Steele and listened as he told them what had happened at his house after Mrs. Fret's phone call the previous evening. When he finished, Mac let out a long whistle.

"What are you going to do?" he asked. "You can't hide the bank statement forever."

Steele shook his head. "I know. I feel bad about Dad. I— I . . ." He stopped, unable to continue.

"You've got to tell him what happened," said Riley. "You've got to tell him about Dirk."

"I know. Why do you think I was up half the night?" Steele clenched his fists in frustration. "It's just that Dad doesn't understand about Dirk. He thinks he'll stop bullying me if I stand up to him."

Mac and Riley nodded sympathetically.

"Besides," continued Steele, "if I tell him, I'm going to end up feeling like it's all my fault."

"Steele, you've got to tell him," pressed Riley. "When he hears how Dirk's been threatening to scare GM, he won't think it's your fault. He'll realize you were only trying to protect *her*."

From the way Riley was looking at him, Steele wondered if she had found out that the money he'd been handing over to Dirk had also kept her and Mac safe from the bully. *No*, he thought, but he quickly looked away before his expression told her he was hiding something.

"Riley's right," said Mac.

"I know! I know!" said Steele impatiently. "I just need to figure out how to tell him."

"What's there to figure out?" snapped Riley. "Just do it!"

Steele could see that she wasn't about to give it a rest, and he was right.

"That jerk's got all your money," Riley went on. "Now he's got you telling lies to your dad. Next he'll make you steal for him."

Steele sighed. "You're right. But I just wish I could think of a way to stop him for good without having to tell Dad."

The three friends walked the rest of the way to school in silence, Steele vaguely aware of the worried glances flashing back and forth between Mac and Riley.

"Oh, Squeal!"

Steele tensed. *Dirk.* Since he'd given the bully most of the money in his bank account, Dirk and the Jerks had left him alone. He should have known they hadn't forgotten about him.

"Still hearing voices in the ground, creep?"

Steele wished he'd never mentioned the voices in the park. When he had arrived at school the next day, the Jerks had pressed their ears to the ground and pretended to converse with aliens, laughing hysterically all the while. Steele had felt his face turn as red as the school's bricks, but he had shrugged to show the other kids that he didn't care what the Jerks said, and had hurried inside the building.

The story had spread like wildfire. Not a day passed without whispering and snickering and rude comments filtering through the playground to his ears.

When Steele ignored him, Dirk pointed at Mac and Riley.

"Look, guys! Steele found the aliens."

"Why don't you shut up?" snapped Riley.

"Puddle scum's mad," taunted Dirk as he pretended to hide behind the Jerks. "Look! I'm so scared I'm shaking."

"Puddle scum! Puddle scum!" chanted the Jerks.

Riley's face turned red.

Steele grabbed her arm. "It's OK, Riley. Don't pay any attention to them."

"I wish they'd come over here," said Mac fiercely, but under his breath so that the bullies couldn't hear. "I'd rearrange their faces."

Snickering rudely, Dirk and his pals smashed their fists against their palms as if they were smashing Steele's face. Then they turned away.

"I wish he'd disappear," muttered Mac, staring daggers into Dirk's back.

Riley was shocked. "Don't ever wish for something like that, even about Dirk the Jerk. Imagine how horrible you'd feel if it came true. Just like that girl in Chicago who told her brother she wished he'd never come home again. Well, she got her wish. Her brother disappeared yesterday afternoon outside his school."

"You're making that up," accused Mac.

"I am not," said Riley. "If you listened to the news for a change you'd know what's happening in the world."

"Ah!" said Mac. "I watch *Space News,* so I know what's going on out there." He raised his arms toward the sky. "Which is more than I can say for you."

"You'd be surprised how much I know about space," said Riley.

"Yes," agreed Mac. "I would." Then he added nastily,

"Since the only two things in the sky you could identify last week were the moon and the sun."

"Another missing kid," whispered Steele, oblivious to his friends' bickering. He couldn't help thinking about the two Libertyville girls, and the Toronto boy, Ryan Massey. "Counting the boy in Chicago, that makes four kids who have disappeared in just four weeks." He turned to Riley. "I watched the news last night. Are you sure it happened yesterday?"

"I saw it," insisted Riley. "The boy's name was David something."

They continued walking. As they passed the original school building, heading toward the students' entrance in the newer wing, the longest, blackest limousine Steele had ever seen pulled up to the curb just ahead of them.

Mac whistled.

"Cool!" whispered Riley.

Time seemed to slow and then come to a full stop. Every head in the schoolyard spun toward the sleek car. Steele felt the strangest feeling wash over him—as if the entire street were locked in suspended animation, holding its breath, waiting for something of great significance to happen. He stared at the car windows—twelve on the passenger side alone, and all tinted blacker than the inside of a wolf's mouth at midnight. But nothing was visible through the opaque glass.

After what seemed like an age, a door near the back of the limousine opened and a pair of black boots emerged, followed by a girl dressed from head to toe in black. Her knee-high black matte boots, crisscrossed along their length with wide black bands, fit her like a pair of long socks. She wore an ankle-length black coat. Her long hair was the colour of a witch's hat. Under the open coat, she wore more black: a short skirt, tights, and a T-shirt with a glowing design on the front. Steele stared at the design but couldn't decide if it was a silver serpent, or a green serpent breathing silver fire. Dangling from the girl's pale earlobes were miniature black bat earrings. And around her neck, moulded to her throat as snugly as flesh, was a wide chain mail choker. It reminded Steele of silver scales, and he shuddered.

Seemingly oblivious to the students' reaction to her arrival, the girl reached inside the limousine and removed a black backpack. Slinging it over her shoulder, she paused for a moment and gazed at the white columns framing the arched main entrance to the school. Then, eyes locked on the building, she breezed purposefully along the sidewalk toward the half-dozen broad steps that led to the front doors. As if they had been turned into zombies, the kids slowly moved aside, opening a path for the new girl. She moved among them as if they were invisible.

Just as she drew alongside Steele, the girl's eyes shifted abruptly to him and lingered there. They were the most extraordinary blue Steele had ever seen—a spellbinding, neon blue—and he felt bewitched, as if he were being pulled into the wild, unearthly blueness and couldn't lift a finger to save himself. He tried to tear his eyes off the girl, but they wouldn't obey. Then she blinked, and Steele found that he could control his eyes again. He looked away, but not before he saw the girl's eyes suddenly change from blue to silver.

Steele's flesh crawled. The girl's eyes gleamed like molten silver. Steele felt a chill grab hold of him, and he could feel his teeth chattering. He glanced over at Mac and Riley but could tell that they hadn't noticed anything peculiar. He looked back at the new girl, but all he could see was her black coat disappearing through the main doors—the doors that only teachers and visitors to the school were allowed to use.

With a sound like a mournful wind in the trees, the other kids let out their breaths in unison. Steele turned toward the street. The long black limousine was gone.

"She's cool," said Riley. "I hope she'll be in our class."

"Her limo's cooler," said Mac. "Right, Steele?"

Steele wanted to tell them about the girl's silver eyes, but he was afraid they'd think he was losing his mind.

"She gives me the creeps," he said instead.

Mac and Riley exchanged questioning looks.

"What's wrong with you?" asked Riley. "You don't even know her and you're acting as if you hate her."

"I don't hate her. I just said she gives me the creeps."

"I know," agreed Mac sympathetically. "It's her black clothes." Then he added, "I don't care if she *is* one of those weirdos who wear only black. If she asks me to go for a drive in that limo, I'm not going to say no."

"You mean Goths," corrected Riley. "I don't think so. Her fingernails aren't black and neither are her lips."

"Whatever," said Mac. "She must be rich. I wonder what it feels like to be able to buy whatever you want," he added, unable to hide the note of envy in his voice, or the greedy expression that spread across his face.

They fell silent, each thinking of things that money could buy.

Finally Mac turned to Steele. "I bet she's a rock star," he said.

Steele followed Riley into the grade six classroom and stopped short when he spotted the new girl parked in the third seat from the front, in the row by the windows. Mac bumped into his back, and other kids bumped into him, and so on until there were ten noisy students trying to force their way into the room at the same time.

Mac gave Steele a shove, propelling him forward.

"Sorry," Steele mumbled.

He was surprised and disappointed to discover that the strange girl was in his class. While she looked like an eleven or twelve year old, something in her manner had made him assume that she was older.

"She's not a rock star. A Gorgon is more like it. Why do I have this really bad feeling about her?" he whispered to Mac.

"It's probably because you don't have any sisters, so you act goofy around girls to compensate for your inability to relate to them," Mac whispered back.

"Shut up," hissed Steele. "Who asked you?"

"You." Mac grinned. "Chill, Steele! What's wrong with you? You're weirding out over a girl."

Mac slid into his seat and shot a paper airplane across the room at Riley. He made awesome paper planes—sleek jets that streaked through the air like bullets, and larger, slower aircraft, like this one, that circled lazily before landing on Riley's desk. His aircraft had earned him a lot of praise from classmates, not to mention a lot of detentions from teachers.

Steele's eyes followed the flight of Mac's paper plane without seeing it. Then he shrugged and pretended to read his science notes. If Mac thought he was being weird now, imagine what he'd think if Steele told him about the girl's eyes! He felt her eyes on him now and forced himself not to look at her. He was relieved when Mr. Stone raised his hand, the teacher's signal for silence in the classroom.

By morning recess, the new girl was a sensation. Someone had found out her name was Maddie Fey, and now the school was abuzz with rumours of who she was and where she had come from. In the corridor outside the grade six classroom, students swarmed about her like bees, asking questions and trying to get a closer look at the scaled choker about her neck, or catch a glimpse of the exquisite bats clinging to her earlobes as if alive. But the new girl deftly eluded her curious fellow students. Steele watched as she melted effortlessly through the crowd, as if either she or they were as insubstantial as air.

Instead of heading outside with the stream of students, Maddie Fey went in the opposite direction. Steele saw her disappear into the library. At lunchtime, and again when the last buzzer sounded, she picked up her backpack and walked out through the main door as if she were the school principal or one of the teachers. As the doors swung shut behind her, the sleek black limousine pulled up, gliding to a stop at the curb.

"She's a witch!" whispered Melissa Graven, one of Steele's classmates, elbowing her way to the front of the crowd of kids pressed against the classroom windows watching Maddie Fey in awe. "Under her clothes her skin is green like mouldy cheese and wrinkled like a rotten green apple."

Steele didn't believe that Maddie Fey's skin was green and wrinkled, but he couldn't stop thinking about her, especially her eyes and the silver scales covering her throat. Nor could he shake the uneasy feeling that had been building in his gut since the moment she had looked into his eyes—the feeling that Maddie Fey had purposefully singled him out from the other kids.

//Λ\\

"But why?" he muttered to himself as he walked home from school. "What's she doing at Hillcrest? And why did she stare at *me* and no one else?" Over tea and blackberry scones in the living room, Steele told his grandmother all about the sinister new girl. "She hasn't spoken to anyone—not one single word all day. Nobody knows anything about her—who she is or where she's from. Melissa Graven said she's a witch. Maybe she's right."

He picked a crumb from his jeans and held it out to entice Pyrus from his hiding place among the multicoloured yarn. "You should have seen her eyes, GM. She was looking straight at me when they turned from blue to silver. It was freaky. And then I felt cold, like I was being turned to ice. And, GM, I swear the cold was coming from her."

He wasn't quick enough to see Pyrus's tongue lash out and snap up the crumb, but he felt the sandpapery touch on his finger, and saw that the crumb had vanished.

As he waited for his grandmother to digest what he had told her, he watched Pyrus inch away from the skeins of wool, its skin turning blue and red to match the Persian carpet. Steele reached down and ran his fingers along Pyrus's length, absentmindedly tracing the salamander's perfectly formed scales. Then he snatched his hand back as if his fingers were burning. His pet's scaly hide made him think of Maddie Fey's neck.

"Riley said that a boy in Chicago disappeared yesterday," he said after a while, almost to himself. "Just like Ryan Massey."

He placed the empty cups and saucers on the tea tray and moved toward the kitchen. At the doorway, he turned back to his grandmother. He was positive the old woman was smaller than she'd been yesterday.

"I don't know what it is," he said. "But I've got a really bad feeling about Maddie Fey."

A Distant Tomb

Arjella is located at the centre of the Milky Way galaxy near a globular cluster its inhabitants call Oraz. There are more than two hundred billion stars in the Milky Way, most of them with their own planetary systems. There are over three hundred billion galaxies in the known universe.

Somewhere in all that vastness, we would find a place to incarcerate the Tsilihin.

The Mages looked out toward a far, unexplored section of the galaxy, where a massive nebula was rotating and contracting, accelerating the cloud's particles and heating them to the temperature required for nuclear fusion. The nebula was transforming itself into a new star.

They raised their arms and pointed toward the nebula, so far in the distance that they alone could see it. They gazed at a boiling cloud of molten fire that had escaped the gravitational pull of the new star's rotation and was fixed in orbit about the star. These broken bits of condensed fire clouds would, in time, form the crusts of the infant star's planets and their satellites.

That is the site we chose as a tomb for the enemy.

—Excerpt from *The Wardens' Logs*

Chapter Five

Voices in the Park

The next morning as Steele pulled on his jacket, he heard the sound of paper crinkling in one of the pockets. He reached in and pulled out an envelope with Mrs. Fret's name printed in block letters on the front. He opened the unsealed flap. Inside were two crisp $20 bills.

He had given up on the guitar lessons, knowing that he could hardly ask his father for money. Especially since his dad thought Steele had the money in the bank. But if Dad hadn't done it, who had put the twenties in his pocket?

Could it have been GM? He walked to the living room door and peered in at his grandmother. He couldn't see her head above the back of her chair, but the chair was rocking back and forth as usual, and he heard the distinct *click! clack!* of knitting needles over the sound of the radio. He paused in the doorway; he could hear the radio announcer talking to someone about the boy Riley had told him and Mac about yesterday—the boy who had disappeared in Chicago on Tuesday afternoon. Steele shuffled closer to the radio, but the announcer had already moved on to a new topic.

Steele stuffed the envelope into his backpack, part of him wishing that he hadn't found it. At least then Dirk couldn't get his hands on it, and Steele's life would be a lot simpler.

Now he'd have to think of a way to avoid the bully. He placed his guitar case inside the front door and left for school.

He had just turned onto Bathurst Street when he spotted Dirk lurking outside the school. Quickly, Steele ducked out of sight, putting a large bush between him and the bigger boy. He knew the bully was waiting for him—and would try to take his guitar money. But Steele was determined that the Jerk wasn't going to get his hands on the money in his backpack. He waited, peering through the thin branches of the bush until he saw Dirk aim several savage kicks at one of the parking meters outside the school and stomp angrily toward the students' entrance. Steele glanced at his watch: 9:01 a.m. Then he dashed across the street and ran all the way to school.

"Sorry, Mr. Stone," he said, doing an about-face as the teacher nodded toward the door. Steele knew the drill, but he wasn't worried. He was a good student and had only been caught for coming late eight times in all the years he'd been at Hillcrest. He reported to the office and, with a twinge of guilt, filled out a form explaining why he was late.

I was late for school because my grandmother had an epileptic seizure and, since my dad was at work, I had to stay home and keep a spoon in her mouth so she wouldn't swallow her tongue.

He dated the excuse and signed his name: *Steele Miller.*

"Sorry, GM," he whispered, wondering if telling so many lies in less than a week would show on him in some strange way, perhaps make his nose grow like Pinocchio's. His nose was certainly twitching, and he forced himself not to reach up to his face and pinch the end just to be sure it wasn't.

Back in class, Steele felt Maddie Fey's eyes burning into him as if his nose really had sprouted, or as if she could see right into his soul. It gave him the creeps.

"How old is the universe?" Mr. Stone's eyes moved from student to student, stopping when they reached Steele.

"Between twelve and fifteen billion years old, about three times older than our sun," answered Steele. It was an easy question.

"Very good, Steele. "What do you think, class? Was it a comet or an asteroid impact that destroyed the dinosaurs?"

Steele spoke up. "An asteroid. Or else it was the lethal atmosphere after the impact. All that dust blocked out the sun, and there was acid rain, and fires that destroyed most forests and grass."

"But how do we know it was an asteroid and not a comet?"

"Because of iridium, which is rare on Earth and not found on comets. There's iridium in a layer of sediment in the Earth's crust that came from something that crashed into us about sixty-five million years ago. Asteroids have lots of iridium, so it makes sense that it was an asteroid."

"Excellent," said Mr. Stone.

Steele swelled with pride at the teacher's praise. Then he noticed Maddie Fey staring at him as if surprised that he had known the answers. *She's weird,* he thought, quickly dropping his eyes.

At recess, Dirk's Jerks were waiting for him in the schoolyard just outside the door. The thought flashed through Steele's mind that they knew about the guitar lesson money that he had transferred from his backpack to his back pocket.

"Trying to hide from us, Squeal?" they said, forming a tight ring around him and shepherding him toward the far fence.

Dirk was waiting there, his beefy hands thrust deep into his cargo pants pockets, a scowl distorting his face. Two of the gang kept their eyes peeled for the schoolyard monitors.

"Hand it over, Squeal." Dirk pulled one hand out of his pocket and thrust it palm upward at Steele.

"What?" asked Steele.

"Don't play games with me," snarled Dirk, his expression cold and derisive. "Give me the guitar money!"

"I don't have any guitar money," lied Steele. Despite the chill in the air, he felt sweat trickling down his spine. The envelope seemed ready to burst out of his back pocket.

"You're lying!"

Steele shrugged. "I'm not lying. I already gave you all the money my dad put in my account for the lessons."

Dirk grabbed the front of his shirt and held his fist an inch from Steele's nose. "Listen up, you little creep. If you're lying to me, I'll splatter your brains all over Toronto."

"Yeah! You better not be lying . . ." jeered the Jerks, pressing closer and jamming their knuckles hard into Steele's ribs.

Steele twisted free from Dirk's grasp and spoke through clenched teeth. "I'm—not—lying."

Dirk put both hands on Steele's chest and gave a vicious shove. Steele flew backwards and landed on his backside on the ground. As if they had rehearsed it a hundred times, the Jerks scattered, leaving a wide space about Steele. Then Dirk looked about at the kids who had been watching the encounter with wide eyes, and raised his voice.

"Aw, look, guys! Poor Steele's listening to the little aliens. Steele! You need some serious help, man." He leaned down and hissed in Steele's face. "I don't care if you have to steal the money from your batty old grandmother. Just get me the money. Pray your old man makes a deposit before next Thursday."

Steele turned away, his nose wrinkling in disgust at the sour smell of Dirk's breath. Ignoring the laughter that spread through the schoolyard like a bad wind, he pushed himself to his feet. Mac and Riley ran to his side, their eyes angry and frightened at the same time.

At that moment something drew Steele's eyes to the library windows on the second floor. There, framed against the glass, was a slim dark figure. Steele felt himself flush. He recognized the figure.

It was Maddie Fey, and she had seen Dirk knock him sprawling.

His encounter with Dirk and the Jerks did nothing to weaken Steele's resolve to get to his guitar lesson. Just before the final school buzzer sounded, he excused himself, grabbed his jacket from his locker, and dashed home. He collected his guitar case from the front hall and ran all the way to Mrs. Fret's studio. He breathed easier after he handed her the envelope.

That day Steele played like he'd never played before. At times, he felt as if his fingers were acting on their own. It was pure magic, and for a little while, he forgot all of his troubles.

"You've been practising." The guitar teacher beamed at him when the lesson came to an end. "That was excellent, Steele."

Steele couldn't hide the grin that stayed plastered to his face as he left the studio and rode the elevator to the ground floor. He felt good, as if he'd done something grand. He looked around but didn't spot the bully anywhere outside Mrs. Fret's studio. But he decided to take the long way home, just to be on the safe side. As he hurried along the street, he peeled half the wrapper off a chocolate bar and bit into it, feeling immensely pleased with himself at avoiding Dirk. In fact, he was so pleased that he let his mind wander, and before he knew it, he found himself at the bottom of the ravine, on the path beside Taddle Pond. He stopped short, alarmed that he hadn't checked the dark areas of the park.

He was just about to retrace his steps to where the path joined Wychwood Park when he heard a menacing voice coming from what seemed to be the ground ahead.

Come here, little boy! Down into my dark place!

At the same time, he heard another sound behind him at the top of the ravine—a sound like metal wheels bumping over the rough ground. Steele spun around and saw an old man limping down the path toward him, pushing a rattling, beat-up shopping cart. For a split second, he was struck by an acute sense of *déjà vu*. Perhaps it was the sound of one of the front wheels wobbling uncontrollably that brought on the feeling, but for the life of him he couldn't remember where he had seen the old man before. What was he doing here? He looked like one of the homeless people Steele saw along the streets downtown—the poor wild-eyed souls who frightened him out of his skin. But they never came into Wychwood Park. Never!

RUN! Steele wanted to obey the voice in his mind, but fear held him frozen in his tracks. He watched in horror as the man hobbled purposefully toward him.

Suddenly several shadows darted from among the thick stands of trees flanking the footpath and launched themselves at the noisy shopping cart, knocking it over onto its side. Out tumbled cans, bottles, and shopping bags that apparently held the sum of the old man's possessions.

"Go! Hooligans!" shouted the old man, flailing his arms at the shadows. His voice was harsh, the words slurred.

But the shadows didn't turn and flee in fear; they had voices, and they laughed horribly before they turned on the old man. It happened so abruptly, all Steele saw was a blur. He heard the muffled crunch of glass breaking as a body fell to the ground on top of the cans and bottles. Then, like black ghosts, more shadows burst from among the trees and raised long black arms over their heads, then brought them down on the fallen figure.

"We don't want your kind around here," hissed one of the shadows, in a voice Steele knew all too well. "You're dirty and you smell like you wet your pants."

Dirk.

"Smelly old man," echoed the Jerks. "We're going to teach you a lesson you won't forget."

Do something! screamed a voice in Steele's mind.

"STOP!" he shouted, praying that his voice would carry outside the mesh fence and into the houses on the far side of the street surrounding the pond. But he wasn't too hopeful. It wasn't as if it were the middle of summer and windows were open. But someone coming home from work might hear and come to investigate. He shouted again and again. "STOP! STOP!"

The Jerks halted their wicked business and rose, becoming as still as the surrounding trees. Then, catching sight of Steele in the weak light near the fountain, they left the old man and moved swiftly toward him. Steele turned and ran, nervously stuffing the rest of his chocolate bar into his mouth and chomping furiously. The Jerks followed, coming faster. He had almost made it to the top of the ravine when they caught him.

One snatched the guitar case out of Steele's grip. The others grabbed his arms and dragged him back down into the ravine, to the fountain where Dirk waited.

"Bring the liar to me," said Dirk.

The Jerks pushed Steele forward; he fell in a heap at Dirk's feet.

"Get up!"

"Yeah, liar, get up," echoed the Jerks as if they shared a brain.

Steele got up slowly. *Don't show them you're afraid,* he commanded himself. *Starting now, stand up to them.*

"Do you know what I do to liars?"

Steele forced himself to meet the bigger boy's eyes. He shrugged. Then, in a flash, he leaned close to Dirk and—*blauk!*—he barfed the chewed-up chocolate bar all over the front of the bully's pants.

Dirk screeched, dropping the bat and sucking in his gut as if that would help.

Even though he was afraid, Steele couldn't help grinning.

The fist caught him on the side of his head just above his left ear, jolting him sideways and sending him sprawling. He groaned, sitting up and pressing his hand against his temple. Through stinging eyes he saw Dirk crouching over him, his hands on his knees.

"You dirty little scumbag. When I'm finished with you, you're going to wish you were dead."

Dirk was shaking uncontrollably, the veins on his forehead and neck swollen as thick as night crawlers. Steele stared at the pulsing veins, fascinated, thinking they were about to erupt through Dirk's skin.

"You're going to die, liar," chorused the Jerks, taking turns kicking at Steele.

"I'm not scared of you," said Steele, fending off the kicks and struggling to rise. "Cowards!"

"Ha, ha, ha!" laughed the Jerks.

"Shut up!" snapped Dirk, grabbing his bat and swinging it viciously.

Steele ducked as the bat whizzed past his head, the wind from it ruffling his hair. It took a second or two before he heard the sound of something cracking into splinters, and realized that the bully hadn't swung at him after all. He had done something much worse.

The bat had gone clean through the guitar case and smashed his guitar. Steele's stomached lurched. *Not my guitar!*

"LEAVE THE BOY! GO!" The command came from the darkness behind Steele. The words were clear, cold, and threatening.

At first, Steele thought it was the old man. But the voice was different—stronger—no trace of slurred speech now. He froze. *The Prince of Darkness!* No, no! This was a different voice—hard, yes, angry, yes, but not evil like the voice he had heard in the ground.

The bullies also froze, wary. They scanned the park for the slightest movement. Then Dirk spat on the ground, his eyes glued on something near the Wytch fountain.

"Clear off!" he snarled. "Mind your own business."

Steele wanted to turn around and see who was back there, but he had to keep his attention on the gang.

Suddenly, Dirk uttered a shrill scream. His lethal baseball bat leaped from his hand as if it had come alive, hitting the ground with a dull *thud* near Steele's feet. For a second, Dirk stared at his hand as if the bat had bitten off one of his fingers. Then, as his eyes switched to the bat, he quailed in terror, his eyeballs rolling back in his head. His high-pitched screeches filled the air and reverberated off the trees. Then he turned and fled toward Wychwood Avenue.

It happened so fast, the Jerks didn't have time to react. They stopped dead, staring after Dirk until he disappeared from sight, their mouths hanging open in disbelief. Steele thought they looked as if someone had taken a pair of scissors and cut black holes in their ghastly grey faces.

For a moment, Steele was dumbstruck. He looked about to see who had frightened the bully, but no one was there. The old man had disappeared—there was no sign of him or his rickety shopping cart. Even the cans and bottles were gone. Besides, thought Steele, the voice hadn't been the old man's.

Steele didn't know what to make of it. Except for him and the Jerks, the park was deserted. He acted quickly, instinctively, knowing that the Jerks were confused and at their most vulnerable without their, until now, fearless leader.

"It was the Wytch!" he whispered, opening his eyes wide to show the whites.

"Shut up!" snarled one of the Jerks, lashing out with fists clenched. "Just shut up!"

Steele sidestepped neatly. "Once you've seen her, you're marked. She'll hunt you to the ends of the earth. Just wait and see, Dirk's going to be next!"

The Jerks exchanged glances. Steele could see that they were uncertain whether to continue beating him up, or follow Dirk's example and hightail it out of the park.

"If you don't believe me, come on, I'll show you where she hides." Steele was enjoying himself now.

"Don't listen to him!" spat one of the Jerks.

"He's crazy!" cried another.

But they backed away.

"Don't go!" begged Steele, trying to control the laughter lurking in his throat. He grabbed one of the Jerk's arms. "Please! I'm scared. Don't make me go through the park alone. I saw the bones." He shuddered. "Soon Dirk's will be there too. There are mounds and mounds of bones. You can still see the blood."

The Jerks' faces were now so pasty they looked like wraiths. Without another word, they turned and took off like mad. One of them stopped to make a grab for Dirk's baseball bat, but thought better of it and ran after his buddies, his voice cracking as he called out to them to wait for him. They didn't stop running until they reached Christie Street.

The sight of his busted guitar case drove away any satisfaction Steele felt over scaring the Jerks with stories of the Wytch. Heartsick, he dropped to his knees on the cold, damp ground and gently gathered up the smashed case and splintered pieces of guitar.

"I hate him!" he whispered, blinking away the tears that formed in his eyes as he walked slowly toward number six Wychwood Park, cradling the shattered guitar like a baby in his arms. "I wish the Wytch *would* get Dirk!"

The Wardens

The Mages sealed the enemy in casings for their long journey, and used magic to ward the seals. The pods were programmed with the coordinates of the condensed fire clouds, and then launched.

By imprisoning the Tsilihin in the fiery core of the distant infant planet, and eliminating the greatest menace ever to darken the skies over Arjella, the Mages believed that they were performing a service for all sentient life forms in the universe. But they also realized that they knew virtually nothing about the alien terrorists, despite having fought them for hundreds of years. So, to ensure that the creatures never escaped, we were sent to accompany them and to watch over their molten tombs until the end of time.

We are wardens, guardians of fire.

—Excerpt from *The Wardens' Logs*

Chapter Six

Bad News

That Friday, the day after the spooky events in Wychwood Park, Dirk didn't show up for school. When Steele learned of the bully's absence, he was so relieved he felt dizzy, as if the ground were spinning beneath his feet. He had lain awake most of the night, feeling sorry for himself and dreading the thought of running into Dirk at school in the morning. Something in the park had scared the bully half to death. Steele had no idea what that something was, but he was sure that Dirk would think Steele had something to do with it. He had seriously considered skipping school, pretending to be sick. But in the end, he decided that he couldn't let his fear keep him home.

During recess, the Jerks were huddled together on their undisputed turf by the wire mesh fence, arguing in harsh whispers and spitting on the partially frozen ground. Despite Dirk's obvious absence, the other students in the playground, including Steele, Riley, and Mac, kept a safe distance away from the bullies.

Steele was still angry at the loss of his guitar and kept sending withering glances at the Jerks. Then he noticed something odd. Every time he looked in their direction, they turned away quickly, as if the gang didn't want him to know they had been staring at him. It was very weird.

Mac too noticed the way the Jerks kept glancing at Steele, and he couldn't resist making an issue of their strange behaviour. "Evil eye! Begone!" he cried, making a cross with his fingers and pointing it at Steele.

"I wish you'd been there," said Steele, after he told Mac and Riley what had happened in Wychwood Park. "Dirk was screeching like a baby. Then he threw his bat practically at my feet and took off like I had morphed into the Hulk or something."

"But," said Riley, a puzzled look spreading over her face, "what I don't understand is, if *you* didn't freak him out, what did?"

Steele shrugged. "I don't know. There was a voice behind me—a horrible, cold voice—" He lowered his own to a whisper. "I told the Jerks that it was the Wytch, just to scare them, but . . ."

"But what?" Mac asked loudly.

"Shh," said Steele. Then he whispered, "I think it really *was* the Wytch."

"Phuff!" spluttered Mac contemptuously. "Are you saying the Wytch scared Dirk? You're not serious?"

"Shut up and listen," snapped Steele. "When I looked around I swear there was no one there. As crazy as it sounds . . ."

"Aren't you forgetting the old man with the shopping cart?" Riley reminded him.

Steele thought about the old man. Then he shook his head emphatically. "No! He was gone. Even the shopping cart and all the junk that fell out of it were gone. And the old man's voice was different. He sounded drunk. Besides, it couldn't have been him. He was no match for them. They were beating the stuffing out of him when I tried to help him."

"Let me get this straight," said Mac. "Something scared Dirk so badly he ran away. And the only people in the park at the time were you, him, and the Jerks."

Steele nodded.

"Duh! You don't have to be Einstein to figure out that it had to be you."

"Get real, Mac. If you were as big and fat as Dirk, would you be scared of me?"

"Hmm," said Mac. "You've got a point. But the Wytch? Steele, do you realize how freaky you're sounding?"

"There must have been someone else in the park," said Riley quietly. "Someone you didn't notice."

The three friends spent the rest of recess in a heated debate over who or what, besides the old man with the shopping cart, could have scared Dirk half to death. But when the buzzer called them back to class, they were no closer to coming up with an answer than they had been when recess began. They agreed to meet at Steele's house at ten the following morning to investigate the Wytch fountain in the daylight and search for clues to help them solve the mystery of Dirk's panicked flight from the park and the menacing voice Steele had heard coming from the ground.

It was only as he was walking home that Steele suddenly realized that Dirk wasn't the only one who hadn't shown up for school. Maddie Fey had also been absent.

"That's strange," he muttered thoughtfully. Then his mood lightened. "Maybe she's not coming back."

///\\\

His father was working late, so Steele spent a quiet Friday evening playing backgammon with his grandmother. GM appeared not to notice him or the board; she smiled her gentle smile and looked out the window at something far off in the night sky, her delicate fingers feeding the continuous, twisted strands of yarn to the restless knitting needles. When it was her turn, Steele threw the dice and moved her red game pieces on the board. Out of the corner of his eye, he caught flashes of colour as Pyrus streaked across the floor to disappear under a chair or a chest of drawers.

By the time the French carriage clock on the mantel struck eleven, Steele could barely keep his eyes open. He crawled about the floor hunting for Pyrus, and finally cornered and caught the salamander.

"Good night, GM," he said, kissing her cheek.

He was halfway up the stairs when he heard the front door creak open, and then his father called out to him.

"Come into the den, Steele! I want to talk to you." He sounded angry.

Steele felt knots forming in his stomach. *He found the bank statement under my mattress.* Steele couldn't talk with his father now; he needed time to think of what to say to him. But he was trapped.

Slowly, he descended the stairs and made his way to the den. His father was standing in the middle of the room, the TV remote in his hand. He glanced at Steele. Steele noticed the haunted look in his father's eyes and the deep lines etched into his brow, and he felt responsible, as if he had physically put them there. *What am I going to tell him?* But he needn't have worried. His father seemed more interested in the late-night news than in discussing Steele's bank statement.

"Here we are," he said. "There's something that I think you should see."

Steele glanced at the screen, and his mouth dropped open in shocked disbelief. Pyrus twisted out of his grasp and shot toward a corner, vanishing halfway there. Steele didn't notice; his eyes were on the woman standing in front of the television cameras, crying and pleading. She was short and stout. Her resemblance to an overweight bulldog was uncanny. Her nose and cheeks were blotchy from crying, but Steele knew who she was. It was Dirk's mother.

The news anchor cut in: *The disappearance of Dirk Humphries has panicked residents in and around the St. Clair/ Bathurst area. Police are stymied, admitting they have no leads at this time. They are asking for your help. If you have any information, contact the Metro Police. Stay tuned for the latest developments in the Dirk Humphries and Ryan Massey disappearances after the national news tonight at eleven. Coming up next, sports with Peter Bridge.*

"Isn't that the boy you were having trouble with two years ago?" asked his father, switching off the television.

Too stunned to speak, Steele could only nod.

His father placed his hand on Steele's shoulder. "I'm sorry, son. I was worried that you'd see the news about Dirk before I could get home. I didn't want you to be alone."

"He—he wasn't at school today, but nobody thought—" Steele stopped, his mind reeling. *Oh my God!* he thought. *Yesterday . . . in the park. Oh, please, don't say he disappeared yesterday.* "When—?" He almost choked on the question.

His father sank onto the sofa and let his head fall back against the cushions. When he spoke, his voice cracked from weariness. "We're still trying to pin down the time. His mother said he disappeared sometime last night. She is, of course, upset, and wasn't very coherent. When I spoke with her, she seemed confused. But I had the feeling she was holding something back."

Steele shivered despite the warmth of the room. That the strange doings in the park yesterday might be tied to Dirk's disappearance was too horrible for words. The bully was gone, but ironically, after wishing for two years that he'd disappear, Steele felt bad. And the evil that Steele had sensed shortly after Ryan Massey disappeared seemed much closer now.

"I was looking forward to doing something together tomorrow," said his father. "But I have to go in to work early. I'll make it up to you, though—I promise."

"It's OK, Dad. It's not your fault." For no reason at all, Steele felt like crying.

His father closed his eyes, but opened them immediately and leaned forward. "This is a terrible business. I want you to keep your eyes open, son. Be especially careful. And keep the doors locked when you and GM are here alone." He ran his fingers through his short dark hair. Then he rose wearily. "Come on. Let's go to bed now. If you're up early, we'll have breakfast together."

Like a sleepwalker, Steele climbed the stairs, his father's strong arm around his shoulders the only thing preventing him from breaking down. *They got Dirk!* He didn't know who *they* were, but he felt sick as the words he had said to the Jerks yesterday evening replayed like a scratched CD in his ears. *Dirk's next! Dirk's next! Dirk's next!*

The Journey

We followed the pods through space, as they moved like silent torpedoes among stars and swirling nebulae, planets, and their moons. We eluded dazzling fireballs and icy, luminous comets that dwarfed our planet. We sailed past the legendary Orpheus, a silent, glowing red giant, a thousand times larger than the infant planet's star. We gazed in wonder at stars that had collapsed and shrunk into white dwarfs. We marvelled at the exquisite beauty of the Eagle nebula as it mushroomed and blossomed, protostars forming amongst colourful columns of gas and dust. For many of us, it was our first sighting of a star maker.

We followed the pods for untold thousands of light years before we reached Oort, a giant cloud formed from over three trillion comets. From Oort, our journey to the condensed bits of fire clouds that in approximately six billion years would form the third planet from the new star was almost over.

—Excerpt from *The Wardens' Logs*

Chapter Seven

Super Sleuths

Pyrus's long tongue flicked Steele's nose and woke him up the next morning. Glancing at the clock on his bedside table, Steele groaned, disappointed that he had overslept and missed breakfast with his father. He dressed quickly, placed Pyrus on his shoulder, and went downstairs. It was nine-thirty. He had chores to do before Mac and Riley arrived, but first he needed to talk with his grandmother.

"You'll never guess who's gone missing," he said and waited, giving her time to digest the news. "Dirk. Remember all the times I wished that he'd die? Well, now he's disappeared, maybe even dead. Someone is taking kids, GM, and everyone's scared. I've got a horrible feeling that whoever it is is coming for me."

GM treated him in her usual manner, as if he didn't exist. Steele didn't mind. He listened to the soft *click! clack!* of her knitting needles and felt comforted. For a few moments he forgot about Ryan and Dirk and the other missing kids. He forgot his fear that something evil was stalking him, and found himself thinking of happier times. He wished he could stay with GM, like this, a while longer.

"Company's coming," he said, getting up reluctantly. "Mac and Riley will be here soon."

Before leaving the room, he turned on the radio and rolled up GM's knitting. Then he went to the kitchen, emptied the dishwasher, cleaned Pyrus's cage, and filled a dish with fresh water. Camouflaged to match the blue sky, Pyrus perched on the windowsill, his green, unblinking eyes following Steele's every move.

By ten o'clock, Steele had finished his chores and was waiting anxiously by the front door for Mac and Riley. Mac arrived first. Steele took one look at Mac's ashen face and knew that he had heard the news about Dirk.

"It's true, isn't it?" Mac asked.

Steele nodded. "Dad told me last night. And it was on TV."

Mac brushed his hand over his face. "I still can't believe it. Who'd have thought Dirk the Jer— I mean . . . Oh shoot! I didn't mean . . ." His snow-white face turned beet red.

They stood in the doorway, strangely ill at ease and at a loss for words. They had feared and hated the bully for two years and had always called him Dirk the Jerk. Now, though, with Dirk missing, it seemed wrong to call him that.

"Don't feel bad, Mac. I feel terrible too, about what happened to Dirk, but I still hate him." He punched Mac's shoulder lightly. "And just because he's disappeared doesn't mean he's stopped being a jerk."

Mac grinned sheepishly. "I guess. But it's sort of confusing, isn't it. I feel that I'm supposed to like him now, and say kind things about him."

Steele tugged on his arm. "Come in. GM will want to see you. After, come to the kitchen. I'm getting stuff for the park."

Mac slipped out of his jacket and threw it on a bench near the door. As they passed the living room, he poked his head through the doorway.

"Hi, GM."

Steele's grandmother occupied the rocking chair by the window. She was rocking evenly back and forth, staring outside at something an immeasurable distance beyond the park, her knitting needles locked in their perpetual rhythm.

GM smiled sweetly, but acknowledged neither Mac nor his greeting. Unfazed, Mac pulled up a chair. Steele continued on to the kitchen, listening as Mac conducted a one-sided, stream-of-consciousness conversation with GM as if it were the most natural thing in the world.

"Steele probably told you about Dirk. Funny, but it didn't seem real before . . . you know . . . Ryan Massey and those American kids missing. But now it's someone from school. And that's really scary. On the way here, it came on the news and my dad had to stop the car. He just sat there, gripping the steering wheel and staring at me with this strange look on his face. I thought he was having a heart attack. Then he said, 'My God! That could have been you.' I don't think he and Mom are going to let me go to school until they find the missing kids. But what I don't understand is, why him? I mean, think about it for a second. If you were a kidnapper, GM, would you take Dirk? Of course you wouldn't! Nobody would. At least, nobody sane!"

He sat in silence for a few more minutes, watching GM's fingers on the knitting needles. Then he excused himself politely and joined Steele in the kitchen.

"She's cool!" he remarked, slumping into a chair and examining stuff in the open toolbox on the table. "Is she OK, Steele? I mean, is she eating enough, or . . . ?"

Steele was busy inserting batteries into a flashlight. He looked at his friend sharply. "Or what?"

"Well, I mean—" Mac was clearly uncomfortable. "It's just that she looks awfully . . . small."

Steele dropped the flashlight.

"What is it?" asked Mac.

"I knew it!" said Steele. "I tried to tell Dad she was shrinking. She really is, isn't she?"

"I know a way to find out!" said Mac. "We can make a mark on the back of her chair where the top of her head is. Next Saturday we'll make another mark."

"That's good!" said Steele, wishing he had thought of it first. "I'll go get some chalk. Wait here and let Riley in."

Steele raced up the stairs to his bedroom, grabbed a piece of yellow chalk from a box on the desk, and sped downstairs. In the living room, he crept up behind his grandmother and peered over the top of the rocking chair. Then he made a yellow chalk mark on the back of the chair just above her head.

Back in the kitchen, Steele felt better about his grandmother. Soon he'd know for sure if she was shrinking. And, if his and Mac's suspicions were true, he'd have proof to show his father—the chalk marks.

Mac prowled about the kitchen, searching for Pyrus among the pots and pans hanging from hooks over his head and in the collection of Staffordshire animals on the open shelves of the ancient Welsh dresser standing against one of the kitchen walls. But he couldn't spot the elusive salamander. Steele watched him and smiled to himself. No wonder Mac couldn't find Pyrus; the salamander was glued to the leg of Steele's black jeans, camouflaged as black as soot.

Mac delighted in teasing the salamander; he laughed uproariously when the ridges on its spine bristled angrily. Pyrus often retaliated by creeping close to the boy and flicking his long tongue at Mac's face and neck at unexpected moments, causing Mac to jump a foot into the air. Steele believed that Pyrus secretly enjoyed his adversarial relationship with Mac. Once, after one of his tongue-flicking assaults, Steele could have sworn that the salamander's mouth was carved upward in a broad grin.

When the doorbell chimed, Mac ran to let Riley in.

"I never knew GM was so tiny," observed Riley thoughtfully, tossing her backpack onto one of the kitchen chairs and reaching down to lift Pyrus from Steele's leg. "If I didn't know better, I'd think she was shrinking."

Then she noticed Steele and Mac staring at her incredulously. "What? Why are you staring at me like that?" She glanced quickly down at her clothes as if to make sure she was actually wearing any. "What?" she demanded.

"You think GM's shrinking too," said Steele. "Mac said exactly the same thing."

"So what? It's only natural to think GM's getting smaller. After all, we're growing taller."

Steele slapped his forehead. "I can't believe I didn't think of that." He caught Mac's eye. "It makes sense."

"Where's your dad?" Riley asked, jumping to a new subject.

"Working. Metro's been on alert since Ryan Massey disappeared. It's going to be worse now, with Dirk missing."

Riley burst out laughing. "Dirk's missing? You're joking! Who'd want to nab Dirk?" She stopped laughing when she saw the serious look on Steele's face. "You are kidding, aren't you?"

"I'm not kidding, Riley. He disappeared yesterday," said Steele. "I'm sorry. I thought you knew."

Riley looked at Mac in horror. "You said you wished he'd disappear." She dropped onto a chair and buried her face in her hands.

Mac sighed. "I didn't mean it. I was angry because he was making fun of *you*."

"Don't cry, Riley," said Steele. "My dad'll catch whoever's doing this."

Riley rubbed her eyes and sniffled. "I'm scared."

Steele sat down and patted her hand awkwardly. "I'm scared too. I bet even Dad's scared."

Mac paced the kitchen floor like a restless tiger. Pausing at the small television on the counter, he flicked it on, then turned to the others. "The big question is, who's abducting kids, and why?"

"My dad thinks it's a cult," said Riley. "He thinks they're brainwashing the kids."

Mac opened the refrigerator and stared inside. "To do what?" he asked, his voice muffled. Since it wasn't his idea, he didn't think much of it.

"Maybe it's a criminal cult," said Steele. "Maybe they're brainwashing the kids to be terrorists, or slaves, or thieves, or drug mules. What I don't understand is, if that's the case, why haven't they turned up?"

"Unless they're moved somewhere else, like to another country," reasoned Riley.

Steele was silent. When he finally spoke, the words were so soft that Riley had to strain to hear, and Mac had to remove his head from inside the refrigerator.

"What if they're connected?" Steele asked.

The three companions stared at each other, watching the blood drain from one another's faces.

"Do you think . . . ?" Riley and Mac spoke at the same time, their voices trailing off.

"They're connected," breathed Steele, this time with absolutely certainty.

"Listen!" said Mac. "We know that two girls disappeared from that place called Libertyville. Where is that, anyway?"

Steele got out the atlas and searched the index. Then he flipped to the proper page. "It's near Chicago." He looked at Riley. "That boy you told us about at school—didn't he disappear in Chicago?"

"David Draken. Yeah, that's right."

"Maybe kids are disappearing in other cities besides Toronto and Chicago," said Riley.

Steele slammed his fist down on the kitchen table, startling his friends. "Excellent thinking, Riley. I can't believe I never thought of that before. . . ."

"This is serious stuff, guys," said Mac. "We've got to be sure of our facts before we go telling your father that there's a connection between the missing kids in Chicago, and Ryan and Dirk. How are we going to prove it?"

Riley jumped out of the chair. "I know! Come on, Steele. Let's go use your computer and get information on the missing American kids, and we can also check if kids in other cities are missing."

Steele was tempted. "No," he said. "We've got our own mystery to solve about those voices. Let's check out the park first, in the daylight. Then we can surf the Net."

Anxious and excited at the same time, they stuffed energy bars, soft drinks, and pieces of Turkish delight into their backpacks and left the house.

On the television screen, the news anchor peered into the

deserted kitchen and recapped the lead story: *In Toronto this morning, a citywide search is underway for thirteen-year-old Dirk Humphries who disappeared from his home in the St. Clair/Bathurst area without a trace sometime after ten p.m. Thursday night. Police are conducting door-to-door interviews in the boy's neighbourhood in hopes that someone saw Dirk after he left, or was taken from, his home. Dirk Humphries' disappearance follows on the heels of another unsolved disappearance of a Toronto boy. Ryan Massey, the eleven-year-old Riverdale boy, mysteriously vanished outside his home on November fifth. Police have turned up no leads in either case.*

Steele and his companions slid down the ravine toward Taddle Pond, their voices high with a combination of fear and exhilaration. It was a crisp, clear day. The winter sun filled Wychwood Park with brilliant whiteness that turned Mac's hair silver and drove away the shadows. The wooden benches, the birch trees, the pond, and the fountain appeared as sharp and clear as if seen through binoculars, and not at all the vague, distorted shapes they had seemed in the black of night.

"OK," said Riley when she reached the bottom of the ravine. "It might help if we knew where everybody was Thursday night."

Steele thought for a moment. Then he walked over to the edge of the pond and turned toward the Wytch. "I was about here. The old man was behind me, coming down the ravine from the west. Dirk and the Jerks were hiding in the trees back there near the old man. I didn't see them when I came down the path, so they must have come along behind me."

"What about the voice that scared Dirk?" asked Riley.

"Over there," said Steele, pointing east toward the fountain.

"Is this where you heard the voices in the ground?" Mac dropped to his haunches near the shore of the pond, between Steele and the Wytch.

"A bit farther. Keep going. Closer to the fountain. There. Stop."

Mac looked down. The path was strewn with matted, decomposing leaves. Quickly, he dug at the partly frozen ground, brushing the leaves aside and scraping away hard mud caked on the path. Underneath the leaves and mud was a rusted iron grate covering a concrete drain.

"Look!" he shouted.

Steele and Riley rushed to the spot and crouched over the grate, which was rectangular, and measured about two feet long by one foot wide. They squinted through the holes into the darkness. Then they stretched out on the ground and pressed the sides of their faces against the cold iron. They held their breaths and listened. Nothing.

Steele removed the flashlight from his backpack, knelt on the ground, and shone it between the square holes in the grate, but the light wasn't powerful enough to illuminate more than a couple of feet down. Beyond the light, it was as black as the inside of a closed coffin. Disappointed, Steele flicked the light off and shoved the flashlight into his jacket pocket.

Frustrated, Mac sprang to his feet and picked up a long whip-like branch that had broken off one of the trees. He walked about, using his switch to swat at dead flowers and stalks of crisp grass. Steele and Riley set to work trying to pry the metal grate off its concrete base using Steele's screwdriver as a crowbar.

"It's not fastened down," complained Riley, red-faced from exertion. "Why won't it move?"

"It's too heavy," muttered Steele, grunting as he wedged the screwdriver under the grate and pushed down on it with all of his strength. The grate wouldn't budge.

They listened again with their ears pressed against the frosty metal, but they heard nothing.

Bored with lopping off the heads of dead flowers, Mac bent forward and wandered cautiously among the trees, scouring the ground for clues. He was just about to give up the search when he saw faint marks on the soggy ground beside the pond between the grate and the Wytch.

"What have we got here?" he said, dropping onto his knees. He caught the fingers of his glove in his teeth and pulled his hand free. Then he reached down and traced his finger along the nearest mark.

Nearby, Steele was listening intently, his ear glued to the grate, as Riley dropped a stone into the drain. He waited to hear the *plop* of it hitting water. He shivered involuntarily.

"What?"

Steele shook his head. "Nothing. It's like the stone's still falling. I didn't hear it hit bottom."

"Freaky!"

Confounded, the pair stood and stared at the metal grate.

"Hey! I found something," Mac shouted triumphantly.

They hurried over and knelt on the ground beside Mac.

"The old man's shopping cart," said Steele, staring at the narrow wheel tracks.

"You said the old man was back there." Mac pointed away from the fountain, past the grate. "But the wheel tracks show he was here."

Steele closed his eyes and pictured the old man pushing his dilapidated shopping cart down the dirt path. Then he saw the shadowy figures of Dirk and the Jerks detach themselves from the trees and fly at the old man, toppling the cart and then knocking the old man down. Steele opened his eyes.

"He'd have had to go by me, and he didn't. Besides, the cart rattled. I'd have heard it."

"Not necessarily," said Riley. "If Dirk and the Jerks were coming after you, you might have been too focused on them to notice what the old man was doing."

Mac agreed. "When you heard the voice, you thought it was the old man. That's what you said. When you looked for him, he was gone, and so was the shopping cart and all the junk that fell out of it."

"Don't you see," continued Riley. "If you didn't hear the old man picking up all those bottles and cans, or the sound of the cart wheeling away, how can you be so sure he didn't go past you?"

Steele shook his head vehemently. "You still don't get it," he said. "If he had picked up the junk, I would have heard the noise. But he didn't. There wasn't time."

"What are you saying?" asked Mac.

"I'm not sure," answered Steele. "I don't know how he did it, but he just seemed to vanish, and so did the shopping cart and all the junk."

"Just like the missing kids," whispered Riley.

They stared at the tracks in silence. And then, suddenly realizing he was kneeling on the wet ground, Steele stood.

"Come on," he said. "Let's check out the fountain."

He and Riley walked a few feet over to the edge of the pond, near the stone basin. Riley jumped over the water into the basin, but Steele stopped and gazed at the Wytch. She was cold and aloof, as unfeeling as the dark green stone from which she had been sculpted. *She's just a statue, a chunk of rock,* Steele told himself. He felt silly for telling Mac and Riley that the Wytch had scared Dirk. He looked at Riley.

"This was a stupid idea," he said, his face burning, but not from the cold. "Let's go back to the house." He turned and his eyes fell on Mac, who was on his hands and knees over the grate, his body as rigidly intent as that of a hunting dog marking game for a gunner.

"What's wrong?" he asked, rushing to Mac's side. "What is it?"

Riley followed him. "I'm freezing," she said, gripping Steele's shoulder as she lowered herself to the ground.

"Be quiet!" hissed Mac.

Steele waited, eyes and ears straining. Just when Steele felt he couldn't stand the suspense or the cold any longer, Mac dropped back to sit on his heels and reached for the switch that he had abandoned on the ground.

"There's something down there all right," he whispered, as if he were only now beginning to believe Steele's strange story about the voices. "I heard it."

Steele studied his friend's face to reassure himself that Mac wasn't putting him on. But Mac looked truly astonished.

"I'm serious," whispered Mac. "I heard something."

"I believe you," said Steele. "Was it a voice?"

"What did it say?" asked Riley.

Mac frowned. "I think it was a voice, but I couldn't hear what it said. It was too faint."

They listened for a long time as the cold air stiffened their wet jeans and set their teeth chattering. Mac poked the switch through one of the holes in the grate, jiggling it about. Suddenly he tensed, staring in horror as the switch slowly began to slip from his hand.

"Aiii! Help!" he cried, sitting back and bracing his heels against the edge of the grate.

"What?" whispered Steele.

Mac wrestled with the switch, using both hands to hold onto it. "Something's pulling on the other end," he breathed. "Quick! Take a look!"

Steele thought Mac looked like a fisherman trying to reel in a whale. He got out his flashlight and shone it into the drain. Then he and Riley leaned over the grate and peered through the grid.

"Maybe it's caught on something," suggested Steele, focusing the light on the switch and following it with his eyes.

Then a scream burst from Riley's throat.

Steele saw a face glowing in the light and coming swiftly up out of the darkness. It was the most horrible face he had ever seen. Its eyes were as red as blood and in its snarling open mouth he saw vampire fangs more than an inch long and as sharp as the point of a carving knife. The skin on the hideous face was engraved with disgusting markings or tattoos, and covered with scars, as if the flesh had been flayed off with a whip and was in the early stages of regeneration. The sudden appearance of the grotesque face scared Steele and Riley, but it was the crazed glaze in its cold, lidless eyes that sent them streaking through the park toward Steele's house, screaming at the top of their lungs.

Mac didn't wait to find out what had frightened his friends. Casting terrified glances over his shoulder as he ran after them, he shouted, "Wait for me!"

The Arrival

Leaving the confined space of our craft for the molten core of our new home was indescribably exhilarating. We were delirious, wild with excitement. For hours, we chased our tails and each other through the pristine fire, gulping down great licking swirls of liquid flames.

Over time, the outer reaches of the burning ball of fire cooled and formed a thin, brittle crust that wrapped itself about the molten lava core. The fire pushed the crust outward and a new crust formed, and so the process continued until the planet's outer crust hardened to contain the molten lava. Millennia passed, and still the planet continued to evolve. The power of the bubbling liquid pressed its cooled dross against the crust, compacting it into solid ultrabasic materials to form its mantle, an almost impenetrable shield between the burning core and the planet's crust.

A billion years would pass before we realized that we were not alone in the fire. Something was in here with us. Its name was Death.

—Excerpt from *The Wardens' Logs*

Chapter Eight

The Note

Shaking from fear and from the chill, the three companions huddled about the fireplace in Steele's living room, their frozen hands wrapped about hot mugs of steaming tea. Steele turned off the radio and moved his grandmother's chair and knitting close to the fireplace, so she wouldn't feel left out. He didn't expect GM to have shrunk while they were in the park, but he couldn't help checking to see if there was a space between the chalk mark and the top of her head.

As they warmed up, they told her about the scary face in the grate in Wychwood Park.

"It was the most horrible monster!" exclaimed Riley. "Its eyes were red like burning coals. I almost died when they looked right at me."

"Its face was worse," said Steele, his mouth turning down in disgust. "It was all sliced and bleeding, and covered with weird markings."

GM stared into the fireplace and smiled at something beyond the burning logs. She didn't react as Steele and his friends shared their adventure with her. She continued to knit without dropping a stitch, as though she hadn't heard a single word they said.

Mac, who hadn't actually seen the monster in the grate, sulked and poked at the burning logs with the fire-tongs.

"It's not fair," he complained. "I'm the one who discovered it, but I didn't even get to see it."

"You wouldn't have wanted to, believe me," Riley assured him. She glanced at Steele. "Do you think it was one of the voices you heard in the ground?"

Steele shrugged. Was it? He didn't know. He hadn't told Mac and Riley about the Prince of Darkness because it sounded too crazy. But if there really was such a creature, he couldn't imagine it could look scarier than the creature he'd seen. Its face was now permanently engraved in his mind, like the bloody cuts and marks on its hideous flesh.

"We've got to tell your dad," said Mac. "He'll find out who's down there."

"Are you serious?" said Steele. "If I tell him what we saw in that grate, he'll never let me go near the pond again."

"But what if something terrible happens?" said Riley, worry lines furrowing her brow. "I mean, what if Ryan and Dirk were taken there and locked in an underground chamber or something? Steele, we've got to tell someone."

Steele looked at his grandmother. "What should we do, GM?"

He didn't really expect an answer, so he wasn't disappointed when none came.

But as he stared at the knitting needles, an idea came to him. "Riley's right," he said. "We'd feel really bad if Ryan and Dirk were being held down there and we did nothing. So we've got to tell Dad. But, let's not tell him about the face we saw. Let's just say that we heard a strange noise coming from under the grate. I know my dad. He'll send a team into the drain to investigate."

Mac and Riley nodded in agreement.

After tea, they pulled GM's chair back to its place near the window. Steele picked up her empty mug and carried it to the kitchen.

"What are we going to do now?" asked Mac.

"I don't know about you guys," said Steele, "but I can't get that horrible face out of my mind."

"I know," said Riley. "I'm going to have nightmares for a long time."

"Come on," said Mac. "Let's go use your computer and check out the missing kids."

Minutes later, crowded together at Steele's desk, they logged on to the Internet and began their search for missing children in cities other than Toronto.

"Start with Chicago," suggested Riley. "That's where David Draken disappeared."

"Good idea," said Steele. "And those two Libertyville girls . . ."

They did searches in Chicago and New York. There were a lot more kids missing than Steele had realized. He and Mac and Riley stopped talking and concentrated on taking notes. Except for a short dinner break, they worked throughout Saturday evening, collecting and printing information on missing kids in other cities. Riley's mother picked her and Mac up around nine, and Steele went to spend some time with his grandmother. But after only a few minutes, he felt a great weariness creep over him. He was in bed and asleep long before his father came home.

In his dreams, Steele heard footsteps coming up the stairs to the third floor. He struggled to get out of bed and hide in the closet in the large laundry basket, but he couldn't free himself from the duvet. It tangled about his legs and chest like a living thing. The footsteps stopped outside the door, and then the doorknob turned and the door swung open. The monster from the grate glided slowly into the room and moved toward Steele, its bloody eyes burning into him. He opened his mouth and screamed as the monster bared its long, sharp fangs.

Steele sat bolt upright and stared into the darkness, his heart pounding. He reached out and switched on the lamp, reassuring himself that there was no one else in his room, but it was a long time before he finally went back to sleep.

Mac and Riley were at Steele's on Sunday morning in time for breakfast, which they wolfed down before hurrying back to their research. They avoided the park, still disturbed by the events of the previous day. Instead, they spent the rest of the day locating, printing, and comparing news reports about children who had been reported missing over the past three months.

Steele's father looked in on them when he returned home late in the afternoon. Steele seized the opportunity and told his dad that they had heard something coming from the grate the previous afternoon. Mac and Riley helped him fill in the gaps in the story. His father seemed really interested in what they were telling him. Then he smiled reassuringly.

"It might be important," he said. "I'll look into it and let you know what I find."

After he had gone, Steele and his friends exchanged satisfied looks. Then they went back to work. By the time Steele's father called them to help prepare dinner, they had found over seventy cases that had two important things in common.

While Riley washed lettuce and endives, and Steele chopped tomatoes, cucumbers, avocados, peppers, and other vegetables for the salad, they took turns telling Steele's father about their project. Steele's dad listened patiently, as only a skilled police officer could do.

"We probably missed some," said Mac, seeming pleased when no one appeared to notice he wasn't helping with dinner preparations. "But we found over seventy cases in Canada and the U.S. where the kids disappeared near their homes or schools, just like Ryan and maybe Dirk. And they all disappeared since school started in September."

Steele took over. "We also found that in all of those cases, the kids were abducted right in front of a parent, relative, or friend."

"Which I think is really strange," said Riley, and then added, "almost as strange as the way Mac always manages to weasel out of doing any work."

Mac flashed her a look that would have withered a freshly watered plant. "Why don't you shut up, Riley?"

"Hey! Stop it!" snapped Steele. He turned to his father. "Well?"

They waited silently, their eyes now glued to Steele's father. They tried to read his expression, but his face told them nothing. He looked at them solemnly before speaking.

"A fine piece of work," he said. "All three of you would make excellent detectives."

The kids beamed with pleasure.

"But tell me, how did you come up with the theory that the abductions in different cities might be connected?"

"It was my idea," said Mac, not at all averse to taking the credit.

"Don't listen to Mac, Dad. He's lying," said Steele. "We were talking about whether the four kids we knew about had been abducted by a cult, and wondering why nobody's seen any of them. Then Riley said maybe they were transferred to another city. And then it hit us at the same time. But, as usual, Riley and I did all of the reasoning."

"You have to reason it out," sneered Mac. "Because your brains are so minuscule they can't hold more than a sentence apiece. But my brain is—"

"SHUT UP!" yelled Steele and Riley together.

Steele's father laughed. "It doesn't matter who thought of it, it was clever of you to follow it up with such meticulous research." He turned serious again. "Now, if you promise to keep this to yourselves, I'll tell you something that happened yesterday afternoon."

The kids crossed their hearts and swore on penalty of death that they wouldn't breathe a word to anyone.

"And if I tell, you can cut my tongue out," swore Mac.

"I don't think that will be necessary," said Steele's father. "Your word is good enough for me."

"My word is my bond," agreed Mac solemnly.

"One of the missing kids turned up yesterday in New York City," continued Steele's father.

"No kidding!" gasped Steele. "Where? What? How?"

"Let me finish," said his father. "Her name is Megan Traft. She disappeared in mid-September. It happened practically on her doorstep. Actually, her mother was watching from the porch window—"

"Megan Traft!" interrupted Mac, his pale eyes as round as saucers. "No way!" He appealed to Steele and Riley. "Isn't that one of the kids we read about?"

"Yeah," said Steele. "Riley put her name on our list."

Steele's father nodded. "Her mother said she took her eyes off the girl for only a second, but when she looked back, Megan was gone. Yesterday morning when her father opened the door to get the newspaper, he found Megan sitting on the doorstep, tearing the paper into long strips." He paused.

"What a strange thing to do. Did she say where she'd been?" Steele asked.

"Did she identify her abductors?" Riley jumped in.

"Why was she shredding the newspaper?" Mac said.

Steele's father raised his hand for silence. "Megan doesn't remember anything. Apparently her mind is a blank. Not just about the abduction—she doesn't seem to remember anything at all about her life. She didn't recognize her father and mother. She doesn't know her name. Another strange thing is that although she looks like their Megan, her parents say she's a stranger."

"I don't understand," said Mac.

"She's mean. Nasty," said Steele's father. "According to her mother, Megan was a happy child . . . didn't have a mean bone in her body. Now she's sullen and prone to fits of temper over the most trivial of things."

"What sort of things?" asked Riley.

Steele's father shook his head. "The police gave only one example, and it's a bit bizarre. Apparently, when her mother asked Megan to wash her hands for dinner, she went berserk, broke all the dishes in the cupboard, and tried to bite her own fingers off."

"Eeuw!" exclaimed Riley, shaking her fingers. "How gross!"

"It's horrible!" cried Steele, his own fingers tingling as if they were expressing dismay at the girl's actions. Then an incredible idea formed in his mind. He sank onto a chair at the table and stared at his father. "You said that Megan's mother looked away for a second." He knew from the surprised expression on his father's face that he was on the right track. "I have to reread the articles, but I remember one or more of the other parents said the same thing. Am I right?"

His father nodded proudly. "Good work, son."

"What's this? You might have told me." Mac did not seem pleased.

"I just thought of it," Steele said apologetically.

Steele wondered if all of the parents had been distracted seconds before their children had disappeared. If so, who or what had distracted them?

"Dad, remember when you said you thought Dirk's mother was holding something back? Did you ever find out what it was?"

His father nodded thoughtfully. "Yes. I spoke with her again yesterday morning. What happened, according to her, is even more bizarre than Megan Traft's behaviour. Mrs. Humphries said that Dirk was pretty upset when he got home Thursday night. He went straight to his room and was sleeping soundly when she looked in on her way to bed. She said she heard a gurgling sound coming from his computer and went over to shut it down. Apparently Dirk's got one of those screensavers that's like a tropical aquarium, with an angelfish and sergeant majors and all sorts of other fish swimming about." He took a deep breath.

"What happened then?" asked Steele.

"Mrs. Humphries said that the angelfish suddenly grew into a huge, vicious shark and started attacking the other fish, ripping them apart and eating them alive. She said the blue screen turned red from the blood of the dead fish."

Steele and his friends stared at each other.

"No way!" Steele gasped. "That's crazy! It's impossible."

"Right!" cried Riley. "The fish aren't even real. It's just a computer program."

Steele's father raised his hand and the kids quieted down. "You're right," he said. "It couldn't have happened. Yet, according to Dirk's mother, that's exactly what did happen. A moment later, she looked back at Dirk and he was gone."

"So," said Mac, "Dirk disappeared while his mother was freaking out over the screensaver."

"Yes," said Steele. "Don't you see? Something distracted her, just like in some of the other cases we found."

"Talk about clever," cried Mac. "Someone distracts the parents with something really creepy, while someone else snatches the kids."

Riley looked confused. "Who's doing these things?" she asked. "And how are they doing them?"

"That's the big question," said Steele's father grimly.

Shortly after Mac and Riley left, the phone rang. It was police headquarters.

"Something's come up," said Steele's father, slipping his arms into his overcoat. "It's going to be a long night. If I'm not back before you leave for school, don't forget to lock up." He looked at Steele for a moment. "I'm really proud of you and your friends . . . all the work you did on the missing kids, and discovering what the cases had in common."

Steele smiled with pleasure. "Thanks, Dad."

He locked the door behind his father and went to talk with his grandmother. He switched on the radio and dropped to the floor next to GM's rocking chair. Pyrus seemed to materialize out of thin air, greeting Steele by flicking its long tongue on his knee. Steele tried to grab him, but he wasn't fast enough. His hands grasped at air. As he peered about for the elusive salamander, he remembered that Maddie Fey had been absent on Friday, the day after Dirk disappeared. For some unexplainable reason, her absence troubled him. Then his ears perked up as a woman's voice came on the radio, and he forgot all about Maddie Fey.

A man, who refused to be interviewed, called the police tip line to report seeing a homeless man pushing a shopping cart on Bathurst Street, north of St. Clair Avenue, shortly after two a.m. Friday morning—around the same time thirteen-year-old Dirk Humphries disappeared from his home in that area. The caller was awakened by the sound of wheels clattering on the sidewalk and he got up to investigate, worried about the recent spate of break-ins in the neighbourhood. When he stepped outside, he saw the old man staring at the Humphries house. Police are interviewing several homeless men who match the description given by the neighbour. We'll keep you informed on the latest developments as they happen.

Steele shivered as he stared at the radio. The news about the old man stunned him. In his mind, there was no doubt that it was the same old man who had been in Wychwood Park the night Dirk went missing. But what did it mean? Steele took a deep breath and blew it out loudly.

"It doesn't make sense," he said to his grandmother. "There's no way the old man could have seized Dirk and carried him off in his shopping cart. No way on earth!"

Later, in his room, he couldn't settle down. The details surrounding Dirk's disappearance gnawed at his mind. Finally, he opened his closet door and removed the smashed guitar and case. He still hadn't worked up enough courage to tell his father what Dirk had done. Deep in a secret place in his heart he had hoped that the guitar could be fixed. But as he placed the pieces of split wood on the carpet beside the flattened body, he knew that it was beyond repair. The neck had broken away and the strings were loose and twisted. He placed one hand on the body, steadying it, and made one last attempt to reattach the neck. But it was hopeless.

Sighing heavily, he gathered up the broken pieces and went to replace them in the closet. He heard something slide along the wood inside the hollow body. He peered through the hole, tilting the guitar until he saw a small scrap of white paper, then tipped the guitar over onto its face and gently shook it. The scrap of paper caught on the strings. Steele peeled it loose and, with trembling hands, unfolded it. Inside was a message written in red:

If you value your life, be at the northeast corner of Dalhousie and Shuter at midnight November 25th. Don't be late and don't even think about not showing up! And above all, don't tell anyone!

The note was unsigned.

Meteorite Rain

As the new star formed out of the exploding nebula, its gravity drew the erupting gas and dust into a disk that spun around it. Large particles of dust attracted smaller particles, and when they collided, their outer layers of ice stuck together, creating bigger particles of rock and ice known as planetesimals.

As small dust particles were sucked into larger particles, the spinning disk separated into rings of larger rock masses. Then the process repeated itself on a grand scale. The gravity of the largest rock clusters overpowered the smaller clusters, and formed seven planets.

During the first five hundred million years of its history, our new planet was bombarded by meteorites as it sucked up the last of the planetesimals. The surface was a barren wasteland, every square mile scarred and cratered.

On the surface, we looked for signs of life. But, one sniff of the poisoned air told us that nothing could live here.

But as we made our way back to the fire, and our constant vigil over the prisoners, life was beginning on the ocean floor.

—Excerpt from *The Wardens' Logs*

Chapter Nine

Midnight Meeting

"November twenty-fifth. That's tonight!"

Steele read the note, and tucked it away, at least twenty times. Then he unfolded it and read it again.

"I'm next," he said. "They're after me. I'm going to disappear—just like Dirk and the others."

He wished he knew who *they* were. At least then he'd know what he was up against. Was the Prince of Darkness one of them? Did *they* work for him? Was the evil, scarred face the face of the Prince of Darkness? He read the note yet again, then glanced at the clock on his bedside table. He was so agitated, he couldn't think clearly or sit still for more than a few seconds. It was already five past ten.

Midnight was now less than two hours away. What would happen if he didn't show up at the northeast corner of Dalhousie and Shuter? Steele had never heard of those streets, and it occurred to him that he had no idea where they were. What if they weren't in Toronto at all? What if they were in Scarborough, or North York, or Mississauga—miles away? Even if he left now, he'd never get there before midnight. Fighting a rush of panic, he bounded down the two flights of stairs and rooted through the junk drawer in the kitchen for the city map.

Spreading the map out on the counter, he found Dalhousie Street, and tracing a finger along the line until it intersected Shuter, he bumped over Pyrus who had crept silently onto the map and become part of it. Steele picked up the salamander and placed it on his shoulder. Then he turned his attention back to the map. He breathed easier when he discovered that the location of the meeting place was only a short distance from the Eaton Centre, right on the subway line.

He refolded the map and stuffed it in his backpack. Then he sat at the table and stared at the phone. It seemed to be waiting for him to call his father and tell him about the note.

"But I can't," he said aloud. "The note said not to tell anyone."

He dropped his head onto his arms. What if he ignored the note, played dumb, pretended he had never found it, and just went to bed? Would they come to the house? Did they know where he lived? Feeling that he had to talk to someone or explode, he left the kitchen and went into the living room, seeking comfort in the company of his ever-silent grandmother.

"I can tell *you* about the note," he said. "They'll never know."

So he pulled the footstool across the carpet and sat close to the old woman. Then he told her, and she smiled out the window at the darkness.

"What would Dad do if he were in my shoes?" he asked when he had finished. He stared at the enormous scarf, his eyes following the intricate patterns as if they might speak to him and tell him what to do.

"What would he do?" he repeated, forcing himself to think like a police officer. But it wasn't as easy as it sounded.

He was just a kid and, at that moment, being a kid sucked.

Pyrus bit his elbow, making him jump practically out of his skin. He tried to catch the rascally salamander, but he couldn't spot him among the brightly coloured birds and animals in the carpet's pattern.

"Do you ever wish you had magic powers?" he asked his grandmother.

Steele did. He wished that he had Pyrus's magic. If he could camouflage himself, he wouldn't be scared to ride the subway in the middle of the night. He wouldn't be scared of anything.

Then an idea came to him.

"I know what Dad would do!" he cried. "He'd make sure he could be followed. He'd leave a trail."

Excited, Steele went back upstairs, sat at his desk, and wrote a letter to Mac. He slipped the note he had found inside his smashed guitar into an envelope along with the letter. On the front of the envelope he printed Mac's name and the following instructions: *TO BE OPENED AFTER 1:00 a.m., Monday, November 26th.* He presumed it would be okay to tell someone, besides GM, after the time specified in the note.

If he disappeared that night, the letter, which he intended to drop in Mac's mailbox on his way to the meeting, would trigger a massive manhunt, perhaps the biggest in Toronto's or even Canada's history; it would give the police their first tangible clue in the missing-kids cases. That is, assuming whoever had planted the note was involved in the other disappearances.

Steele looked at his watch and gulped. It was time to go. Still, he remained seated at his desk, unable to bring himself to move. The only time he had ever been out alone in the middle of the night was when he played his guitar in Wychwood

Park, and that didn't count because he was just across the street, in full view of his house the whole time. Going downtown at midnight wasn't the same. It was dangerous. Bad things happened in the dark. Evil came out at night, when it could slink through the parks and hide among the shadows. Maybe the monster with the scary face hid in dark underground drains by day and, like a vampire, only came out at night. Besides, his father would kill him if he ever found out.

"Don't go," he pleaded with himself. "It's probably just a trick."

Writing the letter had made him feel better, but he still didn't relish the thought of being out on the streets of Toronto at such a late hour. In fact, it scared him half to death.

It was now or never. Steele grabbed a piece of chalk from a box on his desk and dropped it into his backpack. Then he picked up the letter and went downstairs. It was just after eleven p.m. when he slipped quietly out of the house.

Mac lived in Forest Hill, several blocks north of St. Clair Avenue just west of Spadina Road. It was an uphill run and Steele was panting when he finally reached Mac's house and pushed the envelope through the slot in the front door. He hesitated and gazed up at Mac's bedroom window, half-hoping that his friend would look out and see him. But the house was bathed in darkness. Then Steele turned and ran toward the nearest subway entrance. During the ride downtown, he studied the map, memorizing the route to the designated meeting place. At 11:35, he raced up the escalator at the Queen subway station and sprinted east on Queen Street.

Gazing up at the familiar looming towers that broke the skyline of Canada's biggest city, he felt that he was viewing them with new eyes, and he couldn't help but wonder if this would be the last time he'd ever see them.

He had been hurrying for what seemed like ages when he suddenly stopped dead. Perhaps he'd miscalculated the distance to Dalhousie Street. *I've come too far,* he thought, panicked that he wouldn't reach the meeting spot in time.

He was just about to turn back when he saw the street name on a pole at the next intersection. Breathing a sigh of relief, he ran toward the sign, his heart thumping loudly against his chest. Steele swung left on Dalhousie and continued until the sound of traffic faded to a dull hum and he found himself in a predominately commercial area, with a few residential buildings scattered here and there. When he reached Shuter, he jaywalked across the intersection to the northeast corner. Then he walked a short distance along Shuter until he came to a well-concealed alley. He ducked into the shadows and peered along the street in both directions, before checking the time again. It was ten minutes to midnight.

"Please don't show up," he said under his breath, sweating despite the cold winter air on his face.

A siren pierced the silence, growing louder as it came nearer. A police car screeched around the corner onto Shuter like a wild animal, tires blackening the concrete, and sped past the alley, its dome light flashing red like a beacon in the darkness. Steele stared at it, willing it to do a U-turn and come back for him, only letting the thought go when the car turned onto a side street and disappeared. The familiar-looking cruiser made him think of his father, and a desperate urge to run—to get away as fast as he could before it was too late—washed over him.

He peeled back his glove and checked the time again. Five minutes to the appointed hour. He wondered about the note. Who had stuffed it inside his guitar? And when? Steele thought for a moment. He'd only gone to his lessons twice this month, and he was pretty sure that if the note had been inside his guitar while he was at Mrs. Fret's studio, he would have noticed something wrong with the sound, or heard the paper sliding on the wood. But if the note wasn't there last Thursday afternoon, then whoever put it inside his guitar had to have done it between the time he left the studio and the time he reached home after Dirk had smashed the guitar. There were only two people who had the opportunity to get at his guitar. Mac or Riley. Had they done it yesterday or today as a joke?

He didn't think so.

Just as he was losing his nerve and about to get the heck out of there, a clock on a tower somewhere in the area boomed the first stroke of midnight.

Steele's heart skipped a beat.

"One," he counted under his breath.

Bong! "Two. They're not coming."

Bong! "Three." He scanned the street in both directions.

Bong! "Four."

Nothing moved. Steele had never felt so alone. He imagined that all of the houses and buildings were vacant—that somehow the people who lived here had heard about the midnight meeting and fled, abandoning him to the night and whatever was coming for him.

Bong! "Was that five or six? Six."

A taxi, its roof light glowing like a yellow egg, turned onto Shuter from two streets away and slowly approached. Steele sucked in his breath.

Bong! "Seven."

The taxi stopped at the light at Dalhousie and Shuter. The glowing roof light meant it was vacant. Or had the driver merely forgotten to switch it off?

Bong! "Eight. Please change," he pleaded with the light, his eyes riveted on the cab, half expecting one of the back doors to swing open.

Bong! "Nine."

The taxi turned left onto Dalhousie and picked up speed.

"Ah!" Steele let out his breath, his knees knocking together with relief. "They're not coming. It was a joke after all. Wait till I get my hands on Mac and Riley."

Bong! "Ten."

A clattering sound coming from the opposite end of the alley startled him and he wheeled about and peered into the darkness. He could barely make out the bent figure ambling slowly toward him, but there was no mistaking the irregular rattle of the twisted front wheel on the old shopping cart that the figure was pushing. Steele's heart stopped. It was the scary old man Dirk and the Jerks had attacked in Wychwood Park, the night Dirk disappeared! The same old man one of Dirk's neighbours had seen outside the bully's house in the middle of that terrible night!

Bong! "Eleven. The note! He did it! Somehow he put it in the guitar that night in the park. He got Dirk, and now he's coming to get me!" Steele was almost moaning now.

Bong! "Twelve."

The old man paused.

RUN! RUN! screamed a voice in Steele's head.

He blinked the sweat from his eyes. "He's old. I can run faster than him." He turned and flew blindly out of the alley.

Then he skidded to a stop, a low, strangled cry bursting from his throat at the sight of Maddie Fey's long black limousine waiting at the curb like a hearse.

He stumbled backwards, his mind whirling. And then, in a rush, it came to him—her absence from school on Friday, the day after Dirk went missing. Steele had been troubled by her absence, but he had dismissed it. How could he have been so stupid? Maddie Fey had to be involved in Dirk's disappearance. And now Steele was trapped.

He shrugged out of the straps on his backpack and rooted frantically in an outside pocket. Removing the piece of chalk, he scrawled Maddie's Fey's name on the rough brick wall of the first house siding onto the alley. Then, remembering that the note had warned against being late, he walked slowly toward the vehicle.

Ahead, the shadowy black limousine crouched like a monstrous beast about to spring upon its unsuspecting prey. The dark windows didn't give anything away. Steele's skin crawled. He felt cold icy eyes watching him from the darkness on the other side of the tinted windows.

I'm going to go in there and never come out! he thought.

Then a tiny spark of hope ignited in his heart. Mac! He had totally forgotten about Mac and the letter. He knew that as long as Mac got the letter, he'd find Steele.

His heart thumping erratically, he stepped up to the vehicle and knocked softly on one of the windows near the back end, casting panicky glances over his shoulder at the mouth of the alley.

When nothing happened, he almost bolted, and would have if he hadn't heard a soft click near the right front tire. He looked along the monster's length and noticed that a door near the front was opening soundlessly. He swallowed, tasting metal, and realized that he had bitten his lower lip and drawn blood. As he crept along the side of the car, he tried to see through the windows, but it was so dark inside the vehicle that it was like trying to peer through granite. When he reached the open door, he poked his head tentatively inside.

Sharp claws grabbed his arm and dragged him into the blackness.

Death

Death toyed with us. It hid in the fire, became one with it, and stalked us through the thick molten lava. We were not afraid. We are immortal beings—the highest life forms in the galaxy. We did not know then that we could be killed.

We had been sent to this planet to guard the fire and monitor the pods that had been fashioned as unbreachable tombs for the Tsilihin monsters. The prisoners had transformed in the very fire that was to have been the death of them. The fire consumed their dry leathery hides. It melted their bony armour and turned them into liquid. In time, all physical traces of their known forms were gone. No longer Tsilihin, they evolved into creatures of fire, and when their heat ignited and intensified until it was as white as lightning, they burned great holes in the hulls of their tombs, and escaped.

They were truly terrible creatures now—all fire and rage, and they were loose.

—Excerpt from *The Wardens' Logs*

Chapter Ten
The Black Limousine

Steele's voice cracked, but it was still working. "I don't know what you want—" he blurted out. "But if you're thinking of making me disappear like Dirk, you'd better think again. I left a note with someone. And if I'm not home by one o'clock, you're going to be in big trouble. My father's with the police, and this place will be crawling with cops. They'll find you because I said in the note that I was coming here to meet you, MADDIE FEY."

He clamped his mouth shut and waited. He could hear breathing in the darkness—short snuffling sounds that did nothing to quell the rapid beating of his heart. Something was in here with him.

Steele blinked repeatedly to allow his eyes to adjust, but no matter how many times he blinked, he still couldn't see his hand when he held it in front of his face. It wasn't merely dark inside the limo like the dark in his room when he turned out the light. This was a different sort of darkness, thick and tangible, as if the very air in the limo was black. He felt he could reach out and catch fistfuls of it.

Abruptly, lights flooded the space and Steele could see again. What he saw made him gasp in disbelief.

It was alarmingly clear that he wasn't in Maddie Fey's limousine anymore.

But where am I? He was alone in a large, circular room, perhaps a foyer. The lower wall was panelled in a dark, polished wood. The floor was covered with black-and-white marble tiles, in a chessboard pattern. The light was coming from clusters of long, tapered candles in black sconces mounted high up on the wall. It struck Steele that all of the candles must have burst into flames at the same time.

He tilted his head back and looked up. Directly overhead, a chandelier hung from a chain that dropped from so high up, Steele couldn't see the ceiling where it was anchored. It was so gigantic, standing under it made Steele nervous. As if it had been waiting for a signal from him, the chandelier suddenly lit up like Methuselah's birthday cake.

"Awesome!" he breathed, momentarily mesmerized by the flickering flames of hundreds of candles. Then he shook himself and moved quickly from under the chandelier. *I've got to get out of here,* he thought. *If there's a way in, there's got to be a way out.*

He completed a slow circle and found himself looking into a pair of yellow eyes belonging to the biggest, reddest rat he'd ever seen. On all fours, it was as tall as Steele.

"Ahh!" he shouted, jumping in fright.

"Eee!" squealed the rat, its red hackles rising.

Steele's heart was pounding hard as he slowly backed away. The rat's nearness was overpowering. Waves of heat from the creature's body washed over him, but Steele felt cold and sick and disgusted and afraid all at once.

"G-get away!" he said.

The rat inched closer, never taking its ferocious yellow eyes off Steele. Then it sprang at him, knocking him over and pinning him to the floor. Its thin lips curled back to expose a double row of sharp, pointed teeth.

"What's your name?" The rat's voice was a harsh, guttural sound that seemed to come from deep in its throat.

Steele felt the creature's breath on his face and knew it had spoken, but he couldn't get his mind to accept the notion of a talking rat.

"Speak!" snarled the rat. "Before I tear you limb from limb."

Steele tried, but the only sounds he could make were unintelligible shrieks. The rat dug its claws into his shoulders and shook him roughly.

"S-stop!" Steele said weakly. "P-please s-stop! M-my n-name's S-Steele."

The rat stopped shaking him, but its grip on his shoulders tightened. And for a long, terrible second, Steele was afraid the rat didn't believe him. He opened his mouth, but before he could repeat his name, the rat let go of his shoulders and backed away.

"Get up!" ordered the rat.

Steele didn't know if his legs would hold him, but he made himself obey.

"W-where's M-Maddie F-Fey?" he stammered, placing his hand on the wall to keep from falling down.

The rat bared its sharp teeth. It wasn't a pretty sight.

"She's changing."

Steele turned deathly pale. *Into what?* he gulped, as the room spun and then went black.

//Λ\\

Steele opened his eyes.

The rat reared up on its hind legs, blocking the candlelight. It loomed over him like a nightmare come alive. Its yellow eyes burned wildly and a coating of white froth formed at the corners of its lips.

It's going to eat me, thought Steele, staggering backwards.

He squeezed his eyes shut and waited for the creature to bite his head clean off his neck. When nothing happened, he opened his eyes to slits and peeked at the towering figure.

A silver flask appeared in the rat's clawed forelimb as if the creature had conjured it out of thin air. Its eyes stayed fixed on Steele as it removed the stopper. Then it held out the flask. Long tendrils of steam drifted from the mouth of the vessel, curling and twisting like spectral fingers.

"Drink this!" hissed the rat.

"Get away! Don't touch me!" cried Steele, lashing out with both arms and knocking the flask out of the rat's claws. He knew he was hysterical, but he couldn't help himself.

The rat snarled and ground its teeth. Its clawed forearm raked the air less than an inch from Steele's face, letting Steele know that it could slice him up like a ripe tomato if it chose to. Then its pointed nose twitched, and it dropped onto all four limbs, turned abruptly, and scuttled into the shadows against the wall where the light from the candles didn't reach. Steele held his breath and watched the rat's long, red, hairless tail writhing like an angry snake as it trailed behind.

The instant the rat was out of sight, Steele let out a breath and raced about the enormous foyer, running his hands along the walls and pushing his shoulder against the dark wood panels.

There's got to be a way out of here, he thought, hammering his fist on the wall. *Come on! Think!* he chided himself.

Frustrated, he stood in the middle of the room and stared at the wall.

"That's weird!" He could have sworn that, except for the sconces, the wall had been bare. But now he counted nine arched alcoves in the wood panelling. Standing in each alcove was a tall statue—the first held the figure of a man; the next, a woman. Their blind, unblinking eyes seemed to be staring at him, following his every move. The sensation gave Steele the creeps. But he couldn't stop looking at them. He walked about the room, moving from alcove to alcove, examining each statue. The figures were all of men and women, and they were covered from head to toe in long, black, hooded cloaks. Their faces were frozen in expressionless masks and, up close, they appeared to be looking through Steele, to a place as far away as the world into which his grandmother had gone.

To his surprise, they didn't look scary or evil, only cold, and grave, almost sad. They didn't look at all like Maddie Fey. And yet, they were like her—especially their necks, which were covered with silver scales.

He stared for a long time at the statue occupying the eighth alcove. It was a young woman—years younger than the other figures. There was something vaguely familiar about the tilt of her head and the perfect oval of her face. Steele felt that he knew her.

"Yeah! Right!" he said. "It's this spooky place. It's making me imagine things."

But he couldn't shake the feeling that he had seen her before.

"Who are you?" he wondered aloud, then moved on to the

ninth and last alcove. "Did Maddie Fey lure you here and turn you into stone? Is that what she has planned for—"

He stopped dead, the words stuck in his throat like a fishbone. The ninth alcove was empty.

"It's for me!" he whispered.

He remembered the silver flask, and the noxious smoke that had leaked from its mouth when the monstrous rodent removed the stopper. The rat's words replayed in his mind: *Drink this!*

"They're going to poison me, and then turn me to stone!"

Steele turned away from the empty alcove, his mind in turmoil. "They're going to kill me. I've got to get out of here!"

He couldn't believe his eyes when he found himself staring at a massive sweeping staircase that wound up and up into darkness as thick as soup. Maybe, just maybe, he hadn't noticed the alcoves, he conceded. But there was no way he could have missed the long staircase. It hadn't been there a minute ago. He had just completed a circle of the room, and it hadn't existed.

"Where am I?" he groaned. "What sort of place is this where candles light by themselves, and rooms change, and rats talk and grow as big as people?"

He sank down onto the third step and dropped his head into his hands. He didn't think he'd been drugged or knocked out. He turned his mind back to the moment that the rat's sharp claws, or those of some other creature, had grabbed him and dragged him into Maddie Fey's long black limousine. The next thing he remembered was the candles flickering on by themselves. In frustration, Steele squeezed his head with his hands.

Please, oh please, let me be dreaming, he thought. *Please, when I wake up, let me be home.*

A bell tinkled overhead. Steele twisted about and looked up. Candles burst into flames along the wall, lighting the way to the top of the stairs. Far above, he could barely make out the dim form of the rat crouching on the top step, the candle-light reflecting off a small bell clutched tightly in its claws. Steele shivered when he saw the creature's eyes burning with a fierce light of their own.

"Come," commanded the rat. "She's quick to anger."

Steele started to shake. The last thing he wanted to do was make Maddie Fey angry and forfeit any chance he might have of getting out of here alive, before she turned him to stone. He hurried up the long stairs, his sweaty palm sticking to the smooth wooden banister. As he climbed, his eyes glued on the rat, he gradually became aware of more alcoves in the wall on his right. He risked a quick look.

The figures occupying the alcoves lining the stairway weren't men or women. They were horrible winged monsters—savage things with silver scales on their powerful necks, rows of fangs as long as Steele's arm in their wide-open mouths, and claws like knives on their slashing forelimbs.

"Ahh!" Steele cried, dropping into a crouch and covering his head with his arms.

At the top of the stairs, the rat hissed impatiently.

They're not real, Steele told himself, lowering his arms to his sides and hurrying up the stairs, careful not to look at the monstrous creatures lining the staircase. But he felt their stony eyes on him.

There was another ringing sound. The bell had slipped from the rat's claws and tinkled as it hit the floor. At the same moment, the creature curled its claws, bared its teeth, and leaped down the stairs at Steele, who cried out and flattened himself against the wall under one of the alcoves.

The rat shot past Steele, sharp teeth gleaming, hair bristling—a savage red streak moving down the stairs so swiftly, Steele's eyes couldn't follow him. Steele held onto the wall, his heart pounding out of control.

"Oh God! What do I now?" he asked himself as he huddled there, halfway up the stairs. He wanted to run, but he didn't know where. At last, he gathered up his courage and continued climbing.

He was out of breath by the time he reached the top. He grasped the banister and looked back. The stairway was so long, he couldn't see the bottom step. Shaking his head, he turned and surveyed the large open area before him. It was bare, except for the familiar candle-lit sconces and a monumental, gold-framed mirror hanging by a thick, black chain. Steele walked over and gazed at his image in the mirror. His expression matched the way he felt. His eyes were dark and frightened and his face was gaunt and pale. He looked away.

Out of the corner of his eye, he saw the dark frame of a door that he hadn't noticed before. Cautiously, he approached it, his heart thumping. What would he find on the other side of the door? Maddie Fey? Or someone else? The Prince of Darkness? He had just lifted his hand to knock softly when the door swung open and he found himself on the threshold of an enormous, candlelit chamber.

"Ahh!" He moved back, then took a deep breath and stepped inside. He sensed the door closing silently behind him, like a lid coming down on his coffin. He also sensed movement from within the room—the faint rustle of cloth brushing against cloth.

He was in a large dining room. Swallowing his panic, he let his eyes travel about the room. In the far wall was a gigantic fireplace, large enough for his father and ten other police officers to fit inside, standing erect. A huge log, practically a tree, blazed in the hearth, shooting sparks up the chimney, the light making shadows dance in macabre patterns on the walls and on the black wooden beams on the high ceiling.

In the middle of the room was a long table of dark polished wood. In the dim candlelight, Steele could barely see the other end, near the fireplace. Around the table were a dozen or more high-backed chairs with ornately carved wooden arms and backs.

They look like thrones, he thought.

The seats were covered in red velvet. He hated red velvet. The colour made him think of bloodstains, as if someone had bled to death on the chairs. On the table before each chair was a black place mat, inlaid and edged with silver. On its wooden surface, just to the right of the large, gleaming dinner knife at each place setting, stood a silver goblet studded with gemstones.

Steele's eyes darted from throne to throne but, from where he was standing just inside the door, they were so tall that he couldn't see who was sitting in them. He moved farther into the room until he could see the chair at the head of the table.

There sat the familiar, sinister figure of Maddie Fey.

She watched him, unsmiling, her eyes changing from blue to silver and back again. She looked cold and cruel in a long black gown. Her silver neck glinted in the candlelight. Steele felt like a fool as he realized that when the rat had said that

Maddie Fey was changing, he had meant her clothes. On the floor beside her, its great head resting on the arm of her chair, was a large animal. It could have been a dog, but it didn't resemble any dog Steele had ever seen. For one thing, when it blinked at him, he noticed that it had two pupils in each eye. For another thing, its fur was shimmering silver, like Maddie Fey's icy eyes.

"Come in, Steele," said Maddie Fey, pointing at the throne to her immediate left. "I've been waiting for you."

Her voice was clear and sophisticated, and as cold as the North Pole.

Steele didn't move. He folded his arms across his chest.

"Why did you bring me here?" he demanded in a voice that sounded braver than he felt.

Maddie Fey stared at him for a moment as if sizing him up, deciding what or how much to tell him. Steele waited, wondering what she could possibly say. He let his eyes drift about the table. The other thrones were empty. He looked back at Maddie Fey. But when she finally spoke, her answer left him speechless.

"I brought you here to keep you alive this night."

Life

Charged with guarding the Tsilihin prisoners and protecting this fragile planet from creatures that were utterly and instinctively evil, we watched over the planet from deep within its melted core. Time passed. Centuries became millennia—and still we kept watch. Geological ages came and went, leaving historical data encoded in deposits of carbon, iron, stone, and ice for later life forms to unearth and decipher.

For the next two billion years, stromatolites were the only life forms on the planet. They developed on the ocean floor, from cyanobacteria, simple, single-celled microbes that we brought with us from Arjella.

We were wild with excitement because cyanobacteria are photosynthetic. They produce oxygen. And oxygen was needed to cleanse the poisoned air and ready the planet for life.

Death could not assail the oceans to get at the cyanobacteria. Its life-sustaining fires were swiftly extinguished when it tore and railed at mighty waves to reach the ocean floor. Filled with rage as black as its heart, Death plotted and schemed.

—Excerpt from *The Wardens' Logs*

Chapter Eleven

Aliens

Steele slowly reached out and gripped the back of the throne at the foot of the table to steady himself. He felt as if something was coiled about him, squeezing the air out of his lungs.

"What are you talking about?" he asked.

Before Maddie Fey could reply, the door burst open. Two dark figures sailed through the air as if they had been hurled. They landed in a tangle of arms and legs near the foot of the table. The red rat stood in the doorway, its yellow eyes raking over Steele.

"I caught them trying to break the windows," it hissed.

Steele stared at the tangled figures in disbelief. "No way!" he cried as he recognized the mop of dazzling white hair.

"Mac!" cried Steele, rushing over to his friend. "What are you doing here?" Then he saw Riley. "How . . . ?"

"It's a long story," groaned Mac, untangling his limbs from Riley's and squinting up at Steele. "Where's here?" He got up slowly.

Suddenly he tensed and gripped Steele's arm. "There was this giant monster outside the limo! I swear it was as big as a lion. It caught us and—" He looked about wildly, his eyes finally fixing on the rat, framed in the doorway. "Ahh! There it is! Don't let it get me!"

"It won't hurt you," Steele said, with more confidence than

he felt. He thumped Mac gently on the shoulder. "But what are you doing here?"

"I . . . uh . . ." Mac started to say, then an envelope slipped out of his pocket and floated to the carpet.

Steele recognized the letter. His heart fell as he realized that his plan had failed. Instead of telling the police where Steele had gone, Mac had taken the letter and followed him. Now no one would know the location of the midnight meeting. He felt like yelling, but he knew it wasn't Mac's fault. His friend had only been trying to help.

"You shouldn't have followed me," he said.

Mac, momentarily forgetting about the rat, looked at the envelope guiltily. He picked it up and pressed it into Steele's hand. "I didn't plan on getting caught."

"You didn't plan, period," Riley grunted, pushing herself to her feet and letting her eyes travel over the chairs and long polished table.

Riley sounded the same as usual, but Steele noticed that her face was as grey as ashes, and her eyes were wide and staring. He put his arm around her shoulders. "It's OK, Riley."

Riley shrugged Steele's arm away. "I know," she said, looking about in wonder. "But where are we? How did we get here?"

Maddie Fey sat quietly and watched Steele and his friends, her hand resting gently on the silver animal's head. Then she coughed softly and rose.

Mac and Riley jumped at the sound. They stared at Maddie Fey as if she were a ghost. Mac recovered first.

"What's *she* doing here?" he cried.

"I think she lives here," said Steele out of the side of his mouth.

Riley was staring at the silver animal at Maddie Fey's side. "What's that?"

"This is my hound, Wish," said Maddie Fey. "And that—" She pointed at the rat in the doorway. "That is Nilats, my chauffeur and friend."

Then she tapped her slim fingers against her goblet impatiently. "Your friends should not have come here," she said to Steele. "They must leave at once." She beckoned the rat. "See that they get home safely."

"No!" cried Mac, backing away from the advancing rat. "I'm not going anywhere without Steele."

"That goes for me too," said Riley, eyeing the rat warily.

Maddie Fey ignored them and appealed to Steele. "I have travelled a great distance to find you," she said, her voice low and controlled. "We must talk now, alone."

"I want them to stay," said Steele, moving closer to Mac and Riley. "At least until we've heard what you have to say."

Steele watched Maddie Fey's blue eyes darken in anger and, for a second, he thought she was going to come around the table and strike him. Then she sighed and sank slowly into her chair.

"Very well," she said, the chill in her voice making the temperature in the room drop sharply. "But know this. As long as they remain in your company they are in danger. By leaving now, they might escape the terror that, even as we speak, searches for you."

Steele swallowed loudly and glanced at Riley. She looked as if she might faint, and he wondered if she was thinking of the horrible face they'd seen through the grate in Wychwood Park.

But Mac snorted. "Terror? What terror? Next, you'll be

saying that evil aliens are lurking about outside, waiting to abduct us."

Maddie Fey fixed her gaze on him but did not respond. Then she looked back at Steele.

"Well, Steele, what is it to be?"

"I'm staying," said Mac.

"Riley?" Steele caught her arm gently. "Listen, I don't know what she's talking about. But if she's right . . . I mean, if there's a chance that being around me could get you killed, I wouldn't want you to stay."

Riley shrugged unhappily. "I want to go home," she said. "But if I do, I'll feel awful, like I deserted you or something. I'll stay. But I've got to call home first."

"No." Maddie Fey's voice was sharp. "If you decide to stay, there will be no calling home. This is not some child's game."

"But what about our parents?" protested Riley. "They'll be worried sick."

"Then perhaps you should go home," said Maddie Fey.

Riley turned to Steele. "I'm coming with you."

"Are you sure?" Steele asked her. "Maybe you should go."

"No," Riley said firmly. "We're in this together."

"Then let us begin," said Maddie Fey.

Steele took the chair at the foot of the table. Mac and Riley sat on either side of him, the long table and the empty chairs distancing them from Maddie Fey like a solid wall. An uncomfortable silence filled the large room, as the rat went around the table filling each goblet with something thick and red. Steele and his friends stared at Maddie Fey, waiting for her to speak.

But Maddie Fey remained silent, taking slow sips from the silver goblet, her silver-blue eyes locked on something the others couldn't see. The silence seemed to stretch into eternity. Finally, she set her goblet on the table and pressed a white linen napkin against her lips. It seemed to Steele that the room and everything in it were holding their breaths.

"Well, here we are," said Mac.

Steele rested his elbows on the table, leaned forward in his chair, and said, "Maddie Fey."

The sound of her name seemed to draw Maddie Fey out of her thoughts. She lifted her eyes toward Steele.

"Before, you said that you brought me here to keep me alive tonight. What did you mean?"

"There is no quick answer," she replied sadly. "You will see why when I have finished telling you what I know." Then she paused and looked slowly from one face to another. "Steele must understand why I have been looking for him, and since you, Riley, and you, Mac, have chosen to stay, you should also know what lies before us. Now listen carefully."

Her voice reached along the length of the table, wrapped about Steele and his friends, and held them spellbound.

"A long time ago, just after the birth of your sun, when Earth was nothing but a ball of burning gas and dust, evil creatures invaded my home planet, Arjella—"

"Whoa!" whispered Mac, his eyes as round as saucers. "Aliens!"

"We had no warning," Maddie Fey continued. "The sky turned black, and the invaders were upon us. They were destroyers from an unknown galaxy. That is what they did; that is all they did. We named them Tsilihin. It's an Arjellan word for 'terrorist.' It comes from Msilihin, which means 'nothing,' or 'an absence of existence.'" Maddie Fey waited, but when no one else spoke, she went on. "I will not describe the terrible war that followed the invasion. It is enough to say that it was atrocious. Most of my people and other Arjellans died. The war lasted eight centuries. We finally defeated the Tsilihin, but we were left with the problem of what to do with those we had captured. We knew that they must be shut away, far away, in a place from which they could never escape."

She stopped and stared into her silver goblet before raising it to her lips. Steele was glad for the pause. He needed time to absorb the things she'd just told them. As staggering as her story sounded, he believed it. Maddie Fey took a sip from her goblet and set it back on the table.

"Since there was no place on Arjella that would serve as a prison for the Tsilihin, we sent them here."

"You what!" Mac jumped to his feet, knocking his chair back onto the floor.

Wish lifted his silver head and growled softly.

"Sit down, Mac!" hissed Steele.

Mac righted his chair and dropped heavily into it, muttering under his breath. His eyes shifted from Maddie Fey to Steele and Riley.

"This is crazy!" he scoffed. "Come on, Steele! Riley! OK, so she might be an alien. But if what she said about sending those Tsilly . . . Silly . . . whatever . . . things here is true, don't you think someone would have found them by now?"

"Let her finish," said Riley. "It can't hurt to listen."

"Your friend is right, Mac," said Maddie Fey. "You may as well hear the rest of my story."

Mac folded his arms across his chest, letting his head fall against the back of the chair. He stared at the ceiling as if the firelight dancing on the dark wooden beams fascinated him. But Steele could tell he was hanging on to Maddie Fey's every word.

"To transport the prisoners, we fashioned pods from a metallic element that is abundant on Arjella, but unknown on your planet. It is called *marflow*. It is stronger than steel combined with titanium, but not as heavy. Then we used magic to seal the enemy in the pods, programmed the pods with the coordinates for your planet, and launched them.

"As I said before, Earth didn't even exist six billion years ago. When we chose this as a prison for the Tsilihin, we believed that the pods would hold them until the end of time, while the gravity of the spinning fireball would ensure that the pods remained in its core." Maddie Fey stopped.

Silence, dark and mutinous, settled over the room. Mac and Riley were glaring at Maddie Fey as if she were solely responsible for sending the Tsilihin to Earth.

Which is ridiculous, thought Steele. Six billion years ago she wasn't even born yet. Or was she? He grabbed the neck of his T-shirt, which suddenly felt tight against his throat, and stretched it to keep from suffocating.

Steele saw Mac reach for the bejewelled goblet and gulp down the thick red contents as if he were dying of thirst. Then Mac looked at the goblet and made the sort of face Steele imagined he'd make if he'd just drunk sour milk. Mac swallowed, looked at Maddie Fey, and laughed abruptly. "I still don't believe you," he said, but he didn't sound convincing. "Are you seriously saying that these evil creatures are trapped in the magma at the Earth's core?"

Maddie Fey shook her head. "Some of them are still there," she answered. "But many have escaped."

"What do you mean, escaped?" asked Mac incredulously. "I thought those pods were supposed to hold them."

"We thought so too," said Maddie Fey.

Mac squeezed his eyes shut and tried to concentrate. "Let me get this straight. The creatures you sent here are loose on our planet, right now, at this minute."

Maddie Fey nodded again. "Listen, Mac! We did not simply send these creatures here and leave them. We sent wardens to guard them. Only something went wrong. The wardens have disappeared."

"Just like the kids," Steele said under his breath.

"I was sent here for two reasons. One was to make contact with the wardens. But when I arrived four months ago, all of my efforts to communicate with them failed. I was not worried at the time, because they had been here for billions of years and were strong and fierce, capable of looking after themselves. Besides, we had had no contact with them since they left Arjella to watch over the Tsilihin on your planet. But as I searched for them, I saw some disturbing signs—scorched earth, volcanic activity where none should exist—for which I could find no explanation." She lifted the goblet to her lips.

Steele watched her, watched the gems in the bowl of the goblet wink green, red, and yellow in the firelight. He realized that he was sitting on the edge of his chair eager to hear the rest of her unbelievable story. As if she had read his mind, Maddie Fey's eyes remained on him as she continued.

"I could not locate the wardens, and I had discovered evidence that something had broken through the Earth's surface. I had to face the terrible possibility that the prisoners had survived the fire somehow, had found a way to kill the wardens, and had escaped."

"But you don't know for sure that the wardens are dead," said Steele.

"No," answered Maddie Fey. "But I cannot find them, and I have searched the planet."

"How could you search the whole planet in four months?" queried Mac.

"I have my ways, Mac," answered Maddie Fey, ignoring Mac's rude snort.

"What are these wardens?" asked Riley.

"They are fabulous creatures," replied Maddie Fey. "On my planet, they are called guardians of fire. They are of a very high order and extremely intelligent. They have been guarding the Tsilihin for billions of years, keeping your planet safe."

"I meant, what do they look like?' said Riley.

"A little like your dragons, only much grander. Their scales are gold like the sun or silver like the moon. They have powerful wings and sharp, sharp claws. They are truly magnificent. They are immortal. By that I mean that unless they are killed, they will live forever. So, if they are still living, you may be fortunate enough to see them."

"You still haven't explained how these creatures broke out of their indestructible pods," said Mac impatiently.

"This is what I believe happened," Maddie Fey answered curtly. "The pods held the Tsilihin for a billion years. And then, over time, something happened that no one could have foreseen. The creatures evolved. They grew stronger, and hotter, and larger until the pods could not contain them. When they broke free, they didn't perish in the fire. They became one with it. Now I have named them Fire Demons, because they ate the fire and evolved into new forms."

"Nothing can live in fire," said Riley.

"Actually," said Steele, "there are these tubeworms that live and evolve at the bottom of the ocean right on top of a vent where boiling, toxic chemicals spew from the Earth's core."

Riley looked at him suspiciously. "Are you making that up?"

"He is not making it up," said Maddie Fey. "By imprisoning the Tsilihin in the fire of your Earth, my ancestors believed that it was for the good of the entire galaxy. But, as I mentioned, we did not foresee that, over time, the pods would absorb the heat and, like Steele's tubeworms, our enemy would be able to live in fire. And now . . . I am afraid that they have learned to exist away from the fire."

Steele leaned his head against the back of his chair and closed his eyes. Maddie Fey's story overwhelmed him. There was silence, and then he heard Mac ask how the Fire Demons could exist away from fire.

"I believe they are using children to keep them alive."

Steele's eyes shot open, but it took a second or two for his brain to assimilate Maddie Fey's words. He gasped, "The missing kids!"

He glanced at Mac and Riley, who seemed frozen in their chairs, eyes riveted to Maddie Fey, mouths hanging open.

Then Riley shook her head and frowned. "How are these Fire Demons using them?" she asked. "Are they . . . eating them?"

Maddie Fey flashed her a troubled look. "I do not think the children are being eaten," she said. "At least, not by the Fire Demons, and not immediately after they are taken. No, they have something the Demons need. But I have not yet discovered what it is."

"If all these Fire Demons are wandering around, how come nobody's ever seen them?" asked Riley.

"An excellent question," said Maddie Fey, rewarding Riley with one of her rare smiles. "The reason no one has noticed them is that they look just like you and me. Recently, they developed the ability to change their shapes."

Shape changers!

Steele and his companions stared at Maddie Fey in horror, almost as if they expected her slim shape to burst into flames. And then they all began to speak at once.

"How is that possible?" asked Riley.

"Have you seen them in other shapes?" asked Mac.

"Perhaps that's why they need the kids," said Steele, thinking out loud.

Maddie Fey held up her hand to silence them. "Patience. Your questions will be answered, but not by me. There are others who have more knowledge than I about the Fire Demons' ability to assume the shapes of humans and other things. One of the reasons I invited you here, Steele, was to meet—"

"Invited!" Steele blurted out before he could stop himself. "If I remember correctly, my invitation didn't offer a choice. It said 'show up or die.'"

He looked at Maddie Fey and realized that she wasn't even listening to him. She was staring at the door. He sighed, confused by all the fantastical things she had told them. He felt that he was trapped in a nightmare and couldn't wake up.

He suddenly thought of something Maddie Fey had started to say. "You said that you were sent here for two reasons. One was to contact the wardens. What was the second?"

Maddie Fey took her eyes off the door and looked at him for a long time. When she finally answered, her voice was sad.

"I was sent here to find you, Steele."

Fire and Ice

Four billion and two hundred million years after the formation of the planet, the creatures we named Death breached the mantle and erupted onto the surface with the force of an asteroid impact.

Death's fire raged across our new world, destroying the mosses and ferns and the primitive gymnosperms that were cleansing the poison air. The fires melted the polar ice caps, and sent the planet spinning crazily in its fixed orbit. The fires launched hundreds of trillions of tons of smoke and dust into the atmosphere, forming a black, impenetrable cloud that blocked the planet's star and shut down photosynthesis.

Nuclear winter settled over the planet, bringing with it an ice age that destroyed all life forms on the planet, including plants, amphibians, reptiles, and insects. The deadly winter lasted eighty-five million years. As Death fled, shivering, back to its fiery prison, we despaired.

But in the oceans, under the ice, unaffected by the planet's surface conditions, life continued to evolve.

—Excerpt from *The Wardens' Logs*

Chapter Twelve

Wood

Steele slumped back in his chair, speechless. It was Mac who finally asked the obvious question.

"Why were you sent here to find Steele?"

But just then they heard a soft knocking on the door, and Mac's question went unanswered.

Maddie Fey got up and moved toward the door. From his place on the hearth, Wish lifted his head, his gleaming eyes following her.

Steele noticed, with a feeling of relief, that the rat was nowhere in sight.

Maddie Fey opened the door. A boy stood on the threshold, his hand raised as if he were about to knock again. Steele guessed that the boy was about the same age as he was.

"Where is Sydney?" asked Maddie Fey, looking past the boy into the hall.

The boy seemed bewildered, or nervous. He said something to Maddie Fey, but his voice was so low, Steele couldn't make out the words. Then Maddie Fey whispered to the rat, who had suddenly appeared as if by magic and who reared up on its hind legs. The rat's whiskers twitched as it listened, and then it dropped onto all fours and scuttled away.

Maddie Fey turned toward the table and introduced the boy as Wood Somers.

"It's short for Woodroffe," said the boy quietly. His eyes took in the others seated at the table. "Which one is Steele?" he asked.

"I'm Steele." Steele stood and reached out to shake the boy's hand, but Wood had already turned away and was talking to Riley. Steele found the boy's behaviour odd. But what was even stranger was the way he had asked about Steele, almost as if he had been waiting to meet him. But why then had he turned away? Steele was baffled. He shrugged and sat down again.

"Wood and Sydney Ravenhurst have also been looking for the missing children," said Maddie Fey, looking at Steele as she took her place at the head of the table. "I asked them here so that you could hear their stories from their own lips. But they were being followed, so Wood said they split up. I sent Nilats to watch for Sydney."

"Were they followed by Fire Demons?" asked Steele. He could sense that Maddie Fey was more worried about Sydney than she was letting on. And he noticed that Wish hadn't returned to his spot on the hearth, but was sitting on his haunches near the door, ears flat against his skull, eerie eyes fixed on the doorknob.

Wood sat down in the chair on Maddie Fey's right and straightened the silver-edged place mat. Then he looked at Steele and shrugged. "They wore black."

His voice was so quiet that Steele could barely hear him.

"Wood, while we wait for Sydney, why don't you tell Steele and his friends about your efforts to find the missing children." Maddie Fey stared at the door as she spoke, as if willing Sydney to appear.

Wood sighed softly. "It all started in September, after Syd's twin brother, William, disappeared."

Steele caught his breath. "The girl we're waiting for . . . you're saying her brother is one of the missing kids?"

Wood continued speaking in his quiet voice as if he hadn't heard Steele's question. But Steele knew he had heard, because as he went on with his story, his eyes returned to Steele again and again.

"Syd was with him at the time, but she didn't see a thing. It was just after six p.m. and they were on their way home from the public library. Syd said she heard a shrill whistling sound, like a police whistle, and looked to see what it was. She thought the sound was coming from a small fenced-in garden in front of a brownstone a few houses farther down the street. But she saw nothing. When she looked back, William was gone.

"Syd and I became friends because we do volunteer work at a homeless shelter on Thursdays after school and on weekends. We were discouraged when the police seemed to be getting nowhere in their search for William, so we decided to take matters into our own hands. We'd gotten to know a lot of homeless people since we'd been working at the shelter, and we came up with this plan to organize them to help us find William—"

The door flew open and the figure of the rat filled up the doorway. Wish growled softly.

"What is it, Nilats?" asked Maddie Fey, rising swiftly, her eyes flashing silver.

"She's lost," hissed the rat.

"No!" Wood left his chair and moved quickly toward the door. Steele got there first, but the rat bared its teeth and snarled at him. "Stay back!"

There was something about the combination of raw intelligence and ferocity in the rat's eyes that made Steele want to turn and run. But he stood his ground.

The rat lunged at Steele, driving him back toward the table. *I'm dead!* thought Steele.

"Let him be, Nilats," said Maddie Fey from behind Steele.

The rat skidded to a stop less than a foot from Steele, its red hair bristling and its breath wheezing from its pointed snout. Maddie Fey addressed the others.

"Sydney's missing. I must go with Nilats and find her at once. We will be back shortly."

"I'm coming with you," said Steele, determined not to be left behind like a little kid.

"We're coming too," said Mac and Riley in unison, rushing to Steele's side. "We can help."

Maddie Fey shook her head firmly. "There is nothing you can do, and besides, you will be safer here."

"I'm not staying behind," said Steele stubbornly.

"You will stay here," said Maddie Fey, glaring at him.

"You can't make us stay," snapped Steele.

"Oh, but I can," said Maddie Fey, her voice low and dangerous. Then she sighed. "I do not have time to argue with you, Steele." She looked at the rat. "Take Steele and Wood with you. Mac and Riley will come with me."

The thought of going with the rat made Steele frantic. "Do I have to?" he whispered, aware that he was whining, but past caring.

Maddie Fey ignored him. "Come! We must hurry," she

said, moving toward a door on the opposite side of the room, one Steele hadn't noticed before. Wish trotted protectively at her side.

They stepped out onto a broad, deserted sidewalk. It was still night. He gazed about, several minutes elapsing before he realized with a jolt that they were no longer in Toronto. He was shocked when he recognized the tallest building.

"The Empire State Building!" he whispered, punching Mac's shoulder. "Look at that, Mac! It's the Empire State Building! We're in New York."

"The CN Tower is taller," said Mac, the loyal Torontonian, pretending to be unimpressed by his first glimpse of the famous Manhattan landmark.

"That's because it's got that spike on the top," said Riley.

What's wrong with them? Steele wondered. *They're acting as if there's nothing strange about the fact that we're in New York.*

He tilted his head back and turned in a circle, blinking at the wall of towers surrounding him like a massive picket fence. Unlike in Toronto, where buildings sprawled almost haphazardly over a large area, the towers here seemed closer together and more imposing, as if they were purposely hemming him in.

Mac looked at him questioningly. "What?"

"We're in *New York*!" whispered Steele.

"Duh! So?"

"How did we *get* here, Mac?"

He looked back toward the door that they had just come through. On the street, as silent as sleep, sat Maddie Fey's long black limousine. Stunned, he grabbed his friend's arm.

"Look!" he whispered, pointing at the curb. "The limo!"

Mac and Riley stared at the limo and then at Steele.

"That's odd," said Riley. "How did *it* get here?"

"There's something very strange going on," said Mac, eyeing the limousine suspiciously. "What happened to Maddie Fey's house?"

"Exactly!" cried Steele, growing impatient. "We just left the house, but we got out of the limo."

Mac's eyes widened in disbelief. "Wait a minute," he exclaimed. "Are you saying what I think you're saying?"

Steele nodded. "The house, the limo—they're one and the same."

"I know it's impossible," said Riley. "But it's the only thing that makes sense."

"But how—?" Mac stopped and gazed at the limo.

"Let us go," said Maddie Fey. "Mac, Riley, and I will search the area around the Empire State Building. Keep your eyes open, and tell me immediately if you see anything suspicious. Steele, you and Wood will search the streets toward Park Avenue. If Sydney is still in the area, we shall find her. We'll meet back here in two hours."

"What if she's not in the area?" asked Riley.

"I will find her, Riley," answered Maddie Fey. "Wherever she is."

Steele watched Mac and Riley disappear with Maddie Fey and Wish. Then he turned and took off after Wood and the rat.

The rat set a rapid pace, moving along the sidewalk so swiftly that Steele and Wood had to run to keep up. They reached Fifth Avenue, where the one-way traffic moved continuously, even at this late hour. Steele glanced at his watch. It was just after three a.m. The sidewalk appeared deserted, but he caught furtive movements in the shadows, and he felt an uneasiness growing inside. *Probably just homeless people ducking out of sight,* he tried to reassure himself. But, what if they were Fire Demons disguised as vagrants? He chased the alarming thought away.

He and Wood followed the rat, jogging in silence along the shadowy sidewalk, each absorbed in his own thoughts. They turned right on West 37th Street and continued east, crossing Madison Avenue, until they reached the intersection of West 37th and a wide boulevard. Steele looked up at the street sign and said it aloud.

"Park Avenue!"

Steele pointed north at a huge, floodlit building that looked as if it had been built smack in the middle of Park Avenue. "What's that?"

"Grand Central Station," answered Wood shortly.

Steele didn't realize that he and Wood had fallen farther and farther behind the rat. It wasn't until they were stopped at East 40th and Park Avenue, waiting for the light to turn, that Steele noticed Nilats was half a block ahead.

The light flashed to green. Steele and Wood stepped into the street. Just then, Steele heard a muffled cry coming from behind. He paused and looked over his shoulder, listening for the sound to be repeated, his eyes peering into the shadows near the buildings. He was just about to turn away when he heard the sound again.

"Help!" It was a girl's voice.

Wood must have heard it too, because he suddenly streaked past Steele, running flat out. Steele took off after him, his eyes locked on Wood's back. He cried out in frustration when he saw Wood disappear into an alley as abruptly as if a hand had reached out and snatched him.

Oh, please! he prayed. *Don't let anything happen to him!*

Fear for the soft-spoken boy gave him renewed strength. He forced his legs to pump faster. "Wood!"

Steele reached the mouth of the alley and skidded to a stop. He peered into the darkness, but he saw nothing. Something grabbed him from behind and he tried to scream, but a pair of sharp claws sank into his arms and something rough and hairy clamped over his mouth. The claws tightened as his captor forced him forward into the alley. Steele struggled but he couldn't break free. Abruptly, the thing released him. Even as he fell to his knees on the rough concrete, Steele looked back toward the mouth of the alley. A large shape loomed above him, blocking the light from Park Avenue.

He opened his mouth to cry out.

"Silence!" hissed the rat, showering spittle over Steele's face. "Get behind me and keep still."

Steele's eyes quickly adjusted to the darkness. He turned and stared into the alley. He could just make out four burly forms coming cautiously toward him. They wore black cloaks with hoods that concealed their faces, but Steele saw their eyes glinting in the blackness beneath their hoods. As they approached, the forms spread out to form a barrier across the alley. They were moving swiftly now. But Maddie Fey's chauffeur was swifter. Steele couldn't believe the change that came over the rat. It lunged at the assailants—no longer an intelligent being but a maddened beast, a thing of pure animal instinct. It tore into them, sharp claws scratching, bared teeth snapping.

Steele held his breath at the ferocity of the rat's assault, watching in horror as one of the assailants flew through the air and smashed into the brick wall with a sound like that of a giant ripe tomato bursting, before slipping to the ground.

It was all over in a heartbeat. The four attackers lay in sodden heaps on the ground, their bodies broken and ruined. Steele felt bile rise up in his throat. Nearby, he heard someone gagging and then the sound of vomit splashing on the ground.

"Quick! Find the girl!" hissed the rat.

Steele couldn't see clearly, but he could have sworn that the rat's red snout was coated with something redder than its own hair, something that had a distinctive metallic smell. Dark froth stained the corners of its mouth. Steele felt sick again, but he swallowed the bitter taste when he felt Nilats's yellow eyes on him.

He enjoyed that! he thought, quickly turning away and moving deeper into the alley. He tried to shut his mind to the grisly gnawing, crunching, slurping sounds that came from behind him.

Steele found Wood leaning against a brick wall, gagging and rubbing his head. The boy looked at Steele and moaned softly. Steele noticed his torn clothes and the dark stains that had to be blood. Next to him, a body was lying face down in the dirt. It was too small to be one of the attackers.

Steele crawled over to it and pressed a finger against its neck. There was no pulse. He gently rolled the body over onto its back. The alley was dark, but he didn't need a light to tell him that the body was that of a girl.

He knew he had found Sydney.

New Life

For eighty-five million years Death's black cloud obscured the planet, making it appear like a black hole. But then, as the cloud grew less dense, the planet's star began its magic; the ice melted.

The end of the ice age left the surface of the planet submerged under a blanket of water. All manner of fishes, enormous and minuscule, struggled to exist in the oceans. Some species emerged for a brief second in the random scheme of evolution, and disappeared in the blink of an eye—prey for the giant sharks and other large predators.

Gradually, the waters receded. The mosses, ferns, and conifers burst from the soil, and new forms of plant life emerged—ginkgos, cycads, flowering plants, and grasses and cereals. Then came birds, and mammals, and the great dinosaurs.

But Death went after them and they too were gone.

And then, four billion and two million years after the planet had evolved from a ball of fire, rock, and ice, a primitive life form emerged from the oceans.

—Excerpt from *The Wardens' Logs*

Chapter Thirteen

The Visitor

The rat pushed Steele roughly aside and crouched over Sydney, sniffing rapidly, its bloody snout practically touching her face.

"She's not dead!" said the rat, in a voice that set Steele's teeth on edge.

"I felt! There was no pulse."

"Get her out of here! Back to the limo," screeched the rat. "Before I rip your heart out."

Keeping one wary eye on the rat, Steele gathered Sydney in his arms and struggled to his feet.

Wood had managed to stand, but he was stumbling about the alley, swaying unsteadily. Steele hoped that his companion could make it back to the limo without collapsing. As he staggered toward the mouth of the alley, Steele couldn't help looking for the bodies of their attackers, but there was no sign of them. Even their bones were gone.

"Who were they? What did you do to them?" he dared to ask the rat.

For an answer, Nilats nudged him in the back, prodding him toward the mouth of the alley.

When he reached the street, Steele looked back and shuddered. The rat lifted its snout and sniffed at the air before brushing past Steele and moving quickly along the sidewalk, back the way they had come. The way it scuttled close to the buildings, just like a normal rat, filled Steele with revulsion. Then he tightened his hold on Sydney and followed, moving with surprising speed, as if speed were the only thing that would erase the images of Maddie Fey's rat tearing the assailants apart in an alley far away from Toronto.

Maddie Fey's search party was waiting outside the limousine.

"Look!" cried Mac excitedly, pointing at Steele. "They found her."

Maddie Fey hurried to meet Steele; Mac and Riley followed, their eyes locked on the limp figure in his arms.

"Is she alive?" asked Maddie Fey, taking Sydney's hand.

Steele's breathing was harsh and laboured from carrying Sydney all the way back. Mac and Riley took the girl's legs, trying to relieve him of some of her weight.

"She's alive," said Steele.

"I'll take her," snarled the rat, who had appeared out of nowhere. It snatched Sydney out of their grasp. Then it slung her, none too gently, over its shoulder and disappeared through one of the doors of the limousine. Steele glared at the open door, loathing for the rat gnawing at his heart. He reached for the handle of the second door from the rear.

"Not that door," said Maddie Fey, stepping between him and the door he had been reaching for. She pointed at the open door. "Use that one."

Steele frowned and followed the others through the door the rat had used. *What is so special about that other door?* he wondered.

The door closed behind them, plunging them into blackness.

This time, when the darkness disappeared, Steele and his friends were in a grand library. They exchanged surprised glances and looked about.

Tall wooden bookshelves occupied three of the four walls. The shelves were crammed full of books of every size and shape imaginable. In the middle of the room stood a long, narrow table, with comfortable-looking chairs placed haphazardly about it. The table and the seats of the chairs were stacked with books. Along the fourth wall was a black marble fireplace; a fire burned brightly in the hearth.

"I don't understand," cried Riley, pulling her ponytail in frustration.

Steele wasn't sure that he understood either. In Toronto, he had been dragged inside the limo only to find himself in Maddie Fey's house. A short time ago they had left the house through a door in the dining room and ended up in New York outside the limousine. He didn't know how the house became the limo and vice-versa, but he suddenly knew how they had got to New York.

"The limo doors are portals," he said softly, staring at Maddie Fey in wonder.

Maddie Fey smiled slightly. "Yes."

"Where do they go?" asked Steele.

"That is not your concern," she answered shortly. And then she left the room, followed by the rat, with Sydney slung over his shoulder, her arms dangling behind him like the limbs of a rag doll.

"How did you figure out the doors were portals?" asked Mac.

"I can't believe it took me this long," said Steele. "I guess I was so focused on trying to understand how the house could be the limo that I missed the obvious. When Wood came in, I assumed that he and Sydney were from Toronto, because that's where we entered the limo. But when we got out in New York, I should have made the connection."

"Not necessarily," reasoned Mac. "We'd been here a long time by then. Long enough to drive from Toronto to New York. It's not that far."

"It's at least seven hours from Toronto, Mac. We might have been in Maddie Fey's house for two or even three hours, but certainly not seven. No. We could only do it if the doors are portals."

"There are a dozen doors on each side of the limo," said Mac. "What if each door leads to a different city!"

"Or a different world," said Riley.

They didn't speak for a long time. Then Steele told them about the second door from the rear on the passenger side, the one Maddie Fey had stopped him from opening.

"Whoa!" said Mac. "We've got to get a look in there."

"Are you out of your mind?" asked Riley.

"Come on, Riley. Don't you want to know why she wouldn't let Steele open that door?"

"No," snapped Riley. "I don't want to know."

"I don't want to know," Mac mimicked.

"Do what you want," said Riley angrily. "I'm not going near that door." Then she noticed the platters on the coffee table. "Look! Food!"

Mac's ears perked up at mention of food, and he made a beeline for the coffee table.

But Steele wandered about the library, staring at the tall wooden bookshelves. He tried to read the titles on the spines of some of the books, but they were in a strange language.

Probably Arjellan, he thought. He looked toward the fireplace. Silver candlesticks with long silver candles rested on the mantel, flickering a soft light. On the wall above the mantel hung a picture, a pastoral scene depicting two men sitting on a log, smoking long-stemmed pipes as they gazed out over a flock of fluffy black sheep. Steele moved closer to the painting and peered at the sheep. Now he could see that they weren't sheep at all, but some sort of animal he had never seen on Earth.

On a low table in front of the fireplace the three platters were piled high with an assortment of sandwiches. And in the middle of the table was a large crystal decanter filled with a brilliant yellow liquid. Mac and Riley were busily wolfing down sandwiches as if they hadn't eaten for a week. Steele's stomach growled.

Steele, Mac, and Riley sprawled on the floor about the fire, worrying about Sydney, talking about the attackers in the alley, the missing kids, and the Fire Demons, and washing down sandwiches with the yellow drink, which Riley claimed tasted like green grapes, peaches, and strawberries.

"I've got to phone home," said Riley. "My mother's going to kill me when she hears where I am."

"My dad probably thinks I've been kidnapped," said Mac. "I bet he's hounding the police at this very minute."

Steele knew that his father would be going out of his mind with worry. "Riley's right," he said. "We've got to call home. I don't think we should tell them everything, like about the limo and Maddie Fey and the rat—just say we haven't been abducted and that we'll call again."

He noticed that Wood didn't join in their conversation. He sat in a chair in the shadows near a corner of the room, and was so still that Steele thought he was sleeping. He felt sorry for Wood. Besides being worried to death over Sydney, he must be pretty sore after being beaten by those creatures in the alley. Steele wondered if his injuries were more serious than anyone had thought. Perhaps he should tell Maddie Fey. He realized that Wood was awake when he heard the sound of the door opening and the boy sat forward in his chair.

Steele held his breath as Maddie Fey came into the room.

"Sydney is awake—barely," she said. "She asked for you, Steele."

"She's my friend," said Wood, barely above a whisper. "I'm coming too."

Maddie Fey looked at Mac and Riley. "You'll get to see her later."

Mac and Riley didn't argue. On hearing that Sydney was going to be OK, they high-fived each other, and celebrated the good news by piling more sandwiches onto their plates and topping up their glasses.

Maddie Fey led Steele and Wood along several corridors, down a short flight of stairs, and into a stark white room. Sydney was lying on her back on a small bed. Steele thought it looked like a hospital room, but when he sniffed he couldn't detect the unpleasant smell of formaldehyde and disinfectant that he associated with hospitals.

In the dim light from a lamp on a stand beside the bed, Sydney's dark skin glistened like polished mahogany. The ends of her short black hair were highlighted with different colours—red, yellow, and orange. Steele was surprised that the colours suited her. She was slim, even slimmer than Riley. As if she sensed him staring at her, the girl's eyes fluttered open.

"Steele." Her voice was thin and shaky, and blood trickled from a cut on her lower lip.

Steele moved close to the bed so that she could see him. "Hi, Sydney," he said. "I'm glad you're going to be OK." He saw the scratches on her face and the darker blotches on her neck, and felt anger rise up inside him. "Who did this to you?"

Sydney caught his wrist and clutched it so tightly Steele winced.

"Don't talk," she rasped. "Listen! Please. Found . . ."

"We found you," Steele assured her. "You're with friends now."

Sydney tightened her grip on his arm. "Not . . . meant. Found . . . kids."

Steele looked at Wood on the other side of the bed. "She said something about kids. Is she saying that you and she found the missing kids?"

Wood's shrug told Steele that he didn't know what Sydney was talking about.

He reached for Sydney's free hand. "Syd?"

Sydney's eyes fluttered as she struggled to focus on Wood.

"Wood? Where's Wood?" Her voice was weaker now.

Steele leaned closer. "It's OK, Sydney. Wood's OK. He's right here."

"No!" Sydney pulled on Steele's arm to try to raise herself. Her eyes were round with terror. "Wood? They followed us. Had to split up. They killed him!"

"She doesn't understand," said Steele, looking at Maddie Fey helplessly.

"You better go now," said Maddie Fey, gently prying Sydney's hand from Steele's wrist. "Understanding will come with rest."

Steele backed slowly away from the bed and suddenly

stumbled. "I'm tired," he said, brushing his hand over his face.

"Nilats will show you to your room," said Maddie Fey, without looking around.

Steele awoke sometime later with a start. Something was wrong! He sat up and looked about, momentarily disoriented. He was in a strange bed, in a strange room, and he had no idea how he got there. A soft light burned in a lamp on the mantel of a fireplace in the wall at the foot of the bed. He breathed easier when he recognized the two figures sleeping in a pair of overstuffed chairs on either side of the fireplace.

And then everything came rushing back.

"Mac!" he whispered.

Mac's eyes shot open. "What? What?" When he saw Steele, he looked relieved. "Riley! He's awake!"

"Go away," mumbled Riley.

"What are you doing here?" asked Steele.

"When you didn't come back, Maddie Fey made the rat take us to you."

"But, why didn't you go to bed?"

"We decided it would be better if we stuck together," said Mac. "And besides, we wanted to find out what happened with Sydney." He snuggled deeper into the chair.

Steele swung his legs over the side of the bed. "Well, I've had some sleep, so why don't you take a turn."

"It's OK," said Mac. "These chairs are really comfortable."

Steele looked at Riley, about to offer her the bed, but her soft, regular breathing told him she was asleep again.

"What happened with Sydney?" Mac asked.

"She's hurt pretty bad," said Steele, feeling angry again. "You should see the bruises forming on her neck. They must have been trying to choke her when we heard her shout for help. It's a good thing Wood got to that alley in time."

"Did she say anything?"

"Yeah," said Steele, remembering Sydney's incoherent mutterings. "She kept asking for Wood, but we couldn't convince her that he's still alive—even when she saw him. She said something else. It sounded like 'Found . . . kids.' At first, I thought she was trying to tell me they'd found the missing kids. But I don't think she knew what she was saying."

For a while they sat in companionable silence. Steele settled back against the pillows and stared at the ceiling, wishing he knew how he fit into everything. He had learned a lot since the rat had dragged him into Maddie Fey's limousine, but he still hadn't learned why he was in danger, or why Maddie Fey had come looking for him. After a while, his eyes closed.

The next thing he knew, he was sitting up in bed, his heart thumping loud and hard in his chest. Something had awakened him—a cry from somewhere in the house.

Then he heard another sound, a soft hissing or a sigh, just outside his door. He stared at the door, straining to hear the sound again. But Maddie Fey's great house was now as silent as a morgue.

Then the doorknob began to turn. Someone was coming into his room! Steele froze. The door opened slowly and a dark figure paused in the doorway and regarded him.

"What do you want?" said Steele, struggling to identify the figure. "Is that you, Wood?"

Wood slipped into the room and closed the door. "I came to

make sure that you were all right," he said, his voice barely audible.

"I'm OK," said Steele. "Just tired. All I need is a good night's sleep."

The door flew open and Maddie Fey stood there. Her cold silver eyes shifted from Steele to Wood.

"What's going—?"

"Silence!" Unlike Wood's flat, unemotional voice, Maddie Fey's was clear, and terribly cold.

She extended her arm toward Wood. "You do not belong here."

At her side, Wish's fur spiked, and the hound bared sharp fangs that gleamed like polished glass in the lamplight.

Steele saw that Mac and Riley were wide awake now, their eyes fastened on Wood, their faces frozen in fear. He waved his arms to get their attention. When Mac finally looked at him, he mouthed the word *go!* and pointed at the door. Mac hesitated. He seemed torn between getting away and helping Steele. But then he dropped onto the floor and crawled behind the chair, motioning to Riley to follow suit.

The laugh that erupted from Wood's throat made Steele's hair stand on end. The boy leaped onto the chair Riley had just vacated, and his body began to waver and ripple. He laughed again, a high, ear-piercing cackle that reverberated from the solid wooden beams on the ceiling.

"Your wardens are dead!" he screeched. "We are free. Now I will kill you and the boy!"

His voice certainly wasn't flat and quiet now. His screeching and screaming turned Steele's blood to ice water. Steele looked past Maddie Fey into the hall, expecting to see the rat, but it was nowhere in sight. When he looked back, he cried out in terror. Wood's flesh stretched, and cracked, and split, and then melted away, as he grew bigger and bigger, morphing into a huge roiling, elongated thing of orange, red, and black molten fire. A Fire Demon!

The heat emanating from the creature formed rivers of sweat on Steele's face, singeing his eyebrows and the hair hanging over his forehead. He knew he had to get out of bed and make it through the door, but he couldn't move a muscle.

Mac and Riley didn't seem to have any trouble moving. They crawled along the wall and disappeared into the hall.

Maddie Fey kept her arm extended toward the Fire Demon. She was small, and looked as fragile as a paper doll next to the glowing, looming monster. Steele opened his mouth to warn her away, but he was terrified that his shout would draw the creature's attention to him, so he quickly shut it again.

The chair on which the creature stood burst into flames which rapidly spread to a wooden side table. The logs in the neatly laid fireplace roared into life, spitting and hissing like a pit of burning snakes. The creature's screams filled the air. Steele's face was burning now, blistering from the intense heat, but his fear paralyzed him as if he had been turned to stone.

"Die!" the Fire Demon screamed again at Maddie Fey— releasing the pent-up rage and hatred it had harboured and nurtured during its long imprisonment. Then it sprang at her, flames licking the air about it.

Steele forced himself to move. He slid off the bed and dashed to Maddie Fey's side. He didn't know what he was supposed to do, or if he could do anything; he only knew that he couldn't let her face the Fire Demon alone. He would stand with her—and probably die with her.

"Steele! No!" Riley screamed from the hallway behind him.

But Steele was beyond listening. Something had snapped inside when he saw Maddie Fey's slim, rigid form facing the creature as if she were its equal in strength. He knew they weren't evenly matched. He thought of Dirk the Jerk, and the countless times he had cowered from and pleaded with the bully to spare him. Maddie Fey didn't stand a chance against this monstrous fiery creature, but she didn't turn and run away. If she could stand there, so bravely facing her death, Steele could stand with her so that she would not be alone.

The heat was unbearable. He felt his blood boiling, and knew that his clothes and even his body were seconds away from igniting. Through stinging eyes, he glanced at Maddie Fey. There was no sign of sweat on her face. The girl was shimmering with a dull, pale light—like burning ice. Her long hair blew back from her face, and Steele noticed the tiny black bats on her earrings suddenly open their wings and streak toward the ceiling.

Steele thought he was screaming, but he couldn't hear himself over the shrieks of his companions and the hissing sound of fire exploding from the Fire Demon. He watched, spellbound, as Maddie Fey slowly opened her palm toward the flaming creature. Her expression was so sad, he felt tears spring up in his own eyes. Something shimmering drifted from her hand, filling the air in the room with glowing flakes that looked like snow, but weren't.

Where the flakes touched it, black spots appeared on the monster that had once called itself Wood, dousing its fire and eating through its burning essence. The creature howled and screeched in anguish, biting and clawing at its own fiery liquid flesh to get at the shimmering flakes, tearing great gobs of magma from itself and flinging the molten fragments about the room, where they splattered against the walls and the floor and instantly burst into flames.

Realizing that the girl's powerful magic was destroying it, the Fire Demon drew its fire back into itself, and then, in a last, desperate bid to survive, launched itself at Maddie Fey, fighting through its own bubbling form to overcome her. It looked like a swimmer wading through chest-high water. But the Fire Demon was doomed. Black pinpoint holes continued to appear in its burning flesh, expanding and consuming the creature until it shrivelled into a trail of black ash on the smouldering floor.

Out of the corner of his eye, Steele caught a glimpse of the rat, red as melted lava, scuttle into the room and sweep the cast-off, dripping, blazing pools of the Fire Demon into a large square container with a thick lid. And then Mac was there, blasting the flaming bed with a fire extinguisher.

"Who *are* you?" Steele whispered to Maddie Fey when it was over and the smoke had finally dissipated.

Maddie Fey gazed at him from eyes as blue and as deep as the Atlantic Ocean. Steele noticed that she looked as perfect as she had the day she stepped out of her long black limousine outside his school. Her clothes weren't scorched and tattered like his. He also noticed that the tiny black bats had returned and now clung to her earlobes with delicate miniature claws. He forced himself not to wince when she reached out and gently touched the blisters on the back of his hand.

"I'm a Mage," she said softly, her eyes switching from blue to silver. "Like you."

Evolution]

It took four billion and two million years for humankind to evolve on this planet. Then things accelerated. The first hominid appeared. It was a walking ape that lived on the forest floor, and had hands and feet. Above, in the trees, lived its ape cousin, who had hands on its four limbs. We named the first human Ramidus.

The greatest, most constant, threats to Ramidus were the great cats with hungry yellow eyes that roamed the forest floor, and Death.

But before we could stop it, Death went after the cats.

With the cats wiped out, Ramidus's cousins left their treetop homes and rejoined Ramidus on the forest floor. Eventually, their gene pools merged.

But there were other cats. They and Death found Ramidus, and the killing began again.

—Excerpt from *The Wardens' Logs*

Chapter Fourteen

Worms

Steele backed slowly away from Maddie Fey. A Mage?

He struggled to hold the threads of his being together, but they were coming undone, unravelling faster than if he had pulled one of the strands of yarn in his grandmother's scarf. He backed into a chair and spun around, startled. His backpack was hanging from the chair and he reached for it, realizing as he did so that the chair was the only piece of furniture in the room that had escaped the Fire Demon's fury.

He turned back. Mac and Riley, pale faces streaked with soot, were staring at him from the doorway.

"You're wrong," he said to Maddie Fey. "I'm not a Mage."

Maddie Fey didn't answer.

"Tell me why you called me a Mage," he demanded.

Steele couldn't help noticing how pale and tired she looked. He felt a twinge of guilt as the full implication of what had happened in this room a short time ago suddenly struck him. Maddie Fey had fought and destroyed a Fire Demon! No wonder she looked half dead. He almost turned away then, but he couldn't. He had to know why she had called him a Mage. And he had to know now.

"Maddie Fey—"

"Please, Steele. Not now! I will show you something later," she said. "When you see—"

"When later?" Steele wasn't going to be put off with another *later.*

He heard the beginnings of a growl rumble in Wish's chest. At the same time, sharp claws cut into his shoulder and spun him away from Maddie Fey.

"Get out!" snarled the rat, marching Steele roughly toward the door.

The creature's strong rodent smell filled Steele's nostrils and coated his throat, making him gag. He tried to shrug free of the sharp claws, but the rat's grip was like a vise. At the door, the rat kicked Steele into the hall, where he landed on his face on the floor.

"And stay away from her! Or I'll tear you in half."

"Leave him alone," shouted Mac, glowering at the rat. "Are you OK?" he asked Steele.

Steele's pride hurt more than the kick to his behind.

"I hate that rat," he said through his teeth. "I really hate that rat." He looked along the hall. "Where's Riley? She was here a second ago."

"She took off," said Mac. "Come on! I know where she went."

They found Riley sitting on the floor of Maddie Fey's magnificent library, hugging her knees and looking lost and frightened. Her eyes were red from crying.

"Oh, Steele! You've got to get us out of here." Riley wiped her eyes with her arm. "I can't stand it anymore. And, besides, my mom's going to be so mad."

Steele dropped onto the floor beside her.

"I wish I could," he said. "But I don't think that's an option anymore. I wish I knew if the Wood creature contacted other Fire Demons. When we were looking for Sydney, I lost sight of him for a few minutes when he went into the alley." He patted Riley's shoulder. "You can't go home yet, Riley. I'm afraid they'd find you."

Riley's shoulders shook as she cried silently. Then she shuddered violently. "That thing . . . all that fire . . . I'm so scared."

"I thought you were going to die, Steele," added Mac.

Steele took a deep breath. "Me too," he said. "When Maddie Fey told us about the Fire Demons, they didn't seem real somehow. I don't know what I thought they'd look like, but it was nothing like the monster that took Wood's shape."

"Where's the real Wood?" asked Riley. "Is he . . . dead?"

Steele and Mac looked at each other and shrugged helplessly.

"I don't know," said Steele. "Let's hope he's still alive."

They sat close together on the floor. Steele didn't have to ask them what they were thinking. He knew they were thinking about the real Wood and wondering what had happened to him.

"Oh, no!" Steele cried, shattering the silence and startling Mac and Riley. "How could I have been so stupid?"

His companions looked at him questioningly.

"Maddie Fey! The rat!" He tried to explain. "After Maddie Fey destroyed the Fire Demon, she said I was a Mage. When I asked her what she meant, she looked different—like she was really exhausted. I thought it was from fighting the Fire Demon, but now I realize that she was sad because of Wood."

"Then the rat went ballistic and kicked him in the butt," said Mac.

"If you really were a Mage, you could have shrivelled that rat into a tiny mouse," said Riley, breaking into a grin.

"I'm not a Mage," said Steele adamantly. "If I were, don't you think I would have made Mac disappear long ago?"

They laughed softly, forgetting for a few moments the terrible things that had happened over the past few hours.

"How long have we been here?" asked Mac.

Steele looked at his watch. "I got in the limo at midnight. It's now seven forty-five."

"Only eight hours," said Mac. "It seems as if we've been here forever."

"Is that a.m. or p.m.?" asked Riley.

Steele shook his head. He didn't know.

Maddie Fey walked into the room then, with Sydney at her side, and the three friends' grief and dread and angst came back. Sydney looked like the living dead, with ugly scratches on her face and black bruises on her neck. She walked slowly, as if something inside were broken, and eased herself onto the sofa. Despite her injuries, she managed a weak grin.

"Maddie Fey told me what happened," she said. "How you guys found me. I guess I wouldn't be here now if you hadn't come looking for me. Thanks."

Steele felt himself turn red, but hid his embarrassment behind a question. "Why did you ask for me when you regained consciousness?" he asked. "What were you trying to tell me?"

Sydney blinked back the tears that welled up in her eyes. "I wanted to tell you about Wood. But then I saw him with you and I was scared."

"Why?" asked Riley.

"Because," she said softly. "I saw them kill Wood."

Mac and Riley stared at her, surprised.

"So you knew all the time that the person with us wasn't Wood? You were trying to warn us." It all made sense to Steele now.

Sydney nodded. "I couldn't come right out with it, because he was there in the room. I couldn't risk getting you all killed."

"I guess you know what happened in my room a little while ago."

She nodded again. "I'm glad that monster is gone," she said vehemently, her damaged face twisted with loathing.

"Who were those people in the alley—the ones Steele said attacked you?" asked Mac.

Sydney shivered. "They aren't people. They're filthy worms."

"Worms?" Mac looked confused. He turned to Maddie Fey. "You never told us about any worms."

Maddie Fey shook her head as if Mac's question amused her. "There are a great many things I have not told you," she said. "But I will tell you what I know about the creatures Sydney calls 'worms.'"

"Well?" said Mac bluntly. "Are you planning to tell me today, or next week?"

Steele felt the air about him charge with hostility. Mac was being his usual obnoxious self. He sighed heavily. For as long as they had been friends, Mac's mouth had provoked fights. Unfortunately, Steele was the one who usually ended up black and blue, because he couldn't just stand there and watch his little friend get killed. Miraculously, Mac usually managed to escape without a scratch. Steele often wondered if his friend realized how small he was—or had the thought never crossed his mind?

As if Maddie Fey had sensed his urge to kick Mac, she looked toward him. "It's all right," she said. "I was just wondering where to begin." Maddie Fey moved to stand in front of the fireplace. "When Sydney said those creatures in the alley were not people, she wasn't speaking metaphorically. They are not human."

Steele and his companions stood still, listening intently.

"They are evil things that belong to the Fire Demons. They do not possess intelligence or a conscience. But they are creatures of instinct, cunning and dangerous. And they must hide their malformed shapes under hooded cloaks."

"Are they aliens, like the Fire Demons?" asked Mac.

Maddie Fey smiled sadly. "No, Mac. They are not aliens. They were here before you were born. They were here long before the first humans walked the earth. They were simple burrowing insects. And as humankind evolved, they also changed." She paused for a moment. "And then they were poisoned, first by you—"

"I never—" Mac bristled in indignation.

"She doesn't mean you, personally," said Steele.

Mac ignored him.

"The chemicals you have been feeding the soil for centuries poisoned them, and caused them to mutate into new species. They began to grow, and their appetites also grew. To catch bigger prey, they developed sharp teeth and claws and other things for trapping and killing. Then the Fire Demons poisoned their minds and filled them with greed."

"How?" asked Riley.

"Well, until the Fire Demons found them, they were content to remain in the ground where they had always been. They had no interest in events on the surface or in the people, and other life forms, who lived there. The Fire Demons showed them a world just above, where food was plentiful, and they promised them that world in exchange for their allegiance."

"You mean that those things in the alley . . . those worms . . . were going to eat us?" Steele felt sick.

"I cannot say for certain," said Maddie Fey. "But I think not. I have a feeling they were acting for the Fire Demons. No, the eating would have come later."

"So what do the Fire Demons need the worms for?"

"To snatch the kids," replied Sydney.

"Why do you call them 'worms'?" asked Riley.

"Because they keep coming out of the ground," answered Sydney. "I had never heard of them until my brother disappeared. But according to the homeless communities, they first started appearing in abandoned subway tunnels about a year ago. And now, they attack almost daily. Thousands of homeless people have died fighting the worms."

Sydney's matter-of-fact narration of a war between worms and homeless people sent chills along Steele's spine. He stared at her, suddenly curious to know how old she was. She certainly looked older than him, but then, perhaps New York did that to kids—made them grow up fast. After all, New York was way bigger than Toronto, almost four times as big.

"The ones in the alley were covered in black cloaks and hoods," he said. "What do they look like underneath?"

"Sort of like insects," said Sydney wearily. "With fangs, and tentacles, and lots of legs with sharp pincers or claws.

Some look like scorpions, some look like spiders or flies. And they're big."

"Did the worms kill Wood?" asked Riley.

But instead of replying, Sydney buried her face in her hands and started crying.

"She should rest now," said Maddie Fey. "It is too soon to talk about some things."

"I'm sorry, Sydney," said Steele. "But, please. Just answer one more question. In your room you were trying to tell me something else . . . something about kids. Do you remember what it was?"

Sydney wiped away her tears and stared at him. "Oh my God," she whispered, standing up slowly as if in a daze. "The missing kids. Wood and I . . . we found them." Then, without warning, she swayed and toppled over in a dead faint.

"How can she faint now?" cried Mac. "Without telling us where—"

"Shut up, Mac," cried Riley, rushing over to Sydney. "Stop being such a jerk."

"Sorry," mumbled Mac. "Is she OK?"

"She needs rest," said Maddie Fey. "There is nothing we can do until she awakens. I think we could all do with a little sleep. Come. Your rooms are ready."

Steele and Mac carried Sydney to her stark white room and then followed Maddie Fey to their rooms like defeated warriors.

Steele tried to feel excited about finding the missing kids, but he was too numb to feel much of anything. When he reached his new room, he didn't even bother to undress. He fell on top of the covers and was asleep before his head hit the pillow.

For a long time, nothing stirred in Maddie Fey's house.

Evolution II

We drove Death back and down into the fire and kept it imprisoned for hundreds of years in hopes that Ramidus would survive the cats. We waited and kept watch over Death, our thoughts on the fragile ape-human. We knew that it would die if it remained in the forest; we also knew that it wasn't fast enough or strong enough to survive on the plains.

When many hominid lifetimes had passed, we flew to the surface. There, we watched in horror as packs of wild, spotted jungle cats feasted on the primitive ape. The population had dwindled to the point of extinction. We sighed heavily. We had kept him safe from Death for hundreds of years, but we could not protect him from the cats.

—Excerpt from *The Wardens' Logs*

Chapter Fifteen

Eyes

Steele awoke feeling tense and desperate. He got up and wandered aimlessly about the room. *I've got to talk to Maddie Fey,* he thought, opening the door and slipping into the hall, his eyes peeled for the rat.

At the end of the hall was a small elevator. Steele stared at it for a second, then opened the glass door, slid the brass gate back, and stepped inside. There were only two buttons on a brass plaque beside the door. In the middle of each button was a symbol. Steele didn't know what the symbols meant, but he pressed the top button. The elevator bumped and lurched as it slowly moved upward.

Ages seemed to pass before the elevator ground to a stop, almost jolting Steele off his feet. He slid the gate back and pushed through the door. Then he froze, gazing about in wonder.

He was in a small observatory. Overhead, the sliding roof of the dome was open, allowing a sleek telescope to penetrate the night sky. Maddie Fey was sitting in a large chair fastened to brackets on a raised platform, peering through the telescope. She was so still, so focused on what was out there, that Steele felt like an intruder. He turned to go back to the elevator.

"Come in, Steele," said Maddie Fey, without taking her eyes off the telescope. "I've been waiting for you."

Steele mounted the steps and joined her on the platform. "I need to talk to you."

"I know," she said.

But Steele wasn't sure how to begin. Now that he was actually alone with Maddie Fey and could ask the questions that were burning inside him, he felt shy and childish.

"Er . . . I—I'm sorry about Wood," he said. "It wasn't your fault . . ."

Maddie Fey turned to him. "I know that, Steele. But thank you anyway. I grieve for Wood, but I was enraged at the creature for coming to my home in human form. I was angry with myself for letting that monster trick me into believing it was my friend. But I am no longer angry. It is not a helpful emotion."

She rose and stepped aside. "Here. You look."

"It's an awesome telescope," said Steele, taking her place on the chair. "I've never looked through one this powerful—only Mac's, and it's minuscule compared to yours. But Mac's isn't that bad, you know. It's good enough for us. We can see Mars and Venus quite clearly. Wait till Mac sees this though . . ." He realized he was babbling like an idiot but he couldn't seem to stop. Sweat formed on his palms as he reached for the bars on either side of the instrument to steady himself. Then he peered through the telescope.

The nearness of the stars and planets and their satellites took his breath away. He could see them as clearly as if he were among them. But as soon as he began to scan the sky for planets and constellations he could identify, he knew that he wasn't looking at the familiar sky over Toronto, or even New York.

"Where is this?" he asked, gripping the bars tightly to stop the trembling in his hands.

"I like to see my world," said Maddie Fey. "Look to the left. At ten o'clock. You'll see a blue planet with lots of green and red. It's got three moons. That's my home. That's Arjella."

Steele could have stared into the telescope forever. But already Maddie Fey was typing commands into a computer and the roof was sliding back in place. Reluctantly, Steele sat back in the chair.

"Why did you come here to find me?" he asked.

Maddie Fey looked at him thoughtfully as she slipped a round, flat medallion from under her black shirt. The disk was as red as blood. Steele noticed that even in the dark it seemed to glow as if a fire burned inside it. She pulled the chain over her head and held it out to Steele.

"Here. This is Ees. It belongs to you," she said. "It will show you the things you need to know."

Steele took the disk from her hand and stared at it. At first he thought it was a flat ruby, but from the way it felt it had to be made of some metal or mineral. It was warm against his palm, and as smooth as silk. When he raised the disk toward the light he was surprised that he could see right through it, except for a cloudy part the size of a pea in the middle. His hand tingled. He looked at Maddie Fey questioningly.

"Look into the clouds," she said.

Steele squinted at the dark spot in the centre of the disk. Nothing happened. Just as he was about to toss it back to Maddie Fey, the small cluster of clouds at its core began to rotate, slowly at first and then faster and faster. Through minute gaps in the clouds, he thought he saw a ball of fire.

Without warning, the cloud expanded outward, fast. Now Steele seemed to be standing inside the clouds, with nothing between him and the inferno. He felt sweat pouring down his face and neck. The wave of fire was coming closer by the second. He tried to look away but his eyes wouldn't obey. His shirt erupted into flames. He beat his arms against the fabric, once again feeling blisters forming on his flesh—swelling and bursting as if his skin were burning away. When the fire flowed over him, swallowed him, the pain was so intense that he knew he was screaming, but he couldn't hear a sound. Hot tears sizzled down his cheeks, burning into his face like molten metal.

"Oh God! Make it stop! Make it stop!"

The pain vanished as suddenly as it had struck. Steele glanced down at his body, naked and glowing eerily. His clothes lay in ashes about his feet. Fearfully, he touched his arms, groaning with relief when he felt firm flesh under his fingers. Even the blisters on the backs of his hands were gone. Somehow he knew that he wasn't wearing his old skin. It had burned away when the fire consumed him. He didn't understand what had happened, but he felt as if he had died and been reborn.

Cautiously, he looked about. He was on a flat-topped knoll overlooking a valley that stretched on and on, seemingly forever. What struck him at once was the complete absence of light. No stars winked overhead. There was nothing up there at all. The sky was like a dark, stretched canvas that had been abandoned by an artist overwhelmed by the sheer immensity of it. But despite the lack of light, Steele had no trouble seeing far across the barren landscape. The sensation was so eerie it made his scalp tingle.

There was no colour either. In all directions the landscape was as grey as ashes. There were no green trees or grass, no yellow, red, or pink flowers, no blue rivers. There was only hard-packed grey earth and rocks as far as the eye could see. As he gazed down and across the desolate, bleached-grey valley, Steele realized that the silence here wasn't like the natural silence of his house in the dead of night.

No. This was a heavy, oppressive silence, as unnatural as the empty sky over his head—the complete absence of sound. It was like death. And Steele knew intuitively that nothing lived here—neither flora nor fauna. No people toiled the grey ash fields, no birds flew in the black sky, no crickets chirruped, no bees buzzed, no animals scratched, no bugs skittered under rocks. . . .

There were no rushing rivers to cradle life, no brooks burbling from among the rocks. There was no wind, no breeze to disturb the hard, dry soil. Even the air felt unnatural: it made Steele light-headed. He imagined that his own quick breaths were the first and only sounds ever to intrude on the primeval silence of this strangest of all worlds.

And then he heard something—a familiar sound that wound about his heart like a warm blanket. He tensed and strained to pinpoint the source, his head suddenly whipping toward a large grey boulder perched on the edge of the hill, leaning precariously out over the downward slope. Over there! The distinctive *click! clack!* of his grandmother's knitting needles was music to his ears. Steele ran toward the boulder.

"GM!"

He saw the back of the familiar rocking chair. He walked past the chair and dropped onto the hard ground so that he was facing the old woman sitting there, rocking gently back and forth, her fingers fluttering like butterflies as they manipulated the long knitting needles. He reached out to touch her arm, but his hand passed through something that felt like cold, fine mist and left a dusting of sparkles on his palm.

"Are we dead, GM?" he asked. "Is that why we're here?"

His grandmother ignored him. She wore the secret smile Steele knew so well. Her faded blue eyes were locked on something on the far side of the great grey mountain peaks, where the boy's eyes couldn't follow. Steele stared at her, flinching inwardly when he noticed the two-inch gap between the top of her head and the chalk mark he had made on the back of her chair. So he had been right all along; GM was shrinking.

"Aw, GM! Don't leave me," he pleaded, bowing his head while he wiped his stinging eyes on his bare arm.

The frail old woman knitted feverishly, as if she knew that her time was running out and she must finish the scarf before it did. Steele listened to the familiar *click! clack!* of her needles, then raised his head to look at his grandmother. She had run out of yarn, but her needles continued to click together. She was knitting nothing. The sight tore at Steele's heart.

And then an even more extraordinary thing happened.

GM knitted a star! And then another! Then a blue river gushed from invisible threads passing through his grandmother's fingers and looping about the tips of her needles. The amazing, living scarf grew rapidly.

Steele's mind absorbed everything like a greedy sponge, expanding, becoming heavier as it soaked up the fantastic images that flowed from GM's needles. She knitted the Milky Way galaxy spiralling into blackness, like water being sucked down a drain. She fashioned black holes, like smudged thumbprints in the sky. She knitted thick, roiling clouds of smoke, and Steele could see flames through gaps in the smoke. He knew what it was. A nebula! A star maker!

From her needles came sound and light and colour. And more! Steele felt fresh air on his face as a gentle breeze ruffled his hair. He smelled the sweet perfume of wildflowers mingling with the scent of fresh green grass. And he knew that somehow his grandmother had knitted the very air he drew into his lungs.

From the old woman's knitting needles shot a bird that flapped its wings and lifted into the sky, its throat bursting with song. A speckled fish leaped in the blue river. A whale slapped its mighty tail and dove into a great ocean. A snake slithered through grass and disappeared under a rock. Giant waves crashed on pristine shores, and mighty forests groaned and creaked and pushed skyward. Great beasts tore across the plains, or stalked their prey on soft, lethal paws on the forest floor.

Steele had no idea how long he had been sitting motionless on the soft grass that now covered the hillside before he finally grasped what was happening. His grandmother was now knitting his world!

Suddenly, the *click! clack!* of the needles slowed and the images became clearer, but also darker, as if something had changed or been lost along the way. The world was noisier now. The oceans were no longer as blue, the grass not as green, the air not as pure. Steele gasped when he saw the CN Tower and downtown Toronto erupt from the points of GM's needles and soar into the blue sky. And with it came a smelly haze that drifted up and settled overhead. On the ground, dark figures lurked in the shadows. But he cried out excitedly when he recognized Casa Loma and other familiar landmarks near his home.

With a roar, a spacecraft launched itself from the needles and soared across the Toronto sky. Through its windows, Steele saw a woman. She raised her head as if she could see him, too. Steele stared at her so intently he could actually hear her heartbeat. It mingled with the barely perceptible murmur of a second heart. Two hearts!

And then Toronto and the spacecraft moved swiftly into the distance to make way for another city. At first Steele thought it was New York, but there were too many bridges— he lost count at twenty—and he didn't recognize any of the buildings, not the beautifully ornate building that looked as if it were made of frosting and should be perched on top of a wedding cake, or the curious storybook tower from which the sound of a boy's screams momentarily froze his blood. The boy sounded like Mac.

The Empire State Building grew from the knitting needles, pushing the other city away, and then Manhattan loomed like a painted wall of towers before him. The needles clicked slower still. Steele recognized Grand Central Station, but not the tiny statue of a man in front of it, peering down Park Avenue, his stony gaze fixed on the small group of kids making their way toward the subway terminal.

"That's me!" he cried, squinting to pick himself out from among the kids.

Then, to his horror, a Fire Demon exploded from the knitting needles and began to blast a flaming path along Park Avenue toward the unsuspecting kids.

"Is that really going to happen?" he cried. He knew even as

he spoke that he couldn't lift a finger to save himself from the Fire Demon, let alone his friends.

He glanced at his grandmother and then back at the needles. New York was gone. Now GM was knitting a person. No, not just any person! Him! Was she trying to tell him something? Steele held his breath and waited. He was in a dark place—somewhere underground, perhaps. Mac and Riley were there too. Yes! And Maddie Fey and Wish. Even the sinister red rat was there.

But why were they standing behind him? What was he doing?

An unending procession of Fire Demons burst from the knitting needles, and suddenly he knew what was going to happen next. He knew it as surely as if the knowledge had been planted in his mind the day he was born. He didn't have to look at the knitting to tell him why Maddie Fey had come looking for him. He knew. At long last, he understood why she needed him and no other.

He stared at the knitting anyway, watching as he summoned his Mage power and drew the fire from the creatures into himself. It was the only way to save his friends, the only way to stop the Fire Demons. But he already knew that his special power had limits. He could only absorb so much fire, and no more. Or he would die. And there were too many flaming creatures. Way too many!

He couldn't bear to watch, but he couldn't tear his eyes away from the scarf. And so he saw the fire licking at his clothes and then he began to glow brighter and brighter, until the light coming from within him surpassed the radiance of a new star and he had to throw his arm up to shield his eyes. Then he saw that the knitting was burning too, unravelling in flames.

Sick with despair, he turned to his grandmother, his eyes pleading with her to stop knitting. But the old woman ignored him as she rocked. She smiled her secret smile as great cities, forests, oceans, and all living things disappeared in a ball of fire.

And then his grandmother and her chair too were gone.

Evolution III

Another hundred years passed before we saw Ramidus again. We were astounded to discover that the creatures had managed to survive. Then we learned the reason and marvelled. Ramidus had learned to work and fight in groups, like wolves. The fledgling apes also began to use heavy sticks as clubs.

Ramidus moved bravely out onto the plains. But we shook our heads vehemently and begged it silently to wait. We could see that its build was wrong. It was too slow and awkward to transform itself into a predator. Its jaw was too weak, and its teeth were too dull to tear raw meat from his prey.

We went back to the fire with heavy hearts, convinced that we had seen the last of Ramidus.

—Excerpt from *The Wardens' Logs*

Chapter Sixteen

Sydney

"He's dead! You killed him!" It was Mac's voice, angry.

Steele felt sharp claws digging into his shoulders, shaking him roughly, breaking up his grandmother's images in his head. But it was the stinging slap on the side of his face that scattered them like dead leaves in a blustery wind. He clenched his fists and struck out at his attacker.

"Get away!" he shouted, feeling his fist connect with something hairy.

Steele blinked, momentarily confused, as the face of a giant rat swam into focus. Then he opened his eyes wide and found himself looking up, past Nilats's yellow eyes, at Mac and Riley's frightened faces. He saw the way they shrank from him suddenly, as if they were afraid of him—as if he might actually hurt them.

"What happened?" he asked, pushing himself up on his elbows and glancing about.

When no one answered, he got up slowly, noticing that his friends put more distance between him and them. Then he remembered that his clothes had burned away. He felt his face flush as he attempted to cover his nakedness with his hands. But, to his surprise, he was fully clothed—still wearing the same jeans and shirt that had burst into flames and burned to ashes on his body. He looked about, noticing Maddie Fey for the first time, and Wish, lying on the floor, his large head resting on his forepaws. The only one missing was Sydney.

"Never mind," he explained. "You wouldn't understand."

How could you understand when I don't? he thought. He knew that he couldn't have imagined the fire. No amount of imagination could cause the kind of pain he had felt when the flames engulfed him. He glanced down at his hands. The blisters were gone, the skin unblemished. *I don't understand.*

He was surprised to find that he was clutching the flat, blood-red disk so tightly, the edges had left a sharp imprint on his palm. He looked at Maddie Fey. Then, almost furtively, he pulled the chain over his head and stuffed the disk down the neck of his T-shirt.

Suddenly he noticed that the others still hadn't moved or spoken since Ees had released him. He looked from Mac to Riley. "What's wrong?" he asked.

Riley came over to him and placed her hand on top of his, then quickly withdrew it and stared at the droplets of water falling from her hand onto the floor. Her expression was now a mixture of confusion and wonderment; it mirrored the look on Mac's face. Then Riley's eyes took in Steele's hair and face, still wet from the salty spray of an ocean knitted by his grandmother.

"What happened?" she breathed.

Steele's eyes met hers, but he said nothing. He was as mystified by his wet clothes as she was, because he knew he hadn't been wearing clothes when he saw his grandmother. But at least now he knew why the others had shrunk away from him. Like an old, arthritic man, he eased his body onto a small sofa, one of four that formed a comfortable sitting area in Maddie Fey's observatory. He leaned back, his wet clothes forgotten, and gazed at the giant telescope, thinking of the sky that he had seen through its powerful eye, remembering the alien beauty of Maddie Fey's world.

"Tell us what happened, Steele," said Maddie Fey. "Until you stirred, your friends believed I had killed you."

"You weren't in your room when we went looking for you," said Riley. "We looked everywhere, and then we saw the elevator and took it up here. When we got off the elevator, Maddie Fey was bending over you. We thought you were . . . dead."

Steele ran his fingers through his hair. He wished everyone would go away and leave him alone. He didn't want to answer questions now. He needed to think—to collect all of the images GM had knit and try to make sense of them. He wanted to replay the image of the woman in the spacecraft, and listen to the two heartbeats again. But that would be self-ish, he thought. It wouldn't be fair to the others. They were as desperate as he to rescue the missing kids and stop the Fire Demons, and they might spot something in the images that he would dismiss or overlook. He smiled weakly and looked at Mac and Riley.

"She didn't do anything to me," he said. "She just gave me a disk and I looked inside it."

"Yeah, right!" said Mac sarcastically. "She just gave you a disk that knocked you out for half a day and, from the look of you, she probably tried to drown you."

"Mac, shut up," said Steele softly and not unkindly. Then he pulled the disk from under his shirt and stared at it curi-ously. "Was I really out of it for half a day?"

"Yes," answered Riley. "We tried, but we couldn't wake you up."

Steele held up the disk. "This is Ees. Maddie Fey said it belongs to me." His eyes found Maddie Fey's and held them. "Was it my mother's?"

Maddie Fey nodded.

"Why didn't you tell me before I looked into it?" he asked, even as he realized that it wouldn't have made any difference if she *had* told him, because he wouldn't have believed her.

"Ees was given to your mother when she became a Mage, fifth plane," explained Maddie Fey. "In our society, each plane represents a higher level of achievement. The first plane is the lowest level and the seventh is the highest. Our disks are presented to us when we reach the fifth plane."

"What level was my mother?" asked Steele.

"Because she had a disk, she was at least plane five," answered Maddie Fey.

"What about you?" asked Mac. "When do you get your disk?"

Maddie Fey's blue eyes sparkled. "I have had it for many years, Mac."

Her answer seemed to silence Mac for the moment.

"It must be magic," said Steele, rubbing his fingers on the disk's smooth surface."

Maddie Fey nodded. "Ees is a very potent magic."

"Cool," breathed Mac softly, eagerly reaching for the disk.

"No, Mac," said Steele. "Believe me, you don't want this." He tucked it back inside his shirt. "I looked into the disk and it pulled me inside, right into a roaring fire. And then my clothes caught fire and I was burning. My blood was boiling, and even my eyeballs were sizzling." A shudder shook his body. "I think I burned to death. I think I died in that fire."

He paused and stared at his hands resting on his knees. When he raised his eyes he saw tears spilling from the girls' eyes, and the blood draining from Mac's face.

"When it was over, I felt that everything was new—my eyes, my skin, my hair, everything. It was the strangest feeling."

Steele told his companions all that he could remember, except about the images of him absorbing the Fire Demons' flames. They listened, hypnotized, as his words knitted GM's incredible living scarf in their minds. When he finally finished, his shoulders drooped and he slumped back in the sofa, totally spent.

No one spoke for a long time.

And then Mac's soft whistle prompted the others to react.

"I wish someone would tell me how those things happened to Steele when he looked in the disk," groaned Riley. "And what they mean?"

"I'm sorry it's so confusing, Riley," said Steele. "I still don't know if it was just a dream. It seemed so real; the pain was real enough."

Sometime later Riley and Mac drifted off to their beds. Steele must have slept then, because when he opened his eyes again, he was alone with Maddie Fey. She was sitting on the sofa across from Steele, her legs curled beneath her, her silver hound stretched out on the cushions beside her, its head resting on her lap.

"I saw my mother," he said. "She didn't tell me, and I didn't even think of it . . . consciously, I mean. I just knew who she was. GM knitted her in a spacecraft. It was coming here. I think her eyes were silver, like yours, and I could hear her heartbeat . . ." He stopped, afraid to put into words and make real what he already suspected. "There were *two* heartbeats."

Maddie Fey remained silent, studying his face, waiting for him to continue.

"The second heartbeat. It was me, wasn't it?"

"Yes," said Maddie Fey.

"But, that means . . ." He couldn't say it.

"It means the man you live with is not your father," said Maddie Fey gently.

Steele looked at her in despair. He felt that losing his father meant losing himself. "It's not true," he whispered. "It can't be true."

Maddie Fey leaned forward on the sofa. "I know many things, but I do not know everything, Steele. I know of only one trip your mother made to Earth, but she may have made other journeys that were not documented. Your mother brought something to Earth that could destroy the Fire Demons if the wardens should ever fail. We believe it's you."

Steele shook his head violently. "You're wrong."

"Steele, you were conceived on Arjella, your mother's and your grandmother's planet. You were already growing in her womb when your mother made the journey to Earth. She brought nothing else."

"What about GM? She came here too. The other heartbeat could have been hers."

"Your grandmother had been here for many years before your mother came."

Steele stared at her. He believed her, but he wanted to hate her for saying the words.

"You said my mother was a Mage, fifth plane or higher. Now that I have Ees does that mean I'm at the fifth plane?"

Maddie Fey shrugged. "I am not sure, Steele. As a Mage, you should have been able to look in the disk and see images, but I have never known anyone who actually entered the world inside the way you did. I do not know what to make of it. You are untrained, and yet . . ." Her voice trailed away.

"What about GM? Is she a Mage?"

Maddie Fey nodded. "A very powerful Mage, so I've been told."

"Why did my grandmother come here?" Steele asked after a while.

"I heard that she relinquished her powers and left our order."

"But why would she do that?" asked Steele, shaking his head.

"You will have to ask her," said Maddie Fey.

Steele wondered what had happened to make GM turn her back on her own world and stop being a Mage. And what had happened to make her stop speaking and take up knitting.

"I can't ask her," he said. "She hasn't spoken a word in over eight years."

Maddie Fey looked at him sharply, but her voice sounded sad. "I'm sorry, Steele."

"Yeah," said Steele, keeping his thoughts about GM shrinking to himself. "How many Mages are there?" he asked.

"Twelve, usually," replied Maddie Fey. "When your grandmother left us, there were only eleven Mages until they discovered me."

"Does GM know who my real father is?"

Maddie Fey got up and looked at Steele. Wish slid off the sofa and watched his mistress. "I do not know your grandmother, or what she may know about your past. Your questions are for her, Steele." She moved toward the elevator. "It's late. I'm going to check on Sydney. We'll talk in the morning."

Steele sighed. He wondered if his grandmother knew about Ees and that she'd been with him inside the disk. Did she know about the Fire Demons and what was going to happen to him?

Long after Maddie Fey left, Steele remained on the sofa. He knew Maddie Fey was anxious to learn where the missing kids were being held. He tried to recall an image he had seen in Ees that had troubled him. It was important, something he should warn the others about. But it eluded him.

He stayed on the sofa letting his thoughts drift aimlessly, and was still there in the morning when the rat shook him roughly awake.

He found Maddie Fey with Mac and Riley in the dining room. Riley was munching on a piece of toast, while Mac's head was bowed over a plate heaped to overflowing with eggs and sausages and pancakes, as well as other breakfast treats. Steele's stomach growled, reminding him how long it had been since he ate. He wondered vaguely where the kitchen was, and who did the cooking. He couldn't quite picture Maddie Fey standing over the stove with a wooden spoon in her hand. The thought that it might be the rat stole his appetite.

The only one not eating was Maddie Fey. On the table in front of her was a tall, clear glass resting in a delicate silver-handled holder. It was half full of something pink and steaming. Wish was asleep on the hearth, his silver head resting on silver paws. The hound's ears twitched as Steele came through the door. He raised his head and stared at Steele appraisingly, double pupils glinting like ice.

The others looked up too. Sydney wasn't with them.

"How is she?" he asked.

"No change," said Mac. "She's still out cold."

Steele went to a sideboard and helped himself to a piece of toast. Then he filled a glass with something that he hoped was hot chocolate, and took his place at the foot of the table.

Maddie Fey toyed with the silver handle on her glass. "It's been almost two days since we brought her here," she said. "I am afraid that our chances of rescuing the missing children grow slimmer with each passing hour."

"There must be something we can do," said Steele. "What if we just wake her up?"

"We tried calling her," said Riley. "And shaking her gently. But she wouldn't respond—"

"Gently!" interrupted a voice from the doorway. "You shook me so hard my teeth rattled."

"Sydney!" cried Riley, rushing to the other girl and giving her a hug. "Are you OK?"

"I think I'm going to live," said Sydney dryly, returning the hug and then joining them at the table.

As Sydney looked from face to face, Steele couldn't help staring at the scabs forming over the deep gouges on her face and wondering if her face would be horribly scarred.

"I feel really bad," continued Sydney. "You guys must have been going out of your minds . . . waiting around for me to wake up and tell you how Wood and I found out about the missing kids."

"Never mind *how* you found them," said Mac impatiently. "Just tell us where they *are*."

Riley's elbow nudged Mac in the ribs, and Sydney's eyes flashed. But then she frowned thoughtfully.

"You're right, Mac. They're being held in an underground waiting room of an abandoned subway station."

"Do you know if your brother's there?" asked Riley.

Sydney shook her head. "I'm almost afraid to hope. If he's not, I don't know what I'll do."

"Where is this place?" asked Maddie Fey.

"Under Grand Central Station," said Sydney. "About seven levels down."

The others stared at her.

"How did you find them?" asked Mac, conveniently forgetting his impatience of a moment ago.

"There's this homeless girl I know. Her name's Emily. I met her at St. Mary's, a shelter where I work." Her eyes grew cloudy, then filled with tears. "Wood worked there too."

Steele wanted to say something to take away her sadness, but he was afraid he'd only make things worse.

Sydney wiped her face with her napkin. "Emily knows most of what's happening on the streets and underground. She's one of my friends."

"Wood . . . I mean, that Fire Demon that was . . ." Steele paused, not knowing how to say what he meant without hurting Sydney.

"It's OK, Steele," said Sydney. "I'm not going to cry."

"That creature who came here as Wood told us about your plan to organize homeless people to search for your brother. It's brilliant!"

Sydney smiled with pleasure. "Thanks! I think so too, if I do say so myself. But I just thought up the idea; Emily did all the work. When I told her I was talking to homeless people, she threw a major fit. I didn't know that before I could ask the homeless to help me, I had to get permission from the Mole Mayors."

"The what?" asked Mac.

Sydney glanced at Maddie Fey. "I thought you were anxious to go after the missing kids."

"I was. I am," answered Maddie Fey. "But I have been thinking. Now that you have told us where they are, I suggest that we leave here just after dark. If worms are guarding the children, they are probably nocturnal. Their minds may be more preoccupied with burrowing and feeding than on their captives. Besides, there will be fewer people on the streets in the evening, and many buildings will be deserted for the night. Fewer lives will be at risk if the Fire Demons strike."

"Go on, then," Mac prompted Sydney. "Finish telling us about these Mole Mayors."

"They're the leaders of the homeless in the five boroughs," answered Sydney. Then, noticing the blank look on the Canadians' faces, she explained, "New York has five boroughs." She started to tick them off on her fingers. "Manhattan, Queens, the Bronx—"

"Never mind about the boroughs," interrupted Mac. "Why are they called Mole Mayors?"

Sydney didn't seem to mind the interruption. "They're not real moles," she said. "They are people. Journalists started calling them Moles because they live in underground tunnels. The name just sort of stuck. Emily took me to meet them, and they agreed to organize their people to help me find William."

"Are you saying there are people living *under* New York?" asked Steele incredulously.

"You'll see for yourself," said Sydney. "You heard Maddie

Fey. We're going down into the tunnels tonight to get the missing kids."

"Whoa!" said Steele. "Are these the people you said were fighting the worms?"

Sydney nodded. "But that doesn't mean they're not dangerous, Steele." She planted her elbows on the table. "The tunnels beneath New York are one of the most dangerous places in the whole country. You've got to watch out for the rats; they're as big as raccoons and they don't run away from you. And then there are the drug addicts, and murderers." She paused. "And then there's the place where the cannibals live. Emily says it's called Neverland."

Evolution IV

Still, we did our best to keep Death away from Ramidus, and when we resurfaced again, we gazed upon it like proud parents. Not only had it survived on the plains, but the hominid had changed. Its head was larger. Its jaw was heavier. Its teeth were longer and sharper. We could not see through its skull, but we believed that its brain was bigger. Our human ape was getting smarter.

And then Death broke loose and fell on Ramidus and consumed it. The stench of burning flesh as the hominid burned stayed in our throats for millennia.

— Excerpt from *The Wardens' Logs*

Chapter Seventeen

The Distraction Theory

Steele and Mac and Riley gulped at the same time and exchanged horrified glances. The thought of having to go down into dark tunnels under the city where they might run into giant rats and cannibals paralyzed Steele. Mac and Riley looked green, as if they were going to throw up.

"Two kids disappeared in Toronto," said Steele. "A boy at our school went missing last Thursday night." He didn't know how many days had passed in Maddie Fey's house, but he guessed it had to be more than three. "My friends and I think we've discovered how he and the other kids were taken."

"We figured it out in a day," crowed Mac.

Sydney ignored Mac and stared at Steele in surprise. "Maddie Fey told us about you," she said. "How you were the one who was going to help us stop the Fire Demons and the worms. But this is the first I've heard about kids missing in Canada."

"Not just New York and Toronto," said Riley. "We found some in Chicago."

Sydney nodded. "I know about them." She glanced back at Steele. "Tell me what you discovered."

"OK," said Steele. "But first, Wood said that you heard a

whistle from a garden and looked to see what it was. When you looked back, your brother had disappeared. Right?"

Sydney nodded again.

"What did you see in the garden of that brownstone?" he asked.

"Nothing."

"You saw *something*," Steele insisted.

Sydney frowned. "There was nothing to see." She suddenly tensed up, her hand flying to her mouth. "Wait! You're right! There *was* something, but it was so stupid, I thought I had imagined it."

"What did you see?"

Sydney took a deep breath. She seemed reluctant to explain, perhaps in case they laughed at her. "OK! I saw a squirrel— just one of those grey squirrels. They're everywhere in New York. But . . . and this is going to sound stupid . . . for a second, I thought I saw it sit up, the way squirrels do, and grip the bars of the fence and . . . it bent the iron bars, and then it bared its teeth at me and its mouth was all foamy. It was horrible. It looked so fierce, I freaked." She stopped and stared at Steele. "It was over in a second. . . . How did you know?"

Steele couldn't hide his excitement. "In a lot of the cases we found on the Internet, something distracted the parents just before each kid disappeared. The boy at my school disappeared from his bed while his mother was distracted by the screensaver on his computer. The angelfish morphed into a shark and went berserk and ate all the other fish."

"That's gross!" cried Sydney, making a face.

Riley jumped in. "We don't know what happened in the other cases, but each report said the parents looked away at something, and when they looked back, their kid was gone."

"But what does it mean?" asked Sydney. "I can understand that it's easier to abduct someone if you distract the parent, or whoever's there. But I can't understand how you can make squirrels, and even computer-generated fish do the distracting. No one can do that."

"The Fire Demons can," said Maddie Fey quietly. "It appears that they can do more than change their shapes. They are animators. They can take the bodies of those they kill, and inhabit them. When I fought that creature in your room, Steele, I couldn't understand how I could have been fooled into believing that it was Wood. I began to feel uneasy only after you and Wood left Sydney's bedside. And my uneasiness grew. I sent my magic hunting through my house, into every room and every dark corner. It wrapped about the Wood creature as it made its way to your room. And then I knew."

"What? What did you know?" cried Steele.

"I sent my magic hunting for humans. It found all of you, but when it touched Wood, it found only a dead human body."

Steele shuddered, struck by the enormity of the idea: a being that could assume the shapes of animate and inanimate objects at will, inhabiting a dead body and making it appear alive or, like a virus, invading Dirk the Jerk's computer, taking over the angelfish and morphing into a shark.

Maddie Fey was right. These Fire Demons didn't simply change from their own shapes into other things. They did something much more malevolent. They changed the natures of the shapes they took—such as invading the body of the grey squirrel and making it strong enough and vicious enough to bend iron bars.

"So, it wasn't a real squirrel I saw bending those iron bars," said Sydney. "It was one of these Fire Demons in the shape of a squirrel."

"No," said Steele, understanding. "It was a Fire Demon animating a dead squirrel."

"How do you know that?" asked Sydney, looking at him with something very close to respect in her expression.

"It's the only thing that makes sense," said Steele. "Otherwise there would have been a shark *and* an angelfish on Dirk's aquarium screensaver. The Fire Demon took over the angelfish and then morphed into a shark."

Sydney dropped her head onto her arms. "Things are so crazy, it's too much," she whispered. "Sometimes I don't think I can go on."

Steele chuckled softly. "If it makes you feel better, I've been thinking that a lot lately." He looked at Maddie Fey. "Remember when the Wood creature told us about Sydney's plan to use the homeless to search for her brother?"

"Go on," said Maddie Fey.

"I'm having trouble understanding how he could have known that. I mean, it had just taken over Wood's body."

"Oh, I think it does more than simply take over a body. I think it must be able to take the mind as well. When that creature came here as Wood, the reason we weren't suspicious was that it had Wood's mind, and in a strange way *was* the real Wood. Otherwise I would have spotted it in a second."

"It makes sense," said Steele. "But once it got into the house, why did it wait so long before it tried to kill me?"

Maddie Fey looked thoughtful. "Perhaps it came to spy, to learn things about us. Or perhaps it only realized it had to kill you after Sydney tried to warn you about him that night in her room. If you figured out what she was trying to say, the game was over. Also, if he came here to kill you, he certainly wasn't going to do it in my presence. He knew I am a Mage. And because he took the real Wood's mind, he also knew about you or, at least, that I had been searching for a boy Mage. I think he discovered that you had not yet learned to wield Mage powers, and he decided that he must destroy you before you became a serious threat. He waited until he thought you were alone and unprotected. Then he struck."

Steele nodded. It was a good thing Maddie Fey had decided to use her magic and search for living humans that night. It had saved his life.

They broke up shortly after that. Sydney was clearly exhausted, and Maddie Fey ordered her back to bed. The girl went without protest. Then Mac and Riley wandered off in the direction of the library, and Maddie Fey seemed to simply disappear.

Needing to be alone, Steele rode the elevator to Maddie Fey's observatory. He was hoping for another glimpse of his mother's world, but his hopes were dashed when he saw that the sliding roof was closed. He decided to go to his room and spend an hour reading. It might help take his mind off the tension mounting in the house.

In his new room, he reached for his backpack and opened it. He had stuffed it with junk snacks before setting out for the midnight meeting, and had remembered to tuck in a book that he was reading. He reached into the main compartment and something bit his finger. He snatched his hand away, then set the pack down on his bed and peered inside. Pyrus darted out and disappeared into the dark blue and gold duvet cover.

Steele smiled. "How did you get in there?" he asked, shaking empty snack wrappers into a wastepaper can. "It's a good thing I brought food. Otherwise, you would have starved."

The sight of Pyrus made him think of home. At that moment, he missed his father and grandmother fiercely. But when he thought about his real father he felt only emptiness. "Dad's my real father," he said to Pyrus.

He found his book and settled down on the bed, feeling strangely at peace. He slept then, clutching the unopened book in his hand, Pyrus curled up at his side.

"Come on, Steele! Wake up!"

His eyes blinked open. Mac and Riley, dressed in long black cloaks, were standing by the bed, their faces as white as snow inside black hoods.

"What is it?" he asked, still groggy with sleep.

"It's time to go," said Riley, tossing a similar cloak on top of him. "Hurry up! They're waiting."

Mac sat down on the edge of the bed. "Maddie Fey said we have to walk. I said 'why not use the limo,' and she just gave me this really penetrating look and walked away."

"What if the limo's just an illusion?" said Steele. "Or the only way to get from Maddie Fey's house to the outside world? Maybe it can't travel anywhere."

"Weirder and weirder," said Mac. "But if you're right, where *is* Maddie Fey's house?"

Steele shrugged. "I know it sounds strange, but it makes sense in a crazy sort of way."

"Why don't we just ask Maddie Fey?" suggested Riley.

"Oh, sure," said Mac. "She'd probably say 'it doesn't concern you.'"

Steele got up and stretched to take the stiffness out of his limbs. "Grand Central Station isn't that far to walk. I saw it when we were out looking for Sydney."

"It's not the walk," said Riley. "He just doesn't want to go into those tunnels."

"Speak for yourself," snapped Mac. Then he jumped as something flicked at his arm. "What's that?" He looked at the bedcovers suspiciously.

"It's Pyrus," said Steele, catching his pet and stuffing it into his backpack. "I found him in here. He ate all my snacks."

"Stupid salamander," snorted Mac, rubbing his arm.

Reluctant to leave Pyrus behind, Steele slipped his arms into the straps on his backpack and swung the long black cloak over his shoulders. His friends couldn't help laughing at the hump on his back from the backpack.

Before they left the room, Riley gripped Steele's arm. "I don't know about you guys, but I'm really scared. I'm not sure I can do this."

Steele wondered if he was brave enough to follow Sydney and Maddie Fey into the tunnels, but he suppressed his fear and smiled as Riley. "You won't be alone. We won't let anything happen to you." He wished that he believed what he was saying.

"I need to call home," said Riley. "I need to tell my mom where I am."

Steele shook his head. "You can't," he said. "Not yet. Calls can be traced. We can't let anyone back home know that we're in New York. If they find out, it'd be all over the news."

On the sidewalk, Steele hesitated, peering into the shadows. He saw, or imagined, furtive movements in doorways and recesses of the buildings flanking the street. He shivered, despite the mild New York winter air, and hurried after Maddie Fey and the others.

Maddie Fey walked beside the rat, who would have looked almost human in its black cloak if it hadn't been for its red tail trailing on the sidewalk. Wish trotted ahead, his silver ears raised like antennae. Riley followed Maddie Fey, sticking as close as her shadow. Steele caught up to Mac and Sydney and fell into step beside them. Mac grabbed his arm and slowed until Sydney had taken half a dozen steps away.

"How are we going to rescue the kids?" Mac asked him. "Tell me that. We don't even have a plan." He hissed through his teeth. "I think this is a really bad idea."

Steele could feel Mac's fear. "You saw what Maddie Fey did to that Wood creature," he said. "I don't think she brought us along to fight. She probably wants us to be there to get the kids away if something happens."

"She might have told us," said Mac. "We're kids, Steele. All this talk about worms and Moles and cannibals . . . as if we're grown-ups. It's stupid. We're just a bunch of kids."

"We might be kids," said Steele. "But we've got Maddie Fey and her magic."

They reached Park Avenue and turned left. Ahead, Grand Central Station squatted in the middle of the street like a fat Buddha. Steele's breath came in short bursts as his eyes travelled over the floodlit building. It was huge! Not tall like the tower directly behind it, but big and solid, and truly grand. Three massive arched windows, framed by Corinthian columns, dominated its facade and extended from its base to its magnificent roof. Grand Central Station was such a powerful presence that it somehow diminished the skyscrapers soaring above it. Long after the glass-and-steel buildings were gone, replaced by newer and taller office buildings, Steele thought, Grand Central Station would still be there.

He focused on the giant clock directly over the entrance to the old terminal. The time was 2:15. The face on the clock had to be at least twelve feet in diameter. Above it, standing with outstretched arms, was the figure of a naked man with a winged helmet atop his head. Steele recognized the figure. It was Mercury, one of the Roman gods. Mercury held something in his hand, but Steele couldn't decide if it was a sword or a sceptre. Behind Mercury was a gigantic eagle, its powerful wings extended in flight; on either side, seated at the god's feet, were a man and a woman. Steele wracked his brain but he couldn't identify them. Beneath the group sculpture, carved into the stone, were the words GRAND CENTRAL TERMINAL.

Steele's eyes fell on something in front of the terminal and he caught his breath. He'd seen that figure before. But where?

"Who's that?" he asked, pointing.

Sydney followed the direction of Steele's arm. "Cornelius Vanderbilt."

"I know about him. He built a lot of public libraries in Canada."

"He also designed and built Grand Central Station."

"What's that building over there?" asked Mac.

"That's the Chrysler Building," said Sydney proudly. "Art Deco. Isn't it grand?"

"It's awesome," said Mac.

Suddenly Steele remembered where he'd seen the statue—in GM's scarf, just before she knitted the Fire Demons.

He called out to Sydney. "Listen, I saw that statue in the disk. I think something terrible is going to happen."

Sydney and Mac looked at him sharply.

"What?" asked Sydney.

"Argh!" Steele balled his hands into fists. "I can't remember. I just saw the statue and felt really funny . . . nervous."

Sydney studied him for a moment. "Come on," she said. "We must tell Maddie Fey about this."

Evolution V

Time leaped forward. The human population had grown so large that there was fierce competition for food. The species branched off and developed into fiercer tribes. The food supply dwindled. And then something happened that sent us fleeing back to our fiery home in horror.

Someone on the surface picked up a long, sharp stick.

Life on our planet became even more perilous than before. With spears in their hands, the beings that we had protected and guarded as diligently as a mother cares for her infant shed their fear of predators and became predators themselves.

With spears, a few hunters could track and kill any animal. They could also kill other humans. Next to Death, the greatest danger facing humans now came from their own kind.

—Excerpt from *The Wardens' Logs*

Chapter Eighteen

The Fire Demons

As Steele hurried to tell Maddie Fey about seeing the statue of Cornelius Vanderbilt, a thundering sound rolled behind him. He wheeled around and stopped dead. Park Avenue was erupting.

The sidewalk behind him buckled and heaved. Then the street cracked along its middle, and split in a wide jagged tear that raced toward him and his companions like a monstrous serpent. Horror-stricken, he watched a blackness pour out of the broken ground and spread like oil over the street, onto the sidewalk, and up the faces and sides of the buildings, until the street and buildings were undulating like living things.

Rats! The blackness was a mass of black rats—as large as cats! And something was driving them from their dark, dank places under the city. Steam and smoke accompanied the rats, issuing from the crack along Park Avenue, creating a blanket of thick smog that hovered about ten feet over the street. Tires screeched and cars were tossed into the air as if they were toys. The ear-piercing squeals of panic-crazed rats almost drowned out the sounds of metal being crushed, and the cries of injured and dying people. Close by, Steele could hear Mac and Riley screaming and he knew that he was screaming too.

A bus careened along the southbound lane of Park Avenue and skidded out of control. Paralyzed with fear, Steele could only watch as the driver leaped from the open door of the moving monster and rolled over and over on the asphalt, causing the rats to surge away momentarily. Then the man pushed himself to his feet and staggered drunkenly toward the sidewalk. The bus continued its sideways motion until its rear end hit a raised section of earth and broken concrete at the edge of the crack. As the bus flipped onto its side and slid toward the sidewalk, Steele heard a loud hissing sound. He stared at the blisters forming and bubbling on the painted surface of the vehicle.

The driver had almost made it to the curb when the bus exploded. The blast catapulted him through the air and smack into a plate-glass window, cracking the shatterproof glass. The bus driver slid down the face of the building and landed in a twisted, broken heap on the sidewalk.

When the driver's head moved slightly, indicating that he was alive, Steele felt tears of relief roll down his face. He cried out to the man as rats filled in the gap that had opened when the driver had leaped from the bus. But then he saw the man disappear under a wave of blackness, his screams cutting into the filthy air like knives.

"NO!" Steele's shout jolted him into action. He raced about in a circle, searching for something to throw at the rats, a stick or a rock, to drive them away from the man. But he knew in his heart that no stick or stone would have any effect upon the rats, and besides, it was too late. He couldn't see the man anymore, and now the living black mass was already spreading toward him and his companions.

Maddie Fey's red rat appeared out of nowhere and moved

in front of Steele, rearing up on its hind legs like a grizzly bear. Then it opened its mouth and squealed—a long, drawn-out squeal that grated on Steele's nerves and set his teeth on edge. At first, nothing happened. But as Steele stared at the seething black tide, it suddenly faltered, and then it veered to the left side of the street, flowing away swiftly like a river swollen from heavy rains. The red rat dropped onto all fours and darted a short distance away, to Maddie Fey's side.

Steele let out his breath and turned to make sure Mac, Riley, and Sydney were still there. He was still puzzled by the rats' aberrant behaviour. He couldn't remember seeing them in his grandmother's knitting. It wasn't supposed to be rats that came out of the ground. It was—

A loud roaring filled the air. Steele turned back, his eyes shifting to the deep rift in the street. He froze, horrified at the violence, but fascinated and repulsed by the flaming creatures that suddenly burst through the wide split. Now he knew what had driven the rats to the surface. Fire Demons! Just like the ones in the disk. He counted four of them. Four gigantic creatures of flame and fury.

"Don't stand there! Run!" shouted Mac, grabbing Steele's jacket from behind and tugging hard.

"People are hurt!" Steele yelled back over the screams and sounds of destruction. "We have to do something. . . ."

Sydney looked at him as if he were out of his mind. "There's nothing we can do. Besides, you've got to get out of here. They're after *you*!"

Steele felt the blood drain from his face. His first impulse was to lash out at her, deny what she had said. Because what she had said was unthinkable. It couldn't be true. Those creatures couldn't be destroying Park Avenue because of him.

How could he live with the knowledge that he was responsible for the screaming and the dying?

Then the sidewalk split at their feet, and he and the other kids were fleeing from the Fire Demons as if flames were already licking at their flesh. They rushed along an elevated section of the street and crossed the broad open space in front of Grand Central Station. As he ran past the statue of Cornelius Vanderbilt, Steele glanced fearfully over his shoulder and saw Maddie Fey, with Wish at her side, standing at the end of the elevated section of street between him and the giant flaming creatures. Steele peered about for the rat, but it was nowhere in sight.

Maddie Fey looked so small and helpless next to the monstrous Fire Demons, Steele's heart fell. *But she's not helpless,* he said to himself, remembering what she had done to the Wood creature. But that was only one Fire Demon—now there were four, and these creatures appeared to be even bigger and more terrible than the one in his room that night.

The sight of them now, wading through their own fire toward her, filled Steele with horror. They were gigantic formless shapes, with fangs and claws of liquid fire. Maddie Fey didn't stand a chance. An army of Mages might be able to stand against these four monstrous beings, but not one small girl Mage.

I've got to stop her.

The thought had barely formed in his mind when his body went rigid. He could sense his companions near him, staring at him in fear, but Steele couldn't speak, couldn't move, couldn't even breathe. He was locked in his grandmother's knitting, facing the Fire Demons, using his power to draw their fire into himself.

But it's not supposed to happen here, he thought. In the knitting, he had been in a vast underground chamber when the end came.

RUN! RUN! He could run away. All he had to do was turn his back on Maddie Fey and run. His friends wouldn't think less of him. They didn't know what he had seen in GM's knitting. They didn't know he was going to die.

No one knew, except him. He knew.

And in the knowing came acceptance of what he must do. Slowly, filled with a desperate recklessness, he darted back across the broad open space in front of Grand Central Station. He had taken only a couple of steps when Mac tackled him, knocked him forward onto the concrete, and sat on his back.

"Get off!"

"I'll get off, as soon as you give me your word that you will come with me through those doors," said Mac.

Steele rested his forehead on the cold concrete. "I can't."

"Then I'm not letting you up."

"Listen," said Steele, knowing that he had only minutes to convince Mac to let him go. "Maddie Fey said I was a Mage. She was right, Mac. I am a Mage. Ees showed me in GM's knitting. Let me up. Maddie Fey needs me. She can't stop four of them by herself."

"Are you for real?" asked Mac, but he was wavering. "If I let you up and you go and get yourself killed, you better stay dead, Steele, or I'll kill you. You hear me?"

Maddie Fey didn't even glance at Steele when he stopped beside her, but she knew he was there and he could tell that she wasn't at all pleased.

"Go back," she said in a voice that would have made hell freeze over.

"No," answered Steele, wondering what he was supposed to do now.

He looked at Maddie Fey. Her arms were raised and extended out in front. Quickly he copied her, raising his arms and extending them. He glanced back at the girl Mage. Her open palms were aimed at the Fire Demons, and flakes of white were coming from her hands and fingers and drifting purposefully toward the advancing flames. Steele opened his fists and turned his palms outward, and waited for the white dust to appear.

Nothing happened.

"Tell me what to do," he hissed.

"Go back."

"I can help you fight these things."

"You will kill me if you do not leave now," said Maddie Fey. "I need all of my concentration to do this."

"Please! Let me help."

Steele squeezed his eyes shut and concentrated on his hands, willing the powerful white flakes to burst from his fingertips and blast the evil monsters to smithereens. He opened his eyes and stared at his hands. Nothing. What was wrong with him? *I'm supposed to be a Mage.* He felt panic rising inside him. The creatures were almost on top of them, their heat melting the pavement at his feet, their screams of rage like a high wind in the trees. Steele realized that he should be sweating, or blisters should be forming on his face and hands, but curiously he didn't feel anything physical, though he felt frustration, anger, and sheer terror.

"Go," said Maddie Fey. "Stay and you will surely die. I don't need you."

Steele's arms dropped like lead weights to his side. He felt as if Maddie Fey had just plunged a knife into his heart. Then he turned and ran.

Mac was waiting just outside the terminal entrance. He slapped Steele on the back sympathetically.

"Where's Riley? And Sydney?" cried Steele breathlessly, suddenly noticing that the girls had disappeared.

"It's OK," said Mac. "Let's go. They're inside."

Steele took one last look toward Maddie Fey, and then he followed Mac into Grand Central Station.

Word of what was happening less than a quarter of a mile away had not yet spread through the building. The terrible sounds hadn't yet penetrated its thick stone walls. Inside, it was business as usual for this early hour. Steele looked about the grand concourse and spotted Riley over by the information counter. She was alone.

Steele hurried over to her. "Where's Sydney?"

Riley smiled weakly and her voice shook when she spoke. "Looking for Emily. She said for us to wait for her here." Then she gripped Steele's arm tightly. "I can't do this," she wailed. "I'm so scared. I want to go home."

Suddenly Steele also longed to go home, to reclaim his old life—to sit with his grandmother quietly, to hear the familiar sound of his father's voice, to laugh, really laugh, with Mac and Riley. But he couldn't go home yet, perhaps ever. And what would he find there? His father wasn't even his father. The hurt he still felt was a thousand times worse than when the rat had slapped his face. It hurt even worse than when the fire in the disk had burned his flesh to the bone. This hurt went deeper—to his heart and his mind.

Steele's eyes drifted about the train station. It was a giant, echoing building. He felt small and inadequate within its vastness, like an ant on the kitchen floor. Over his head, the entire ceiling was painted like the night sky, showing all the constellations that were visible with the naked eye from Earth.

As he wiped his clammy hands on his jacket, he realized that he was growing increasingly tense and afraid. Where was Sydney? If the Fire Demons were really after him, then as long as he hung about Grand Central Station, everyone here was in danger. He stared at the solid walls. It was a great, huge, strong building, but after what he'd seen the monsters do to Park Avenue, he didn't think this building could stop them.

"There she is!" cried Riley.

Steele spotted Sydney running toward them, clinging tightly to the hand of a bedraggled-looking girl with short, spiked blonde and black hair. At the same time he caught an unusual movement out of the corner of his eye. A man was purposefully crossing the marble floor, coming toward him. Steele stared in disbelief—it was the bus driver. The man *hadn't* been killed or seriously injured in the explosion. In fact, he looked as fit as if nothing had happened to him at all.

Except for the split that suddenly opened in his chest, and the tiny fingers of flame spilling out like guts and licking at his clothes. As if the abrupt shredding of the man's chest were a signal, the three colossal windows over the main entrance to Grand Central Station exploded, showering the grand concourse with shards of glass.

And then the screaming began.

"Run!" shouted Steele, giving Mac a hard push with one hand and grabbing Riley's arm with the other.

Sydney's eyes opened wide in terror when she saw her companions racing toward her, pursued by the flaming monster.

Without slowing, she and Emily skidded on the marble floor and veered toward one of the tunnels that led to the escalators and the subway tracks. The others followed, running for all they were worth, heads bent forward, arms raised to protect their exposed flesh from the flying splinters of glass.

Just before he disappeared into the tunnel, Steele let go of Riley's hand and glanced over his shoulder. A woman was flailing at her flaming clothes and hair and running senselessly about the concourse, screaming as she fell to the floor in a ball of fire, her limbs thrashing wildly—screaming even as the fire died. Finally she went still. Steele stopped. As his friends continued running, he stared at the ruined and charred thing that, only moments ago, had been an innocent living being, and felt vomit flooding his throat.

The Fire Demon glided across the beautiful Tennessee marble floor, heading directly for Steele, like a hound following the scent of a fox. In its wake, the blackened marble floor bubbled like thick soup, and all about it, people were dying.

Evolution VI

Over time, the brutish, dim-witted human's brain expanded until he could communicate with simple words. He learned to use fire for cooking and for warmth. He also discovered how to use fire to keep wild animals at bay. His larger brain helped him invent tools to make his life easier. He attached a sharp-edged stone to a stick and waved his stone axe triumphantly.

His larger brain saved the primitive being from extinction. It told him to flee when Death broke through the walls of its prison and came for him. He fled fast and far away. Death went berserk when it found only abandoned huts. In a great flaming rage, it went after weaker beings and burned them to ashes. Only the fittest survived on this planet.

—Excerpt from *The Wardens' Logs*

Chapter Nineteen

The Mole Tunnels

Steele clamped his hand over his mouth, and gagged, the dead woman's screams echoing in his head. As he forced his stricken limbs into a faster, steadier pace, he couldn't help thinking of his father and of all the terrible, unspeakable things he must have seen during his years as a Toronto policeman. Had he ever seen a person burn to death? Could anything be more horrific than that? Steele couldn't think of anything. And for the first time in his life, he thought he understood the reason for the haunted look he sometimes saw in his father's eyes. He wished with all of his heart that he could go to his father now, tell him everything, and then, like a little kid, let himself be held in strong arms and comforted until he finally dropped into a dreamless sleep.

But that could never happen again. The man he lived with wasn't even his father.

A blast of heat foreshadowed the approach of the Fire Demon. It slammed into Steele's back and propelled him forward faster than his legs could carry him. He landed on his stomach on the hard floor, the wind knocked out of him. Gasping for air, he scrambled up, frantically feeling behind to assure himself that his backpack wasn't in flames. It was cool to the touch, and he could feel Pyrus squirming against his

back. He shook his head, puzzled. Then he hitched his backpack more securely on his shoulders and barrelled down the
passage like a wild thing. His weariness slipped from him like
a cast-off blanket, and in its place a spark of hot, boiling
anger began to glow.

Steele leaped onto the escalator and raced down the moving steps. At the bottom he stopped and looked about for the
others. He spotted them in the distance, racing along another
passageway toward another bank of escalators. Steele followed, his footsteps echoing eerily in the deserted passage.
From behind and above came the sounds of screaming.

Mac was waiting for him at the entrance to one of the
gates. "Come *on,* come *on!*" he said, grabbing Steele's arm
and dragging him onto the platform, where several other
people waited for the subway train and a lone cleaner half-
heartedly swept the floor.

Steele resisted Mac's sharp tugs on his arm. He was sick of
running, sick of being terrified out of his skull, sick of feeling
helpless. And if he ever, ever had to watch another person die,
it would kill him as surely as if his heart stopped beating.

"A Mage without power."

"What?" asked Mac.

Steele looked at Mac as if he had just become aware of him.
"Back there," he said, "when I was with Maddie Fey. Mac, I
didn't feel anything. I tried to call up my power but I didn't
feel anything. There *was* no power."

"What did you expect?" said Mac. "Did you think that all
you had to do was hold up your hand, and fire or something
would come blasting out and fry those monsters? I don't
think it works that way, Steele. I think maybe it'll happen
when you're not expecting it."

"But what if I'm not a Mage?"

They jumped when Riley called out to them impatiently from the other end of the track. "Hurry up, you guys. We're waiting."

"What happens if the kids are gone?" asked Mac. "What are we going to do if we meet the worms? What are we going to do without Maddie Fey?"

Steele didn't have the answers.

Then Steele remembered the city that he hadn't recognized in his grandmother's knitting. "Mac, in GM's knitting, I saw three cities—Toronto, New York, and then another city I couldn't identify. There were a lot of bridges spanning a river. I counted over twenty. And then there was a big white building, with towers and pointed things on the top, and a huge clock. Then I saw this place that looked like a fairy-tale castle. It had a really high tower, and a dome on the top. There were screaming kids in that tower. I think it was on fire, but I'm not sure. If the kids aren't here, maybe they're in that tower. We've got to find out which city that was."

"If the kids are gone, then we'll ask Sydney. She'll know if it's a U.S. city," said Mac.

Steele nodded in agreement. He felt that there was something else about the tower that he should remember, but he couldn't dredge up the memory. *It'll come to me,* he thought, storing it away until later.

"Don't laugh," said Mac, after a while. "But I've been thinking about the great fires that destroyed cities like London and Chicago. Toronto burned down once, and even the Parliament Buildings in Ottawa."

"Yeah," said Steele. "But remember, most of the buildings were made of wood back then."

"That's not my point," said Mac. "I think most of the really big fires were set by the Fire Demons."

"You're a genius," said Steele, surprised that the idea had never once entered his mind. What if the Fire Demons had escaped dozens or even hundreds of times before now?

Steele suddenly found himself thinking about Maddie Fey. He hoped that she was still alive. His last glimpse of her was still fresh in his mind. Perhaps it would never fade. She had looked as frail as down, standing alone directly in the path of the towering, flaming creatures. Had she escaped from the Fire Demons? Or had they escaped her shimmering power and burned her to a crisp? What about Wish? And the rat, Nilats? Where had he disappeared to?

"Please let them be alive—even Nilats," he whispered, seeking a thread of hope within, but finding none.

They joined the others near a barricade of wooden planks stacked almost to the roof. An hysterical giggle came from the shadows behind Sydney, and Steele felt hostile eyes watching him. Sydney turned to the girl standing as still as a statue in the shadows behind her.

"This is Emily, the girl I told you about," she said, drawing the girl forward into the dim light.

Emily acknowledged the others with a thin-lipped smile and a sharp nod, but her eyes were unfriendly; they darted restlessly about the cavernous tunnel, never lingering on anyone or anything for more than a heartbeat. Steele thought she looked unnaturally pale, sickly.

"She knows her way around here," continued Sydney. "She's going to take us down to the waiting room where the kids are being held. Remember what I said before. This isn't going to be a walk in the park. Our lives will be in danger every step of the way, there and back. We have to move quickly, so make sure you keep up. And if you can't, say something at once. If you get lost down here, you'll never be found." She pointed at the barricade. "We're going behind there. Emily and I will go first. The rest of you wait here. Don't watch us. Don't look suspicious. Follow us, one at a time. And keep quiet."

The two girls sauntered nonchalantly toward the barricade, slipped behind the planks, and disappeared.

"You go," said Mac, elbowing Steele's ribs.

Steele jumped.

"And remember! Act natural," cautioned Riley.

For a moment, Steele stared at the barricade, wishing that he could see through the stack of planks to whatever waited on the other side. Then he squared his shoulders and forced himself to walk slowly along the side of the tracks until he reached the barricade. Oblivious to the indifferent look of the cleaner and the people waiting on the platform, he ducked behind the planks. Expecting to see Sydney, he was surprised to find himself staring at a door.

The door was made of steel, or another heavy metal, and painted a dull grey. The surface was badly scratched, its hinges so rusted, Steele wondered how Sydney and her friend had managed to get it open. But to his surprise, when he pulled on the handle, it swung outward as easily as if the hinges had been oiled.

Sydney was waiting inside, a blazing torch clutched tightly in her hand. Steele looked about for Emily, but she was nowhere to be seen. Suddenly, he felt uneasy. He couldn't put his finger on the reason for his uneasiness, but neither could he shake the feeling that something was wrong.

Be careful! he cautioned himself.

When all of the companions were gathered inside the door, Sydney removed torches from brackets on the wall and passed them around, setting them ablaze by touching them with her own torch. Then they followed her along a straight, narrow tunnel. Presently, they came to a T-junction and turned right. After only a few minutes the tunnel ended at another metal door, even more rusted and neglected-looking than the first one. Steele was relieved to see Emily waiting for them. As they approached, the girl raised her knuckles to the door and knocked once, then twice, and finally three times.

Steele heard the muffled sound of bolts sliding back and the faintest *screech* as the door swung open. Steele gasped. Blocking the entrance to what appeared to be another tunnel, arms folded across its massive chest, was a huge—

"Troll!"

Steele hadn't realized he had cried aloud until Mac drove his elbow into his ribs. "It's not a troll," he whispered. "It's a woman."

"I knew that," said Steele, thankful that the dim lighting hid the blush he felt in his face. *She looks like a troll,* he said to himself, realizing that his mouth was hanging open and he was staring at her rudely, as if a third eye had suddenly popped open in the middle of her forehead. But he couldn't help it. She was the hugest, fattest woman he had ever seen.

Her small, sharp eyes resembled dried black currants stuck in a cookie-dough face. She had no eyebrows, and her nose was a flat lump. *Like a squashed mushroom,* thought Steele. Fat jowls hung from her lower jaw, completely hiding her neck. Despite the dim torchlight, Steele could see coarse black hairs sprouting from her sagging chin and above her upper lip.

She wore an old green army jacket over a black shirt that was tucked into a pair of green overalls that had been patched and re-patched in a dozen places. On her gargantuan feet were two mismatched, thick woollen socks. From holes in both socks, her big, blue toes protruded like fat slugs. Steele made a disgusted face and quickly looked away.

Was this monstrosity one of the people Sydney had recruited to help find William? Were all the Moles as revolting as her? Steele shuddered at the thought of what else might be waiting in the darkness behind the woman.

"Password," demanded the woman through teeth that were blackened stumps. Her speech was slurred as she bent and leaned toward the children, peering at them over their torches. Steele couldn't help noticing her dirty, broken fingernails and the stains on the front of her tent-sized black shirt.

Emily stood on the tips of her toes and whispered the password in the woman's ear. The giant shuffled—reluctantly, Steele thought—from the doorway, backing against the concrete wall, rolls of fat jiggling like Silly Putty on her neck.

Steele squeezed past, trying to avoid physical contact with the woman. She gave him the creeps. He hurried down the tunnel, water sloshing about his boots. He was desperate to put as much distance between himself and the woman as possible. For a reason that he couldn't explain, he was afraid that the gargantuan sentinel would realize that she had made a mistake in letting him pass, and call him back or come after him.

His fears were realized when a strong arm wrapped about his neck and he felt himself being dragged backwards, away from Mac and the others. Pyrus wriggled frantically as the old woman crushed Steele and the backpack against her chest. Steele's torch slipped from his hand and dropped onto the wet floor, where it sizzled and sputtered out. Black smoke rose from the doused torch, filling the narrow tunnel and making Steele's eyes water.

"Not so fast!" hissed the woman, her breath hot on Steele's neck.

Steele opened his mouth and yelled as something sharp pierced the skin on the back of his hand, but the woman's stranglehold on his neck blocked the sound in his throat. He felt something warm spreading over his flesh, and looked from the bleeding nick on his hand to the wicked knife clutched tightly in the woman's hand, the tip red and sticky.

Eyes riveted on the sharp knife, Steele snarled and struggled, writhing and wriggling like an eel on a hook, but the woman was strong and his struggles were in vain. Abruptly, the woman removed her arm from around his neck and gave him a rough shove in his back that almost floored him.

Afraid of what she might do next, Steele glanced quickly over his shoulder. The dim light from a single light bulb above the door distorted the woman's features, turning her into a hideous, ghostly thing.

"Can't be too careful," she hissed, grinning insanely at Steele as she dipped a finger into the blood on the tip of the knife and then wiped finger and blade on her filthy shirt. "Go on, little bleeder! No fire in you!" Then she cackled like a witch. "Have a good day now, you hear!"

Steele turned and ran smack into Mac, who had become alarmed when he realized Steele hadn't followed the others, and had returned to find him.

220 J. FitzGerald McCurdy

"What happened to you?" Mac caught Steele's arm. Then he paled as he noticed the blood on Steele's hand. "What happened?" he repeated.

"I thought I was going to die," gasped Steele. "And Pyrus, too. Please, Mac, look in the backpack. See if he's OK."

Mac unzipped Steele's backpack and reached inside. "Ouch!" he exclaimed. "The little monster bit me."

"Whew!" sighed Steele. "Thank goodness."

Relieved that his pet was still alive, Steele tore a strip off his T-shirt and wrapped it around his hand to stem the bleeding, his fingers trembling uncontrollably. Mac retrieved Steele's torch from the floor and tried unsuccessfully to relight it.

"She stabbed me," said Steele, who was still in shock. "She grabbed me from behind and tried to kill me."

"No way!"

"It's true!" Steele shuddered. "Ugh! It was horrible. *She* was horrible. What a disgusting creature."

Mac nodded. "The bearded hag."

At that moment, Steele noticed movement in the shadows behind Mac's shoulder, just beyond the circle of torchlight. Someone was there, lurking and listening. He put a finger to his lips, a warning to Mac to be quiet. Then he grabbed his friend's torch and took a quick step toward the dark figure.

It was Emily. Steele noticed that her face was even paler than before, her eyes wilder.

"What are you doing sneaking around?" demanded Mac.

Emily laughed scornfully. Then she spat on the concrete floor and disappeared into the shadows.

"What was that all about?" asked Mac, shaking his head in bewilderment.

Steele knew. Emily had heard them talking about the old woman and she hadn't liked it. The contemptuous look she had flashed at Steele before she spat on the floor and fled spoke volumes. Steele heard her unspoken words clearer than if she had yelled them in his ear. *You think you're better than us.*

"We shouldn't have said those things about the woman," he said softly.

Mac snorted. "Why not? They're true. And, don't forget, she *did* try to kill you."

Steele nodded, but he was troubled. Had the woman really tried to kill him? It had certainly seemed like it at the time, but now he wasn't so sure. And what was it she'd said about fire? He looked down at the bloody rag covering his hand.

"Forget about her," urged Mac, interrupting his thoughts. "Let's get out of here."

After several confusing turns in the long, multi-branched tunnel, they came to a narrow catwalk spanning more tracks. At the end of the catwalk, they descended a steep metal stairway to another level. Ahead, Sydney's voice echoed faintly from the walls. Anxious to hear what she was saying, Steele moved closer.

"It's a maze down here," said Sydney. "There are hundreds and hundreds of natural tunnels, and man-made drains and passages under New York. We're going down to the seventh level, but there are more levels than that. Below the Chrysler Building, there are bomb-proof tubes set into the rock more than seventy-five storeys down."

"Cool!" breathed Mac. "I'd like to see what's down there."

"No, you wouldn't, Mac," said Sydney. "Even Emily hasn't

been that far down, and she's been here for almost two years."

"You *live* down here?" Riley asked, staring incredulously at Emily.

Emily nodded; she still hadn't spoken a word.

"She doesn't like talking about it," cautioned Sydney. "But she's not the only one down here. It's like a city. There are thousands of people living in the tunnels under Grand Central Station. And thousands more under Penn Station, and in other places where there are tracks, and tunnels, and sewers."

Steele listened, amazed. He knew that there were tunnels under Toronto for the subway, gas mains, telephone cables, sewage, and drains. But he had never wondered about them, or learned how many there were. He tried to visualize the vast network of tunnels as the New York girl described them, but the system was so complex and convoluted he finally gave up.

Back at Maddie Fey's house, he had been stunned when Sydney said that homeless people lived in the tunnels, but it hadn't seemed real until now. Steele suddenly sensed their presence all about him. He glanced up into the darkness and felt eyes staring back at him—hating him with a passion that chilled him to the bone. He peered into shadowed nooks and recesses and caught the furtive movements of darker things. His ears picked up new sounds—shuffling, brushing, muffled sounds—that filled him with dread.

"People are always finding things down here," continued Sydney. "Once, road builders found a huge sailing ship under a street near the harbour."

"How many people live underground?" asked Steele.

"No one knows for sure," answered Sydney. "I read somewhere that there are more than 100,000, but Emily thinks it's closer to 25,000."

"Why?" asked Mac, cutting straight to the chase. "Why do they live down here?"

Emily flashed him a crooked smile, but it was Sydney who answered. "Where else can they go? They're homeless. Nobody wants them up top. I told you there are bad people down here. Farther down, that's where the really scary ones are. There's this guy who calls himself the Prince of Darkness . . ."

Steele sucked his breath through his teeth. "What?" he shouted, grabbing Sydney's arm and spinning her around until she was facing him. "How do you know about the Prince of Darkness?"

Homo Erectus

And then, suddenly, a new human species walked the plains, standing as straight and tall as the trees in the forest. *Homo erectus* had a magnificent brain. It allowed him to develop new tools and weapons, cover his naked body, and travel across the planet. He cooked his food, and his long, sharp teeth became obsolete and eventually disappeared.

Homo erectus was an extraordinary species of human. We knew that, if we could keep him safe from Death, from this race would flow all future races of humankind.

But as the humans were evolving, so too was Death. As it became more cunning, we grew increasingly uneasy.

—Excerpt from *The Wardens' Logs*

Chapter Twenty

Deeper into the Tunnels

"Stop! You're hurting me!" Sydney wrenched her arm from Steele's grasp and gaped at him as if he had lost his mind, which Steele feared wasn't far from the truth.

"Tell me!" He was shouting now, but he didn't care. He had to know more about the Prince of Darkness.

"What do you want me to tell you? I don't know anything about the Prince of Darkness."

"You said he lived down here. How do you know that? Who told you?"

Sydney thought for a second, and then she turned to Emily. "You told me."

Emily nodded slowly, her restless eyes darting from one dark place to another, never lingering on one spot for more than an instant.

"Have you seen him?" pressed Steele, turning to Emily.

Emily shook her head.

"Do you know anything about him?"

The girl shook her head again.

Steele wanted to shake *her*, to shake answers out of her. He was sure she knew more than she was letting on.

"Why are you asking about the Prince of Darkness?" Mac asked Steele. "How do you know this person?"

"The voices I heard in Wychwood Park. They were talking about someone who called himself the Prince of Darkness, and they sounded scared. And I mean *scared*. Then another time, I heard his voice. He actually called me."

The companions fell silent, shocked at Steele's revelation. Suddenly Steele thought the cavernous tunnel seemed much colder than when they had entered.

"That was back home. It can't be the same Prince of Darkness," said Mac, his voice booming louder than usual in the silence. "It's . . . impossible."

"It's not," said Steele, wishing he were a million miles above ground. "Don't ask me how I know, I just do." He shivered uncontrollably as he turned to Riley. "Remember that face we saw under the grate? I think it was him."

The others stared at him, stunned. Only Emily nodded, a knowing smile on her thin lips.

"Come on!" said Sydney. "You're making me real nervous, Steele. If this Prince of Darkness is involved with the missing kids, I hate to think of what they've been through. Please, oh please, let William be OK."

They set out again, descending deeper and deeper beneath the city. They followed Emily down metal ladders, along pipes, over catwalks, and through tunnels the Moles had carved out of concrete walls and foundations with pickaxes. Steele was light-headed from the stench of sewage seeping through the walls, and he cringed at the sound of cockroaches crunching under the soles of their boots.

Riley was just ahead with the other two girls. Steele saw her reach for Emily's hand and clasp it gently, then he heard her ask the homeless girl about school.

Emily stiffened and snatched her hand out of Riley's grasp.

"I hate school," she said, speaking for the first time. She grabbed Sydney's shoulder, her eyes darting wildly. "She's a spy. She's here to take me away—"

"No one's going to take you anywhere," Sydney said soothingly, patting Emily's arm. "Her name is Riley. She's from Canada. She's with him." She tilted her head at Steele.

Emily's eyes flitted to Steele and then to Riley. She smiled slyly. "You better watch out, pretty girl. There are bad people down here. If you get lost, they'll catch you. Then they'll cook you, and eat you. No more Riley." She giggled and quickly covered her mouth with her hand, as if her sudden outburst might be punishable under some unwritten law of the tunnels.

Riley grew pale. "Thanks for sharing that with me," she said, dropping back a step to keep pace with Mac.

Trailing behind the others, Steele stopped and wiped sweat from his forehead. Beneath his jacket, the back and front of his T-shirt were soaked. He couldn't understand why he was sweating, when a short time ago his teeth had been chattering. *What's wrong with me?* He looked up at the ceiling, acutely conscious that New York City was up there, just over his head. All that weight, all those buildings! It was depressing. He felt the tunnel walls closing in on him, trapping him, leeching the air from his lungs.

"I hate this place," whispered Mac, falling back beside Steele. "It's creeping me out. What did Sydney say about the rats down here? They don't run away, they run at you."

Steele heard him. He hadn't seen any rats since Nilats had scared them away on Park Avenue, but he'd heard them scuttling along the floor in the darkness. He found it hard to believe that he was under Grand Central Station in a subterranean world where thousands of human beings lived in sewers and tunnels with predatory rats. Steele's mind rebelled at the thought. He felt ashamed about the tunnels, but if someone had asked, he couldn't have explained why.

He waved his arm in a vague arc and spoke to Mac. "How can we allow people to live like this?"

He heard Mac take a deep breath and blow it out slowly. "It's wrong—people living in sewers and holes in the ground."

"Like animals," said Steele.

"Yeah," agreed Mac. "But at least animals care for their own."

Steele wished he could talk to his father—or at least the man he knew as his father. "My dad's always saying that the way we treat old people, and the sick and homeless, shows how civilized we are."

Mac snorted. "Who said anything about being civilized? *They* messed up big time, but we're the ones who are going to be paying." He didn't bother identifying "they."

Steele knew, and nodded solemnly.

As they descended deeper and deeper, the tension grew and they fell silent. Steele's eyes smarted from the sharp smell of urine that permeated the lower tunnels. When they reached the seventh level, Emily led them through a narrow arch into a small recess. She whispered something in Sydney's ear and disappeared back through the arch and into the darkness.

"She's gone ahead to check things out—make sure the kids haven't been moved."

"How many kids were there?" asked Riley.

"About 150," said Sydney. "At least it's some of them."

"150!" cried Mac. "But we found only about seventy missing kids in total."

"I think it's closer to 300," said Sydney, sinking onto the floor and closing her eyes.

Steele couldn't bring himself to sit on the hard concrete floor. He couldn't stomach the filth, or the thought of insects crawling over him, or rats scratching his eyes out. Mac and Riley must have shared his thoughts, because they also chose to remain standing.

Holding Mac's torch, Steele paced back and forth along the length of the recess, forcing himself to breathe naturally and fighting the panic inside him. He almost had a heart attack when Mac sneaked up behind him and touched him lightly on the back.

"While we're waiting, let's test out your magic powers. I have a feeling we're going to need them."

"It's no use, Mac. I tried."

"Try something different. Try turning me into something," said Mac.

"Like what?"

"I don't know. Think of something. Just don't make it something sissy, like a toad. Something fierce, like a lion."

"OK." Steele passed the torch to Riley. Then he pushed his cloak off his shoulders, removed his backpack, and placed it carefully on the floor. "But, Mac, if this backfires, promise you'll take Pyrus with you."

"Nothing's going to happen," said Mac.

"Just promise, OK?"

"OK, I promise," said Mac.

Then Steele scrunched his face and concentrated on turning his friend into a lion.

"It's not working," said Riley. "Maybe you should start with something simpler."

"I know," said Steele. "I'll try to make you rise into the air. That doesn't sound too difficult. Stand back a bit."

Mac moved back and waited.

Steele raised his arm and pointed at him. Then he closed his eyes and imagined his friend lifting off the ground. "Is it working?" he asked moments later, eyes still shut.

"Not exactly."

"It's no use." Steele opened his eyes. "I told you I haven't got any power."

"Don't give up," said Mac, almost desperately. "You can do it. We just have to work at it a little harder. Just at the end, I thought I felt my feet start to lift off the floor."

"Shut up! You're just saying that to make me feel better."

"No. Honestly," protested Mac. "Try it again, only this time do it with your eyes open."

So Steele stared at Mac and concentrated on imagining that he was filling Mac with helium, like a balloon, and making him rise slowly toward the ceiling—but his mind wandered, and his hand, as if it had a mind of its own, reached for the blood-red disk inside his shirt.

Steele couldn't breathe. His mouth was opening and closing spasmodically, like that of a fish out of water. He saw Mac staring at him, a panicked look on his face. Steele felt his body convulse as if he were vomiting, but nothing was coming up. Mac and Riley rushed to help him, but went flying backwards as if they had run face-first into an invisible wall. Riley dropped the torch in a shower of sparks.

Blood gushed from their noses, and Steele could see them yelling but he couldn't hear them. His fingers were groping at the neck of his jacket, trying to rip it open. He was suffocating. His body was wracked by paroxysms of pain. Mac pounded his fists against the unseen barrier, and shouted for help. At that moment, Steele collapsed in a heap on the floor, writhing in agony, and then felt himself go still.

The barrier gave way, and Mac lost his balance and tumbled over Steele.

"Steele! Steele!" He scrambled to his knees and tried to lift Steele's head.

Steele felt his body tense and he began to cough, breathing great gulps of air into his lungs. He looked at Mac, who was staring at him in awe.

"Wha—"

"You did it!" cried Mac. "You almost killed yourself, but you *did* it!"

Steele sat up and took one look at his friends' bloody noses. "I'm sorry. I don't know what came over me. I'm really sorry."

"No, no," said Mac, bristling with impatience. "You didn't punch us in the nose, if that's what you're thinking. You created a barrier around yourself."

Steele eyed him suspiciously. "I did?"

"Didn't you feel anything at all?"

Steele shook his head. "I couldn't breathe. It felt like the air just vanished. I remember looking at you and wondering why you were OK. Then I guess I thought I was having a stroke or a heart attack. But—" He looked from Mac to Riley. "What happened to your noses?"

Mac and Riley explained how they had run into Steele's invisible barrier.

Steele picked up his backpack, and slipped his arms into the straps. Then he picked up the torch and slumped against the wall. He felt weak. "Why would my powers turn on me and smother me, when all I was doing was trying to make Mac levitate?" he puzzled softly. *Maybe the powers don't like it when you play with them. Maybe I am only supposed to summon them in a real emergency.* Steele wished he could talk this over with Maddie Fey.

If he had real magic, like Maddie Fey, could he use it to find the other missing kids, and stop the Fire Demons without having to absorb their fire? Could he look inside their minds and read their black thoughts? What if their thoughts were so horrible, his mind snapped? What if they were waiting for him to get into their minds so they could trap him?

An angry *squeak* from the shadows broke Steele's train of thought. He raised the torch and looked about. Then he saw the shining eyes of a large brown rat darting toward Sydney. And it *was* as big as a raccoon.

"Uh, guys?" he said softly, not daring to take his eyes off the rat.

"What is it?" hissed Sydney, jumping up and stomping on a particularly fat cockroach that had dropped out of her hair.

"We've got company," said Steele. "Get out of here fast!" He jabbed the torch at the rodent's bared teeth. Instead of retreating, the creature snarled and advanced toward him.

Sydney saw the rat. "Back away now, Steele," she said. "Act like you're not afraid, but keep moving back.

As Steele stumbled back, the rat sprang at his throat.

It happened so quickly, Steele didn't have time to react. He felt the rodent's claws stick to his jacket as if they were connecting with Velcro, and heard the creature's grunts and squeals and its sharp teeth snapping as its head burrowed toward his exposed neck.

"Aiiii!" Steele dropped his chin and hunched his shoulders. At the same time, he brought his free arm across his chest and brushed frantically, trying to dislodge the rat before it caught the scent of Pyrus in his backpack. But the creature tore fiercely at his clothing. Recklessly, Steele brought the torch closer and thrust it at the rat, using it to flick the creature away. It worked, and Steele prayed that the smell of burning hair was coming from the animal and not from his own eyebrows.

The rat dropped to the floor and lay there, momentarily stunned. Steele closed his eyes and jumped.

Splat!

The others stared at the smashed rat in disgust. Then they rushed out of the recess into the larger tunnel.

Emily appeared a moment later. She held her sides, her thin shoulders heaving as if she had run a long-distance race.

"What is it?" asked Sydney, handing the girl a water bottle.

"War!" cried Emily, refusing the water, her restless eyes filled with despair. "The worms are killing Moles!"

Steele felt a chill. Back in Maddie Fey's house, Sydney had told him and his friends about the daily wars between the Moles and the worms, but it hadn't really sunk in until now.

"What about the kids?" he asked, his heart beating rapidly. "Are they still down here?"

Emily nodded, but didn't look at him. "It's bad," she whispered. "We've got to go through the worms to get to them."

Sydney held up her torch and turned to her companions, her face as hard as stone. "What are we going to do now?"

"We are going to war," said a quiet voice from the shadows.

The Great Failure

When Death came and took our favourite species of human, we were inconsolable.

We had discovered Neanderthal a century or two earlier. This gentle species had branched off from its *Homo erectus* cousins and had migrated far away. Over thousands of years, Neanderthal evolved into a cold-weather creature, with the pronounced cheekbones associated with harsh climatic conditions. They existed at the same time as *Homo sapiens sapiens,* but they were stronger and had much larger brains.

As with all of the creatures we had watched over since the beginning of time on this planet, Neanderthal was ignorant of our existence. We looked on proudly as he developed tools and fashioned spears for hunting, and for defence against the early *Homo sapiens,* who were fierce hunters and fighters. We watched him bury his dead—the first species to do so—and sprinkle fresh flowers and place treasured possessions on the burial mounds of a loved one.

We had great hopes for Neanderthal. We did not realize our hopes were false.

—Excerpt from *The Wardens' Logs*

Chapter Twenty-One
Arming for Battle

Maddie Fey stepped into the torchlight, Wish gleaming like a star at her side.

Steele had never thought he'd be so glad to see anyone in his entire life. He was afraid to take his eyes off her for fear she'd disappear.

"How—?" he started to ask, but she raised her hand and he fell silent.

"I destroyed two of those creatures, and another fled down into the earth. But one eluded me and is loose somewhere above. . . ."

"It's in Grand Central," said Sydney. "Or at least that's where we last saw it."

"Why are they after me? How do they know about me?" asked Steele, dreading the answer.

Maddie Fey looked at him, but it was Sydney who spoke first.

"It was Wood," she said. "It had to be Wood . . . before the worms killed him . . ."

"That can't be," said Steele, his eyes moving to Maddie Fey. "Because, that first night, in your house, you said that you got me there to keep me alive. That means they were already searching for me."

"I suspect they learned about you from the wardens," said Maddie Fey.

"What do you mean?" asked Steele. "Why would the wardens tell them about me? I thought they were on our side."

Maddie Fey sighed. "They are, as you say, on our side. But they have known of you for some time now, and I can only guess, but I think the Fire Demons have found a way to get at their thoughts. I will not know for certain until I have found the wardens."

"But how do the wardens know about me?"

"Steele . . ." Maddie Fey's voice held a warning.

"No, please. Tell me."

"Very well," said Maddie Fey. "There is only one person who could have told them. Your grandmother."

Steele shook his head in shock, and then he laughed. "No way! I know you're wrong because GM hasn't said a word in eight years. She hasn't even been outside."

"There are other ways to communicate, Steele."

"What! You think my grandmother's been talking to the wardens telepathically? That's crazy!"

"Perhaps," said Maddie Fey. "But we can talk about this later. Now we must free the missing children before the Fire Demons return." She turned to Sydney. "Let us go."

"We're going to need weapons," said Sydney. "The Moles have several armories down here. Emily can take us to the nearest one."

Emily nodded slowly, her chest rising and falling in time with her rapid breathing, her eyes blinking and tearing as if to wash away images that were stuck in her eyes like grains of sand. Then she turned and led them toward a gate and, like a shadow, slipped through the twisted bars. The others followed closely in tight-lipped silence, their eyes trying to pierce the dark places on either side, their ears alert for the slightest sound. But they saw nothing, heard nothing. It was as if the humans and rats and cockroaches that shared the tunnels had fled.

Steele's thoughts kept returning to the incredible things Maddie Fey had said about his grandmother. He simply couldn't grasp the notion that GM had been communicating with the wardens with her mind. He was also troubled. Because if Maddie Fey was right, then GM must know what happened to the wardens. If so, how on earth could he get her to speak? He sighed deeply, feeling more confused than ever.

Soon the concrete floor gave way to corrugated metal. They squeezed through a jagged tear and dropped onto the bottom of a cylindrical storm drain. The thought that at any moment water might come roaring through and sweep them into the Hudson River prodded Steele to quicken his pace. The sound of their boots on the ridged metal boomed in his ears like war drums.

They hadn't gone more than a quarter of a mile when Steele saw two burly figures blocking the drain ahead.

"Who's there?" One of the figures stepped toward them, his voice harsh. "Password?"

Emily said the password, and the figures shuffled aside.

As he hurried past, Steele caught a clear look at the two figures. They were men clad in dirty, patched or torn jackets and trousers. He noticed that their eyes were as wild and restless as Emily's, and their hands shook like leaves in the wind. He guessed that the source of the trembling wasn't fear but long addiction to drugs or alcohol. One of the men went into a fit of coughing, then dabbed at his lips with a soiled rag.

"Go away from here," Steele said to the men. "Find a safe place and hide. The worms are coming."

The man with the chronic cough looked at Steele. In his crazed, restless eyes Steele read the story of his sorry life. He read despair where once there had been hope and promise. He read corruption and madness. When he couldn't bear it any longer, Steele dropped his eyes and turned away, feeling sick and afraid.

Emily and the others had stopped before an archway. Inside was a brick wall. The homeless girl passed through the archway, dropped onto her knees and began pulling loose bricks out of the wall. Steele knelt and helped her. When they had made the hole big enough, Emily crawled inside and the others followed.

Inside the armory—a recessed cave-like chamber that had been chopped out of one of the thick concrete blocks that supported the massive weight of Grand Central Station and the network of tunnels and subway tracks overhead—Steele's eyes widened as he gazed upon rows and stacks of crude weapons, resting on a layer of large green garbage bags. There were spears made from wooden broom handles, broken golf clubs, and lead pipes, the ends tapered and filed until they were as sharp as ice picks. Wooden staves affixed with serrated blades had been transformed into bayonets. Iron fireplace pokers had been melted down and fashioned into swords, the edges honed to razor sharpness. There were piles of axes, stacks of bows and bundles of arrows, rows of pitchforks, and off in a corner of the armory, a small mountain of knives of every shape and size. There were guns too, of every type imaginable, and boxes of ammunition.

As the kids made a beeline for the guns, Sydney's voice

stopped them in their tracks. "No guns. And don't pick something you want," she said. "Pick something you can use."

A voice in Steele's head told him to choose a pitchfork,
mainly because it was the only weapon here that he could
wield without possessing great skill. But as soon as his eyes
fell on the stack of swords, his mind was made up. He had to
have a sword. He tested several before a dull black metal one
caught his eye. He stared at it for a moment. It was a sword
all right. But it was not a crude, melted-down fireplace poker.
It was the real thing. Carefully, he picked it up and gently ran
his thumb along the edge, crying out as the blade sliced into
his flesh as easily as if his thumb were made of water. He
wiped his bleeding thumb on his jeans and swung the sword
in a wide arc. He liked the feel of it in his hand; it wasn't too
heavy, but it was solid. He wondered how it had found its
way here, ending up in a tangled heap of makeshift swords, in
an armory seven levels beneath New York City.

Satisfied with his choice, Steele turned to the hill of knives
and picked out two long throwing blades encased in leather
sheaths. He pushed the sheathed knives down into his socks,
making sure that the tips were securely wedged into his
boots.

"I'm on the archery team at school," said Sydney, coming
up beside him, a short bow strung over her neck and her arms
overflowing with arrows. For a moment, she eyed Steele's
sword longingly. Then she sighed. "I really want a sword, but
I'm too good with a bow and arrow, and it wouldn't be fair."
She knelt on the floor and began stuffing arrows inside her
backpack.

"Quickly!" warned Maddie Fey from the doorway. "We
must go now."

Riley came up to Steele, a pitchfork clutched tightly in one hand, her torch in the other, and at least a dozen knives stuck in a belt about her waist. Mac was waving two short swords that Steele thought looked more like carving knives.

Steele scanned the armory to see what else he could use, rejecting the garbage can shields as too cumbersome. Seeing nothing, he joined the others and followed close on Emily's heels as she flew along the damp, cold tunnel.

At the juncture of three passageways, Emily stopped and peered into the darkness as if, for the first time, she has lost her bearings. The others crowded about her, waiting silently, their bodies rigid, their faces hard and anxious.

"This way," said Maddie Fey, moving quickly to the left, unaware of the surprised look on Emily's face.

A few minutes later, they came to a massive pair of doors. Emily held up her hand, and examined the floor in front of the doors, searching for signs that would tell her others had passed this way before them. Then she lowered her hand and nodded at Sydney.

"Leave your torches here," said Sydney.

The others obediently dropped their torches onto the concrete floor. Emily stepped up to the doors, grasped a pair of iron handles, and pushed. The doors swung inward. Their rusted hinges creaked loudly in the silence. Pale light streamed through the opening. Steele stepped through the doorway, blinking in surprise.

They were on a wide platform that paralleled several rows of train tracks. The litter-strewn pilings and rusted tracks told Steele that many decades had passed since any train had stopped here. He tilted his head back and looked up, gasping at the wondrous construction. The ceiling of the ancient railway station buried deep under New York City rose up and up until its highest reaches were barely visible. Intricate designs of birds and woodland animals were carved into the stone. Stone leaves and vines twined about colossal columns—now cracked and crumbling—that, miraculously, still supported the weight of the ceiling. An American flag hung from the ceiling, the rotting fabric shredded into long strips. From cracks in the ceiling, pale daylight spilled into the cavernous station. But Steele knew they were far underground; he wondered how daylight found its way into this place.

Ahead, at the opposite end of the platform, Steele saw a light flickering in the darkness. As they approached, he could distinguish over a dozen dark figures huddled about a fire burning in a battered old oil drum. Near the drum, more figures poked long sticks at something in a gigantic tub over a smaller fire.

They're not looking at us, thought Steele, feeling the hairs on the back of his neck tingle. *But they know we're here.*

As if they had read his mind, the figures about the fire turned toward him, and watched in silence as he and his companions approached.

Then Steele heard a sound that made his blood curdle. It was the clatter of metal wheels on the concrete platform, and it was coming from behind him. He couldn't mistake the irregular rattle of the wobbling front wheel.

"IT'S A TRAP!" he shouted, his body pivoting toward the source of the clatter.

His heart stopped when he saw the bent shape behind the old shopping cart, limping toward him like the Grim Reaper. It was the old man he had seen in Wychwood Park the night Dirk disappeared, and again on the night he had gone to meet

Maddie Fey. Quickly, he looked over his shoulder. The dark figures had abandoned the flaming oil drum and were also moving, coming swiftly toward them, their hands gripping long, pointed stakes.

"We've got to get out of here!" Steele said through clenched teeth, desperately trying to conjure up a plan that would get them safely away. But he couldn't see a way out. He and his friends were caught, sandwiched between the old man and a group of spear-wielding figures in black cloaks who looked about as welcoming as a pit of rattlesnakes.

"Jump!" he shouted, gripping his sword and leaping off the platform onto the tracks. His weapon flew out of his hand as he tripped on one of the pilings and landed on his shoulder. He grimaced and bit his lip at the pain.

"This way!" he shouted at his friends, wondering what was the matter with them. Why weren't they following him?

"STOP HIM!" screamed Emily.

Although Steele had never completely trusted Emily, he was still stunned by her betrayal. She had led them into a trap. He swallowed the bitter taste of despair and let his eyes travel along the platform. That's when he spotted Mac and Riley, looking about frantically as the enemy came at them from both ends of the platform.

"Riley! Mac! Over here! Run!" he cried.

He heard Maddie Fey call his name, and he thought Wish might be howling, but he was already running, following the tracks away from the old man, past the dark shrouded figures, who were now shouting angrily, past the flaming oil drum and the large steaming tub. He couldn't help gagging when he spotted four grisly limbs sticking out of the tub.

Horrified, Steele forced himself to run faster. Behind, the

sounds of running footsteps assured him that at least one of his companions had made it onto the tracks. He prayed that it was Mac or Riley, hopefully both.

But when the pursuer grabbed the back of his cloak and spun him around, he saw that it *wasn't* Mac or Riley. It was Emily. Steele reacted instinctively, clenching his fists and aiming a punch at her face.

"Traitor!" he shouted.

"No, no, no!" Emily cried, her eyes all whites. She pointed ahead, into the wide black mouth of a large tunnel. "There! Listen!"

Steele strained to hear, afraid that he wouldn't be able to detect anything above the sound of his own heart beating. But howls and screeches came from deeper in the tunnel. He looked questioningly at Emily.

"Worms!" she explained. "They're coming."

The realization that he had been running toward, and not away from, the worms made Steele weak. Then he felt ashamed. Emily hadn't betrayed them after all.

"Sorry," he mumbled, but the homeless girl didn't hear him. She was already racing back to the platform and the others.

Steele started after her, his eyes darting to either side of the tracks. Then he looked ahead toward the tunnel at the opposite end of the platform, just as a host of ragged people burst from its black mouth. They were Moles, and they were fleeing for their lives. Steele gauged the distance between him and the platform. He had to reach it before he was trapped between the worms coming behind and those who were driving the Moles from the tunnel ahead.

Steele ran faster, his eyes locked on the mouth of the opposite tunnel, waiting for his first glimpse of the worms he had heard so much about. What he saw terrified him. He opened his mouth and screamed, but no sound came from his throat. Behind the Moles, like water bursting from a dam, came the most hideous creatures he had ever seen.

Until now, Steele's only encounter with some of the worms had taken place in a dark alley on the surface. Then, the creatures had worn cloaks to disguise their insect forms, and Steele had been fooled into assuming that they were humans. Before he had got a good look at them, Maddie Fey's red rat had struck, turned them into bloody pulp and, Steele was convinced, then eaten them. Later, Sydney had described them as big insects with lots of legs and fangs and tentacles and other sharp appendages for skewering and killing their prey. But neither his encounter with the creatures in the alley nor Sydney's description had prepared Steele for the sight of the things that slithered or twisted or shuffled or crawled from the mouth of the tunnel.

They were as large as adult humans and they came in all shapes. Some were fat and spongy, totally white bodies spotted with slime. They looked like inflated maggots with ripsaw teeth several inches long. Others were encased in grey or black chitinous plate, as impenetrable as armor. There were winged creatures and spider-like things with sharp, stabbing beaks that dripped venom, and swollen beetle things with cruel-looking barbs sprouting from crooked limbs. They buzzed and hissed as they ripped and jabbed at one another with fangs, claws, pincers, and stingers in their frenzy to get at the Moles.

Shrieks and screams reverberated off the carved stone walls and ceiling as the worms surged out of the tunnel and onto the platform behind the lame old man with the shopping cart, and two small figures, huddled against the wall, arms wrapped tightly about each other.

Riley! Mac!

Then everything seemed to happen at once. Driven onto the platform, the Moles turned to face the worms. As the armies clashed, the old man's shopping cart flew into the air, cartwheeled over and over, and crashed onto the abandoned railway tracks. Steele searched for his friends, but Mac and Riley were gone. And so was the old man.

Extinction

One brisk winter morning, as we drove Death back into the volcano from which it had escaped, we came across a vast area of scorched and blackened earth. And there, charred almost to ash, was our beloved Neanderthal. Death had caught him unawares and eradicated him—wiping him from the face of the earth as swiftly and completely as if he had never existed.

We gazed silently at the ruined earth and whispered secret words to guide the gentle human's spirit on its long journey to another, and we hoped kinder, world.

Worried that future races of humans would point their fingers at *Homo sapiens sapiens,* and accuse this early race of exterminating Neanderthal, or assimilating him, we sealed his charred remains in rock. Perhaps far in the future, scientists will study his DNA from fossil remains and compare it with that of *Homo sapiens sapiens.* If so, they will discover that the *Homo sapiens sapiens* had assimilated into its gene pool the DNA of every species of hominid that came before it, except that of Neanderthal.

—Excerpt from *The Wardens' Logs*

Chapter Twenty-Two

The Mole Wars

The sight of his friends disappearing in a wave of worms spurred Steele into action. Gripping his sword, he leaped onto the platform—and immediately slipped in a puddle of water and fell to his knees. He looked toward the spot where the black-cloaked figures had been poking at the four-legged creature in the large tub. Nausea washed over him. The tub lay on its side, empty, its grisly contents splay-limbed on the platform. The creature looked like a large dog, but it was difficult to tell because it had been skinned and gutted for cooking, and its head was missing. Steele retched and quickly looked away—only to find himself in the thick of battle.

A snarling, yellow-eyed creature bounded toward him. Balanced on its hind limbs, it stood taller than Steele's father. Six additional limbs, ending in sharp claws, protruded from either side of its armoured belly. Stiff black bristles or quills coated the creature's limbs. Steele was petrified. His instincts screamed at him to turn and run away, back into the tunnel. But the shrieks of the worms coming from that direction were louder now. There was nowhere to run.

Steele raised his arms protectively, and seemed almost surprised to see the black sword in his hand. Without thinking, he swung the sword at his attacker, then froze, appalled, as the sharp blade sliced into the creature and blood the colour of mud oozed from its swollen abdomen.

The worm howled and buzzed in pain, but neither the pain nor the widening gash in its belly could stop it. It charged at Steele, forelimbs clawing the air. Its sharp claws raked across Steele's arm, knocking him over. Ignoring the sticky wetness that soaked into his torn shirt and cloak, Steele scrambled to his feet. All about him Moles and worms were locked in mortal combat. Afraid that despair would overwhelm him, he forced himself to forget the larger battle and concentrate on trying to stay alive. Through a gap in the battle, he caught sight of Maddie Fey, standing motionless, looking calm and collected in her long black cloak, as a knot of worms advanced toward her. Then she raised her arms. Fire exploded from her fingers, slamming into the worms and swallowing them up in an instant. The creatures' screams hung in the air even as their bodies disintegrated into ashes.

Steele looked back just in time to fend off another attack by the injured worm. He stabbed and slashed at the worm's legs, severing several clawed toes that wriggled and twitched until he kicked them aside in disgust.

The pain of losing its toes inflamed the worm. Jaws snapping, claws slashing, it smashed into Steele, knocked him over onto his back, and pinned him to the floor. Steele felt Pyrus squirming against his back and hoped he hadn't injured the little salamander. He clenched his teeth, and twisted and turned, kicking and biting as though he had been transformed into a worm himself, but he couldn't free himself from the creature's grasp. He cried out as sharp pincers broke through the flesh on his chest and shoulders.

Then the worm's body went rigid. A gurgling sound came

from its throat, and it fell forward onto Steele, dead from an arrow in its neck. Steele frantically wriggled out from under the dead worm, heart racing from his narrow escape. He brushed the creature's muddy blood from his clothes, tightened his grip on the sword, and scanned the battlefield for Sydney. Her arrow had just saved his life. But he couldn't spot her and, besides, there were scores of worms advancing purposefully his way.

Whether the battle raged for hours or days, Steele couldn't have said. After a time, his muscles ached, he could barely hold onto his sword, and his instincts were dull and sluggish. Still the worms came at him, and the body count of Moles and worms mounted steadily.

Another worm came at Steele. This creature had huge protruding red eyes and a long blunt snout. Its jaws were open and Steele could see the rows of jagged teeth. On the ends of its two long forelimbs were sharp pincers, like those of a lobster, only twenty times bigger. As the creature reached for him, Steele crouched and rolled under its belly. Then he slashed at the worm's hind limbs. The blade sliced clean through the thick flesh so effortlessly that Steele wondered if he had missed altogether. But then the worm roared in pain and fury, and snapped its giant pincers. As it spun toward Steele, its dismembered hind legs fell away; the creature lost its balance and toppled onto its back, helpless, its pincers snapping at nothing.

Steele leaped to his feet, stepped up to the monster, and raised the sword above his head, his hatred for the worms seething inside him. But, as he gazed at the creature, he couldn't bring himself to deliver the death blow. He thought of what the worm had been before the Fire Demons had found it and subverted it. What had Maddie Fey called it—a simple burrowing thing?

"Steele! Behind you!"

Sydney's warning came in the nick of time. Steele spun about just as three worms, all grotesque, all different, all with claws like scissors and fangs like spikes, came at him.

Steele screamed, then looked behind and saw three more worms sneaking up on him.

"Over here!" shouted Sydney, peering from behind a concrete barrier off to Steele's left. She notched an arrow and let it fly.

The arrow hit its mark. One of the worms behind Steele crashed forward onto its face and went still.

Steele took a deep breath and was preparing to make a run for the barrier when another worm anticipated his plan and moved to intercept him. Frantic, he glanced to the right. There was no escape that way. The tracks were swarming with worms gushing from the mouth of the tunnel Steele had vacated a short time ago. There seemed to be no end to them. They surged toward the platform, trampling the bodies of their fallen comrades, but were repelled by a large group of Moles clutching sharp wooden stakes and pitchforks.

Twang! The arrow struck the worm nearest Sydney. The worm paused, spitting and hissing like a maddened cat as it clawed and tore at the arrow in its shoulder. Seeing that the injured worm was momentarily preoccupied, Steele made a break for the barrier. But he never made it. Something huge grabbed him from behind and wrapped several pairs of powerful limbs around his chest in a crushing embrace. The sword slipped from Steele's grasp and clattered to the floor.

And then Maddie Fey appeared like an avenging spirit, her

eyes like frost on a windowpane. Steele stared at the blood-red disk she held in her upraised hand and trembled at its terrible power. A wind whipped from the disk and swiftly gathered force. Then it hammered into the enemy worms still spilling from the mouths of the tunnels and drove them back into the darkness. The creature squeezing Steele to death suddenly released him and lunged at Maddie Fey. But she was ready for it. Her magic caught it and tossed it into one of the tunnels as if it were made of straw.

Weak and shaken, Steele collapsed onto the platform, his head shaking back and forth in despair.

With the worms' advance halted, the Moles seemed to find new strength. They rallied and marched on the remaining worms, chasing them off the platform and onto the tracks. They didn't stop their pursuit until the echoes of the creatures' howls and shrieks and hisses faded away, and silence settled once again over the ancient railway station.

The sight of the Moles driving the worms back into the mouths of the tunnels brought tears to Steele's eyes. It was over.

Slowly, painfully, he pushed himself to his feet. When he felt that he could stand without falling down, he slipped his arms out of his backpack and reached inside. Pyrus brushed against his hand. He gently caught the salamander and pressed it against his chest, shielding it as he checked for injuries. Finally, he sighed with relief. The salamander was OK. Quickly, he stuffed Pyrus into the backpack and replaced it on his back.

He flushed guiltily when he noticed Sydney and Emily staring at him. He hadn't heard them approach.

"What was that?" asked Sydney, staring at his backpack.

"Nothing," he answered, dropping his eyes and reaching for his sword.

"There's something we have to tell you," said Sydney. "It's not good, Steele. We looked along the platform, but there's no sign of Mac or Riley. They're gone."

Steele felt his eyes stinging again as he nodded. "I saw them, and then this old man . . . and the worms . . ." He couldn't continue.

Sydney patted his shoulder sympathetically. "Don't give up hope," she said. "If they're down here, we'll find them." She paused. "Won't we, Emily?"

Emily shrugged, her eyes darting furtively about the platform. "Come on." She tugged on Sydney's arm.

"She's anxious to get the kids out of here," said Sydney. "Before the worms attack again."

"They're gone," said Steele. "Tell her not to worry. They won't be back anytime soon."

But his attempt to comfort Emily failed. She tugged harder on Sydney's arm. "Don't listen. We have to go."

"Are you coming, then?" asked Sydney. "Emily said the waiting room where they're being held isn't that far from here."

Steele looked for Maddie Fey. He saw her standing motionless at the edge of the platform, her slim body rigid, her head tilted to one side as if she were listening to something. Wish stood at her side, his ears standing straight up.

"What?" asked Steele, hurrying over.

He heard faint sounds of howling and buzzing, and as he listened, the sounds grew louder. The worms were coming back!

"Oh God! No," he whispered. "Oh, please God! Not again."

The silence that had fallen over the tracks and platform after the worms had been driven off was shattered now by the shouts and screams of Moles working themselves into a frenzy to face the enemy yet again. Steele looked about and despaired. The Moles were staggering around, their eyes rolling crazily. Steele knew they were physically and emotionally exhausted, in no condition to fight. He also realized that there were far fewer of them than before. Hundreds lay dead all about him, their bodies dwarfed by the large bodies of the enemy.

"Steele!" Maddie Fey's voice brought him up with a start.

He turned to her just as the worms rushed from the tunnels.

"I am needed here, but you must use the fight as cover to rescue the children. Take Emily and Sydney and go now while you can. It's our only chance."

But Steele hesitated, staring at the worms. Something was wrong!

"Look!" he said. "They're not attacking. They're running away from something." He ran his fingers through his hair, puzzled by the worms' strange behaviour. What were they running from?

The worms leaped onto the platform. Steele looked about for Sydney and Emily, but the station was swarming with worms and Moles and he found it difficult to spot the girls. He thought he caught a glimpse of Emily thrusting a pitchfork at a huge worm whose whip-like antennae lashed the air, but then she was gone. A moment later, he saw an arrow— Sydney's?—arc through the air and disappear among the worms. And then one of the creatures staggered to the edge of the platform and pitched forward onto the tracks, the arrow embedded deep in the back of its large head.

Just then the world exploded, and Steele understood the reason for the worms' strange behaviour.

A stream of boiling, bubbling magma shot into the air, spraying the old railway station with liquid fire. The first Fire Demon rose from the cracked earth amid a great column of smoke and ash. The railway tracks buckled and twisted and broke apart, sizzling and hissing. The worms screeched and howled, streaking here and there like giant chickens whose heads had been cut off, smashing into each other and trampling others of their kind as they tried to outrun the flesh-melting heat. Steele stopped breathing as the flaming terror loomed higher and higher. Great, licking flames roared with the sound of a tornado, illuminating the platform and bathing it in a fierce copper light.

Sydney suddenly darted out from among the teeming worms and ran to Steele's side; her skin looked as if it were burning in the orange brightness.

"We're dead!" she said in his ear. "Unless we can think of a way to flood the tunnel and douse its fire."

Steele and Sydney backed away from the living inferno, sweat simmering on Sydney's face, but not on Steele's. Steele thought of what his friend had just said about putting out a fire. He saw Sydney staring at him in dismay as his hand wrapped tightly about the red disk around his neck. Steele took a deep breath and concentrated until his head throbbed and he thought he would pass out.

The Fire Demon moved purposefully toward Steele, its burning eyes cold with fury, its wicked fiery fangs opening and closing in a chomping motion. Behind it, Steele saw another Fire Demon, and then another surge out of the earth. But there was no time to worry about them. He had enough to deal with—the creature bearing down on him. He forced himself to remain calm and concentrated on drawing the air about him into his lungs.

At first nothing happened.

The creature slowed, and the fire where its mouth should be seemed to shift and stretch, as if it were laughing at him. Steele forced down his panic and inhaled deeper, until he felt that his lungs would burst. The Fire Demon stopped and stared at him. Suddenly Steele understood his power. He was killing the Fire Demon by sucking the oxygen from the air—creating a vacuum in which fire could not live.

As Sydney watched, her eyes round with fear, Steele struggled to remain conscious long enough to destroy the Fire Demon trapped inside the vacuum with him. Black fumes drifted from the creature as its fire began to cool.

Then the Fire Demon screeched, coiling and striking at Steele as it began to shrink, slowly at first and then faster and faster, until the fire within it died and it evaporated in a puff of stinking black smoke. Steele gasped, and then crumpled to the floor, his eyes wide and staring. He saw Sydney approach him and kneel beside him, tears streaming down her face. She pressed her thumb against his neck, feeling for his pulse.

At her touch, Steele smiled.

"It worked," he said, so softly Sydney had to bend close to his mouth to catch the words.

"I don't know what you did," she said, "but it worked all right. Now, let's get out of here."

"Wait!" Steele exclaimed, sitting up. "Pyrus! Oh God. I forgot about Pyrus!"

He was aware of Sydney gaping at him as if he had lost his

mind, but he didn't care. He shrugged free of the backpack and quickly unzipped the flap. Then he reached inside and plucked the salamander from the bottom of the pack. Its round eyes were glassy and it appeared to be dead.

"Oh, Pyrus," murmured Steele, pressing his pet against his chest. "I'm sorry. I'm so sorry."

"What *is* that?" asked Sydney, brushing her finger lightly along Pyrus's scaly neck.

"Tsit!" Pyrus twitched, and its eyes blinked repeatedly.

Steele felt tears running down his face. He wiped them on Pyrus's head and grinned at Sydney. "His name is Pyrus, and he's alive."

"Hi, Pyrus," said Sydney, taking the salamander and holding it gently while Steele struggled to his feet.

Steele reluctantly put Pyrus back in his pack, and then turned to Sydney.

"Where's Maddie Fey?"

"She's OK," Sydney reassured him. "There were only two other Fire Demons. She got one of them and the other's gone. The worms are going crazy trying to get away."

They forced their way through the stampeding worms, dodging and twisting to escape being trampled under the creatures' clawed limbs. Steele tried to search for Mac and Riley among the hundreds of dead Moles and worms strewn about the charred platform, but he couldn't find them. He noticed that some of the worms had been ripped to pieces, and he was sickened at the ferocity of the attack. He hadn't spotted Maddie Fey's red rat, but the state of those bodies told him the rat had been here, and it had been busy.

At the far end of the platform they came upon Maddie Fey, holding the unmoving body of Emily in her arms.

Sydney started crying. "She didn't betray us," she said to Steele. "She was trying to protect you."

Steele bowed his head in shame and sorrow. "I know," he said. "She came after me. That's why I turned around."

"Her life was so sad," cried Sydney. "So horribly sad."

"I'll take her." A huge figure brushed past Steele, almost knocking him over.

Steele regained his balance and stared at the giant woman in shock. It was the guard from the tunnel—the one who had caught him from behind and tried to kill him. The woman gently gathered the small body in her enormous arms.

"She belongs here," she said, then turned and walked past Steele toward the entrance to the platform.

Steele and the others watched, not speaking, until she disappeared.

"Come on," said Sydney, sniffling loudly. "Let's get the kids . . . for Emily."

And then, to his surprise, Steele was crying too. He looked down at his own blood staining the front of his cloak and shirt as it seeped from wounds on his chest and shoulders. But he barely felt the pain. He was saddened by the homeless girl's death, and he felt guilty, as if it were somehow his fault. But he was even more angry than sad. He felt Maddie Fey's hand on his arm, but her touch gave him cold comfort, and he shrugged it away. He had almost forgotten about the missing kids, and now thinking about them made him angry and frustrated. If they hadn't gone missing, Mac and Riley would still be in Toronto, safe. Let Maddie Fey and Sydney deal with the kids; suddenly he didn't care if he ever saw them. All he cared about was finding his friends.

Steele smashed his fists against the concrete wall until the flesh on his knuckles was torn and bloody. But the physical pain was nothing compared with the pain in his heart at losing his best friends. *Oh, Mac! Oh, Riley!*

"I'll never stop looking for you," he vowed, pressing his head against the bloodstained concrete.

"Hello, Steele," said a deep voice from behind. "We meet again."

Intelligence

For four million years, we watched humans evolve from herd animals to tribal hunters and warriors. At first, they were creatures of instinct, much like our prisoners. But, unlike Death, whose instincts were purely destructive, humans developed instincts such as mother-love, compassion, curiosity, inventiveness, and competitiveness, all for survival.

But something else had happened to our human over the long years. Something so important it made us tremble in wonder. The once-fragile, ape-like creature had developed intellect. Now humans quickly distinguished themselves from the animals. They used intellect to control their instincts. As they learned to curb their hunting, killing instincts, their natures changed. The human began to reason and to show compassion.

But Death was bent on killing. It clawed and slashed at the walls of its prison, and it took all of our power to keep it in the fire.

—Excerpt from *The Wardens' Logs*

Chapter Twenty-Three

The Missing Kids

Steele's muscles tensed. He spun about, and then shrank against the concrete wall, frightened and confused.

"Y-you!" he spluttered, staring at the black-cloaked figure towering above him.

It was the homeless old man, but without his rickety shopping cart. His voice was different, strong and resonant. Steele couldn't detect any trace of slurred speech now. And he certainly didn't look like one of the homeless. He stood as straight as a poplar tree, all traces of the pronounced crook in his back gone. Steele guessed that he had to be at least seven feet tall. His long, tangle-free black hair fell below his shoulders and was tied back against his neck. His eyes were clear and intelligent, and, despite his age, for he was certainly old, he looked powerful.

Then Steele caught a glimpse of something under the man's cloak, on his chest. A splash of red. He gasped. It was a round disk, as red as blood, exactly like the one under Steele's shirt.

A Mage!

As if he had read Steele's thoughts, the old man nodded, his eyes twinkling, perhaps in amusement.

"Where did *he* come from?" whispered Sydney, picking up Steele's sword and holding it out to him.

Steele shook his head. "It's a long story. I'll tell you later." He took the sword and slipped it back into his belt.

"Hello, Fidus," said Maddie Fey, walking up to the man and taking his hand in both of hers. Her smile was warm.

"Hello, dear child," said Fidus, studying her face before leaning over to plant a gentle kiss on her brow.

Steele studied Maddie Fey too. As usual, not a hair on her head was out of place. Her long black cloak was spotless, whereas his was torn and covered in something brown and sticky. But he noticed that her eyes were dull, and her face was gaunt and pale. He wondered how he could have believed that she wielded the magic easily, almost effortlessly. Just because her clothes and hair were perfect didn't mean that the magic hadn't taken a toll on her.

Maddie Fey turned to Steele "This is Fidus, my friend and mentor."

"You're a Mage," said Steele, feeling very young and ungainly. "Er . . . I saw the disk under your cloak—that is . . . I guess only Mages have disks like that."

"Yes," said the man named Fidus, his sharp eyes moving over the platform, following two Moles who were supporting an injured comrade between them. "Only Mages have disks. They are useless in the hands of anyone else." His eyes rested upon the bodies of the many dead or dying worms and Moles, and he shook his head sadly. "I wonder if the humans who live on the surface are aware that they owe their lives to the very people they shunned and drove from the streets," he said quietly.

Abruptly his head whipped toward Steele and he swooped down on him, clutching his arm and gripping it tightly.

"My stars! I almost forgot. Come with me. Quickly!" The

Mage turned and began to drag Steele away from Maddie Fey and Sydney.

Alarmed by the old man's erratic behaviour, Steele tried to wrench his arm free, but the man's grip was like iron. "What? *What?*" he cried.

If he hadn't felt the pressure on his arm, Steele would have thought that Fidus had forgotten about him. Muttering to himself, the old man strode swiftly toward the massive double doors that guarded the entrance to the platform. He pushed through the doors and then hesitated.

In the pale light that seeped through the open doors from the ancient railway station, Steele saw three passageways. They looked like giant black mouths. The old man looked from passage to passage as if he couldn't make up his mind which one to take.

"Aha!" he exclaimed, then dragged Steele after him as he plunged into the mouth of a narrow passage to the right.

Worried that the old man had lost his mind, Steele looked over his shoulder at Maddie Fey. She and Sydney had retrieved the torches they had dropped outside the doors and were hurrying after him, the flames bobbing as they approached. From their expressions Steele knew that they were as mystified as he by Fidus's weird conduct.

Halfway along the passageway, the man stopped and turned to the wall on his left, releasing his hold on Steele's arm. The moment he was free, Steele backed away, rubbing his aching arm and watching the man warily.

Fidus placed his hands flat against the wall and began to chant; his voice was so quiet, Steele could only hear a low murmuring drone.

The outline of a door appeared on the wall. The old Mage took a step back and pointed. Steele heard a sharp *click,* and the door slowly began to open.

Hardly daring to breathe, Steele peered into the darkness on the other side of the open door. And then something moved and he heard a timid voice.

"W-who's t-there?"

"The missing kids," gasped Steele.

"Steele?" said the voice, stronger this time. "Is that you?"

"It's Mac!" cried Steele in disbelief.

The old man moved aside as Mac and then Riley, grasping sharp knives in their hands, burst from the room and rushed over to Steele.

For several minutes, the ancient passageway deep under New York reverberated with the sounds of excited voices as Mac and Riley were reunited with their friends. After they had lowered their knives, Steele embraced them so tightly they gasped for air. But the more they struggled to escape, the tighter he held them. He had almost given up hope of ever seeing them again. Now that he had them back, he was afraid that if he let them go he'd break down completely.

When Steele finally dropped his arms to his sides, Mac cast a fearful glance at the old man. "He locked us in there."

"It's true," agreed Riley. "He just grabbed us and the next thing we knew we were locked in that dark place and we couldn't get out."

Mac lowered his voice. "He threatened to turn us into cockroaches if we made a sound."

"No," said Riley. "He threatened to turn *you* into a cock-roach, because you wouldn't shut up."

Mac glowered at her.

"It was for your own good," said the old man sternly, but his eyes glimmered, and Steele thought he was trying hard not to smile. "But enough of this. Our work here isn't finished. We must not permit those poor children to spend another night in this terrible place."

"But we don't know where they are," wailed Sydney. "Emily was taking us there when . . ." Her voice shook and trailed off.

Mac and Riley looked at Steele questioningly.

Steele caught their arms. "Emily didn't make it," he said.

Riley squeezed her eyes shut and dropped her chin to her chest.

Mac looked dazed, as if something heavy had just fallen on his head. "All the fighting," he said. "It was bad?"

Steele nodded, thankful when his friends didn't question him further. He watched Riley walk slowly over to Sydney, and a few seconds later the girls were hugging and crying. Steele looked away.

Then he saw Maddie Fey and the old man. They could have been made of stone they were so still. For a second, they reminded him of his grandmother, the way their eyes were staring at something far away. Only he had never seen GM's eyes turn the colour of ice. Steele wondered what was the matter with them. He started toward them, but Sydney's hand on his arm held him back.

"Wait!" she whispered.

At that moment, Steele's body tensed and his eyes gazed blankly into the distance. Sydney cried out and snatched her hand from his arm as if he were bristling with static electricity and she had received a shock.

Hearing her cry, Mac and Riley hurried over.

"What is it?" asked Riley.

Sydney tilted her head at Steele.

Unaware of his companions' concern, Steele tried to make sense of the cacophony that blared in his head as if someone had turned up the volume on a radio. He heard shouts and screams and squeals and scratching. He heard crunches and creaks and cracks. At first the sounds were loud and irritating. But gradually he began to assimilate the sounds and separate them, until he could distinguish the shouts of the Moles as they gathered their dead and laid them out on the platform, from the negligible scratching of a tiny insect as it burrowed inside the concrete wall.

He knew that something strange had happened to him, perhaps taken control of him. He had felt the change come over him just after he glimpsed Maddie Fey and the old Mage frozen in their trance-like states. But what did it mean?

As he followed a rat scuttling somewhere in the distance, he gradually realized that if he could follow the sound of the rat, he could do the same with other sounds. Perhaps he could even direct his hearing to locate the missing kids.

He sorted quickly through the loudest sounds, but he heard no kids' voices. Next he focused on sounds that were farther away. Again, no kids' voices among them. Frustrated, he let his hearing drift among the barely audible sounds, and then he heard a voice in his ear that made his heart leap into his throat.

"Come to me, little boy. I'm waiting."

"Nooo!" Steele shouted, as the voice of the Prince of Darkness filled his head. He looked about wildly, expecting to see a scarred and bloody face rushing toward him. Instead, he saw his wide-eyed companions backing away from him as if he had returned from the dead. But he didn't have time to worry about that now. He looked over Mac's head to where Maddie Fey and the old Mage were talking together quietly.

"I heard the Prince of Darkness," he said, rushing over to them. "He's here."

"Who on earth—?" asked Maddie Fey, turning to Steele, then stopping in mid-sentence and staring at him in surprise.

Steele caught her arm. "Listen! You weren't there when I told the others about the Prince of Darkness. I can't explain now, but something happened to me and I heard his voice. It was as clear as if he were standing beside me. If he's in the tunnels, we've got to find those kids and get them out of here fast."

He could see the questions in Maddie Fey's eyes as she stared at him hard. "Please trust me," he said. "Don't ask me how I know, but the one who calls himself the Prince of Darkness is very, very bad."

Steele held his breath as Maddie Fey looked at Fidus, only releasing it when he saw the old man nod.

"Let us go," said Maddie Fey. "We used our powers to search for the children. It took a while, but we found them."

"All right!" breathed Steele.

Maddie Fey and Fidus moved swiftly back along the narrow passageway. Steele followed closely, his ears burning as he listened to his friends whispering behind his back.

"Did you see his eyes?" asked Sydney.

"Yeah!" answered Riley. "All the blue was gone."

"Talk about freaky," said Mac.

As if he, too, heard the whispers, Fidus slowed and put his arm about Steele's shoulders.

"Being a Mage is not easy," he said. "Your friends are frightened because they do not understand."

"Are my eyes really silver?" whispered Steele.

The old man shook his head. "They are blue now," he said. "Later, I would like to hear what happened to you, how you heard the Prince of Darkness."

When they reached the entrance to the platform, Fidus removed his arm from Steele's shoulders and picked up one of the torches. It had burned out on the concrete floor and was now cold. To Steele's astonishment, the old man pointed a slender finger at the torch and it burst into flames. He passed the torch to Steele. Then he led them along a broad corridor and under a gigantic arch to a long, wide stairway. He mounted the steps quickly, taking them two at a time. Steele tried, and failed, to match his speed. At the top, Steele paused to catch his breath, amazed that the old man's breathing was as regular as if he had taken a leisurely stroll in the park.

Steele looked about. They were in a long, arched tunnel. He looked guardedly from side to side, noticing arched recesses along the walls on both sides. In the darkened recesses he could just make out the darker frames of doorways. As he peered into the shadows, he had the feeling that they were being watched. Without thinking, he pulled his mother's disk from under his shirt and held onto it tightly.

Maddie Fey and the old Mage ignored the doors on either side and seemed to be heading directly toward the large door barely visible in the darkness at the end of the tunnel. Steele wanted to wait for the others, but their whispers had alienated him. Still, he wondered what Sydney must be feeling as they drew closer to the missing kids.

"Steele?"

He looked around at Riley.

"We're sorry for talking about you," she said. "We weren't trying to be mean."

"Right," said Mac, walking up to Steele and punching him on the arm. "You really freaked us out, man. Your eyes looked like white lights."

"It's OK," said Steele, smiling to show that he meant it. But he knew it wasn't OK, because the hurt was still there.

"I'm so anxious," said Sydney. "I can barely stop myself from running ahead and screaming William's name." She looked at Steele. "What if he's not there?"

Steele couldn't think of anything to say to comfort her. "We'll find him," he said finally.

Sydney squeezed Steele's arm. "Oh, please be right," she whispered.

Ahead, a figure detached itself from the shadows and moved into the middle of the tunnel, as if to block the way. Steele glanced back and saw other figures slipping from the darkened recesses and falling in behind them—vague shapes crouched low, their eyes flashing yellow in the torchlight.

"Back there," he whispered to Maddie Fey.

Maddie Fey didn't turn around. She kept her eyes on the lone creature blocking the tunnel ahead. "Yes," she said. "I have been aware of them for some time."

"Maybe they're Moles," Riley said hopefully.

Sydney shook her head. "I don't think so. Moles usually ask for a password. I think we're in serious trouble."

"Be quiet!" The sharp command came from Fidus. "There is something here I haven't encountered before." He turned to Maddie Fey. "Can you feel it?"

Maddie Fey closed her eyes and went still. She remained like that for several seconds. Then she blinked and shivered. "Magic," she said quietly. "Dark magic."

"Who's there?" Fidus addressed the shadowy figure blocking their way.

A chilling laugh erupted from the figure. Then Steele heard another sound coming from one of the darkened doorways off to the side just ahead. He thought it sounded like air hissing through clenched teeth, and he listened for it to be repeated. But he heard nothing. *It was just my imagination,* he told himself. But he continued to grip the disk.

Fidus reached for Steele's torch and raised it in front of him as he moved cautiously toward the solitary figure. "Stay here," he commanded the others.

At the same time, Maddie Fey turned to face the creatures coming at them from the rear. Steele forced his eyes away from the shadowed recess and also turned to look back. The creatures stopped, their gleaming eyes riveted on Maddie Fey, their heads swivelling from left to right.

Then they charged, quick and silent.

Someone screamed, but Steele couldn't tell if it was Riley or Sydney. Quickly, he stuffed the disk inside his shirt and fumbled to free his sword. But when he finally pulled it from his belt, he realized that he didn't need it after all. The creatures were no match for Maddie Fey's great hound. At a command from his mistress, Wish bounded to meet the attackers. The creatures took one look at the silver blur coming at them like a phantom beast, its fangs bared menacingly, and they skidded to a stop on the tunnel floor. Then they screeched in terror and turned and fled down the length of the tunnel.

When the last of the screeches had died away, Steele turned

and looked at Fidus. The old Mage was circling the last assailant warily, Steele's torch in his raised hand. A wailing scream came from the dark figure and it crumpled to the floor. Hearing a sharp hiss, Steele turned toward the shadowed recess.

So he *hadn't* been imagining things. There was someone there. Then he caught sight of movement in the shadows, and before he could question the wisdom of his actions, he raised his sword and ran toward the arched recess.

"Siss!" The threatening hiss came from the darkened recess.

Steele felt invisible hands lift him off the floor and pitch him backwards. He sailed through the air and smashed into the wall on the opposite side of the tunnel. The sword dropped from his hand with a clatter. Steele collapsed, hurt and shaken. Mac and Riley were at his side in an instant. Gritting his teeth, Steele grabbed their arms and pulled himself up. His face was as white as chalk as he looked from Mac to Riley.

"He was here," he said softly, snatching his sword and slipping it back into his belt.

"What are you talking about?" asked Mac. "Who was here?"

"The Prince of Darkness," hissed Steele. "He was here all the time." He pointed into the shadows along the wall. "He was hiding over there."

Mac and Riley exchanged puzzled looks.

"I'm telling you I saw him," insisted Steele angrily.

"You don't have to bite our heads off," snapped Riley. "We believe you."

"Besides, we know you can't fly," said Mac.

"Come on," urged Sydney. "Fidus wants us."

They hurried over to the old Mage, who, along with Maddie Fey, was staring at an unconscious man lying on his back on the floor. Steele guessed that the Mages had been too preoccupied to notice what had happened to him a few moments ago. Fidus drew Steele and his companions into a tight circle about him. "That creature is human," he said. "Not a Mole. He and the others were here to guard the children. He would not willingly give up the name of his master. So I probed his mind. But someone had sealed his mind with magic, and I could not break the seal without killing him." He stared at the unconscious assailant and shrugged. "I was going to turn him into something quite harmless, but I don't think he will bother us for a while."

Then and there, Steele decided that he liked the old man. The Mage was more relaxed than Maddie Fey, less serious, and he had a sense of humour that seemed to be missing in the girl.

"Did you find out anything about the magic?" he asked.

"No," said Fidus, looking at Steele thoughtfully. "Except that the one who wields it is very powerful."

"I'm troubled," said Maddie Fey. "Until now we believed that the worms were stealing children for the Fire Demons. Now we find that someone or something else is involved, and it possesses magic that is so dark and evil, as I searched for it, it was hunting me."

Her words chilled Steele. He told them about the person who had been hiding in the shadows, and he took them over to the arched recess. But whoever had been there was gone.

"And you think it was this creature who calls himself the Prince of Darkness?" Fidus asked Steele.

"It was him," said Steele, suddenly sure.

As the group set out once more, Steele noticed the worried look that passed between Maddie Fey and her mentor.

At the end of the tunnel, they crowded about the large wooden door. Fidus and Maddie Fey traced the outline of the door with their fingers. Then Fidus grasped the iron handle and pushed inward. The door opened without a sound. Sydney raised her torch and stepped inside. Steele and the others followed, and looked about the deserted chamber in disappointment.

"We're too late," cried Sydney. "They're gone."

"Wait!" said Maddie Fey. "It looks like an empty room, but there's something . . ." She turned in a circle, studying the walls.

"It's an illusion," agreed Fidus, walking over to the nearest wall, and bumping into it. "Hmm!" he said, rubbing his nose and staring at the wall in disbelief. "It would not let me pass through."

"It's a maze," said Maddie Fey softly. "The children are somewhere inside . . ." She looked at Steele and his friends. "But there is something else in there, and it is also searching for them."

"Worms!" cried Sydney, her face distorted in horror. "They're feeding them to the worms." She ran at the wall and beat her fists on the concrete, screaming her brother's name again and again. Then she slumped against the wall and sobbed uncontrollably.

Riley ran to her and held her until she stopped crying.

Mac looked around, bewildered. "I don't see any maze," he said. "Where is it?"

"It's not visible," explained Maddie Fey. "But it's there, Mac. It's a vast, complex maze with hundreds of dead ends."

Mac looked even more perplexed. "But who made it?"

"Someone very powerful," said Fidus dryly.

"You and Maddie Fey are magic," said Mac. "Can't you do something?"

Fidus smiled sadly. "Yes, Mac. We can do something, but we have to understand the magic here before we can undo it. That will take time. And I'm afraid time is something we do not have."

Steele refused to accept that they'd come this close to rescuing the missing children only to have them devoured by worms. "There must be some way we can get through the maze quickly."

When Mac's eyes suddenly brightened, Steele knew his friend was about to share one of his brilliant ideas.

"Listen," said Mac. "Everybody knows the way to solve a maze is to start at the end and work your way backwards. So let's—"

"Of course!" shouted the old Mage. "Start at the end!" He thumped Mac several times on the back. "Excellent thinking, young man. Now be quiet for a minute and let me think this through."

Steele paced nervously about the chamber, fidgeting with the flat red disk through the cloth of his shirt, his mind whirling. There had to be a way to get to the kids. But how? He glanced at the old man, wondering how he intended to use Mac's idea. In order to *start* at the end of a maze, you had to *reach* the end. How was he going to do that in time to save the children from the worms?

"Come here, Steele," said the old man, removing his disk from under his cloak. "I will need the power of our three disks for what I have in mind."

Steele and Maddie Fey hurried over, their disks in their hands.

"What are you going to do?" asked Steele.

"I am going to try to enter the maze." Fidus placed his hand on Steele's shoulder. "Take my arm. Maddie Fey will take the other. Do not let go, no matter what happens. And do not speak. Do you understand?"

Steele nodded and did as he was told. He held his breath, waiting for something to happen, as the old man stared at the blank wall. Just when he was beginning to worry that Fidus's plan had failed, he felt a shudder wrack the man's body. And then Fidus roared and struggled so violently that it took all of Steele's strength to hold onto him. He was exhausted by the time Fidus's head dropped forward and his body went limp and still.

Steele felt a cold mist brush his face, and he almost dropped the arm he was holding and fled when he saw a pale wraith drift from the old man's body and rise toward the ceiling. From somewhere in the chamber, he heard his friends trying unsuccessfully to stifle their horrified gasps.

He had no idea how long he and Maddie Fey stood there, supporting the old Mage's weight between them. It seemed like forever. Steele's muscles ached and sweat ran down his neck. And then something happened.

The concrete wall rippled and blurred. Then it faded and disappeared, revealing a larger chamber whose walls also disintegrated into dust that floated lazily down to settle on the floor. Steele looked about. The chamber was enormous now, and on the wall directly in front of him a small door appeared. In the distance, Steele heard the rumble of the subway, and then another sound, much closer—the loud creaking of the door slowly opening. He took a sharp breath and focused on the door.

In the torchlight, all Steele could see in the pitch black beyond the open door were glowing eyes, dozens of them, all staring out of the darkness at him and his companions. Steele felt his eyes watering.

The missing kids! Fidus had found them in time.

The old man's body trembled. His neck tensed and his head jerked up. Blinking rapidly, he pulled his arms free and stood up.

"Get them out of here," he whispered. "I must seal this place before the worms break through."

Maddie Fey and Wish moved quickly to the doorway and led the children into the chamber. The door slammed shut, and Steele heard Fidus chanting strange words under his breath. The old man kept it up until the door began to fade and then vanished.

The children followed Maddie Fey in orderly ranks as they filed into the tunnel. Steele stared at them, waiting anxiously for his first glimpse of Ryan Massey and Dirk. He'd seen Ryan's picture on TV so many times, he felt he had known him all of his life. But as he stared at the children filing past, he was surprised by the dull, glazed looks in their eyes and the surly scowls on their faces. He had expected them to be emotional, crying or excited, anything but surly.

Steele followed them into the passageway and walked along the rows of kids, studying each face. At last he turned away sadly. Neither Ryan nor Dirk was there.

"William!" Sydney's excited cry drew every head her way. She ran toward one of the kids, a tall boy with curly black hair and dark skin, and wrapped him in her arms.

But the boy pushed her away roughly.

Steele caught his breath.

Sydney shook her brother's arm. "William! It's me, Sydney."

The boy bared his teeth and snarled at her.

She turned to the others, her eyes filled with despair. "What's wrong with him? Why doesn't he know me?"

"It's not just William," said Steele. "Look, Syd! They're all like that."

"You'd probably be like that too, if you went through what they did," said Riley.

Steele shook his head. "I don't think it's got anything to do with what they've been through, Riley. Remember what Dad said about Megan Traft, the girl in New York who was abducted and later turned up on her own doorstep? Her parents thought she was a stranger, because she had become mean and nasty." He looked at Fidus. "Something's wrong with them, isn't there."

The old man nodded sadly. "Yes, Steele, something is wrong with them."

"What?" asked Steele and Riley at the same time.

"The Fire Demons stole their memories."

Humankind

We were here from the beginning of this planet's time. We fought to protect it from Death's fire and give life a chance to develop. While many species were eradicated through the process of natural selection and others were taken by Death, our presence ensured the survival of intelligent life. Our logs record the evolutionary history of mankind. Our chart shows how long it took for each species to appear:

Species	Time from the Formation of the Planet
Ardipithecus ramidus	4.595 billion years
Australopithecus anamensis	4.596 billion years
Australopithecus afarensis	4.597 billion years
Australopithecus africanus	4.598 billion years
Homo habilis	4.599 billion years
Homo erectus	4 billion 599.1 million years
Homo sapiens (archaic)	4 billion 599.7 million years
Homo sapiens sapiens	4 billion 599.8 million years

—Excerpt from *The Wardens' Logs*

Chapter Twenty-four

Fidus

Like six black wraiths, and one silver shadow, Steele and his companions and Wish drifted from a hidden tunnel exit and walked through the early morning rain toward the long, black limousine that waited silently at the curb. Behind marched the missing children, their faces mean-looking and cross.

Steele stood aside and watched the children as they filed into the limo. His heart felt heavy when he saw Sydney following her brother like a lost puppy.

"What's going to happen to them?" he asked Maddie Fey.

She looked at him for a long time before she answered. "They will remain like that unless we help them," she said. "We must find their memories and steal them back."

Steele gave her a sharp look. "Are you serious? How are we going to find memories? It's not like they're visible."

"You're right," said Maddie Fey. "Memories are invisible. But that doesn't mean they aren't real. Someone has found a way to extract these children's memories. I do not know how it is done, and I can only guess at the reason. But we can find them, Steele."

But Steele was sceptical. "I just don't see how even you and Fidus can find memories," he said. "It sounds crazy."

Inside the limo, Fidus examined Sydney's injuries, a cut over one eye and a deep gash on her arm. Then he turned to Steele, tut-tutting at the slash wounds and gouges on his chest and the puncture marks on his arms where one of the worms had sunk its sharp claws. Steele and Sydney gritted their teeth while Maddie Fey's rat slathered something green and stinging over their wounds and applied dressings. The short whistling sounds the rat made as he worked told Steele that the creature was enjoying their distress. Later, they debated what to do about the missing children. Now that she had found William, Sydney was reluctant to let him out of her sight, so she argued that they keep the children in Maddie Fey's house until their memories were restored. Riley sided with her, but the others, including Steele, thought they should turn the children over to the police or deliver them to the nearest hospital. Finally, they agreed to let Fidus decide the issue. He declared that they had no right to keep the children.

"They need emotional and physical care that we cannot provide," said the old Mage. "And their poor parents need to know that they are alive."

A short time later, they dropped the missing children off at a hospital. Steele, Mac, and Riley stood by the open limo door and watched them disappear into the Emergency Unit.

Maddie Fey and the old Mage did not appear. And Steele couldn't help but wonder why.

Because Sydney couldn't bear to leave her twin so soon after finding him, she decided to accompany him and the other children and deal with the hospital staff. At the hospital entrance, she turned and waved to her friends. "This isn't goodbye," she said. "I'll see you soon. And, Steele, give Pyrus a hug for me."

Steele and the others waved back. Then she was gone.

"Poor Sydney," said Riley, turning away and pressing her fingers over her eyes to stop the tears. "I'd die if I had a brother and he forgot who I was." She climbed into the limo.

"Is that the door Maddie Fey stopped you from opening?" whispered Mac, pointing to the second to last door on the passenger side.

Steele nodded. "Shh! Her rat's probably got the entire limo bugged."

Mac looked about furtively. "There's no one around. Come on, let's try it now," he urged.

"Are you crazy?" said Steele.

"Listen!" hissed Mac. "If we don't like what's in there, we slam the door shut—"

"Get in," hissed the rat, coming up behind them and shoving them roughly toward the open door.

Steele glared into the rat's glistening eyes before following Mac into the limo. "I hate that rat," he whispered. "I don't understand why Maddie Fey keeps it around." Then he remembered how the rat's eyes had glistened, almost as if they were filled with tears. Had Nilats been crying? Was the creature sad because Sydney had left with the missing kids? *No way,* he thought.

Moments later Steele was surprised to find himself with Mac and Riley back in the round foyer with the black and white marble floor. The room was bright with sunlight. He looked about, but there was no sign of a window. He stared at the aloof figures in the alcoves; he knew now that they were Mages. He almost laughed out loud when he remembered how afraid he'd been that Maddie Fey was going to turn him to stone and stick him in the empty alcove. He counted the Mages again. Ten.

I was sure there were only nine, he thought.

He looked at the last two alcoves. Both were empty. He blinked. Then, for a second he thought he saw the outline of a figure in the ninth. But he blinked again and it was empty.

Slowly, Steele followed Mac and Riley up the long, sweeping staircase, his eyes automatically looking for the niches where the giant, dragon-like creatures had stood. To his disappointment, neither the niches nor the giant creatures—he now suspected they were wardens—were there. *Perhaps they just haven't materialized yet,* he thought, recalling how things had appeared magically the last time he was here.

They searched everywhere for Maddie Fey and the old Mage, but the house appeared to be deserted. In the library, they were relieved to find platters of sandwiches and the familiar sweet, yellow beverage set out on the coffee table. In the black marble fireplace, a fire burned brightly. They spent the rest of the day lounging about the fire, munching sandwiches, and sharing their adventures in the tunnels under New York.

Mac and Riley leaned forward as Steele told them about the battle with the worms and the sudden appearance of the Fire Demons. Then Steele listened while his best friends took turns filling him in on how the old man had tossed the shopping cart into the air and snatched them off the platform before they knew what was happening.

Mac was still bristling with indignation at being taken away from the battle and locked up. "He had some nerve," he complained. "Locking us up like we were little kids. I could have helped you fight those worms."

Steele grinned. "I wish you'd been there," he said kindly. "I really needed your help."

"I have to call home," said Riley, abruptly changing the subject.

Mac nodded. "I'm almost afraid to call my parents," he said. "They're going to be seriously angry."

"I want to talk to my dad," said Steele. "But I think we should discuss it with Maddie Fey before we do anything."

Later, when Maddie Fey and the old man still hadn't appeared, they separated and went to their rooms. Steele was too wound up to sleep. He let Pyrus out of his backpack and tried to feed it a sandwich he had taken from the platter. Then he lit a fire in the fireplace and dropped into a chair with his book. Pyrus turned its nose up at the sandwich and darted about the room, taking advantage of its freedom. Steele tried to keep his eyes on the salamander, but it changed colour faster than he could follow. Finally he gave up and opened his book, but before he knew it, he drifted off.

"Get up!" said Mac, shaking Steele's arm. "We've been summoned to the dining room."

Steele rubbed sleep from his eyes and stared at Mac groggily.

"Come on!" said Riley from the doorway. "We've been sleeping for over twenty-four hours."

Steele pushed himself out of the chair. "Is that true, Riley? Have we really been out of it for a whole day?"

"More than a day," said Riley.

"It seems like I just fell asleep," groaned Steele, stretching his aching muscles.

He stuffed Pyrus back in his backpack, slung the pack over his shoulder, and followed Mac and Riley down the hall. When they reached the dining room, Maddie Fey looked up from her place at the head of the table and bestowed a half smile on them. On her right, Fidus raised his hand in greeting. Wish was curled up on the hearth, and he too raised his head and stared at them intently. This time, Steele and his friends chose places near the head of the table, close to Maddie Fey and Fidus.

When they were seated, Maddie Fey's eyes moved from one to the other. "I have something for each of you," she said, opening a shimmering silver box that was resting on the table in front of her. She reached inside and removed three smaller, slim boxes. Then she looked at Mac.

"When Steele insisted that you and Riley join the search for the missing children, I was convinced that it was a mistake." Maddie Fey's blue eyes sparkled like sapphires. "I was wrong. Steele is lucky to have a friend like you, Mac. You stayed true, even when you were afraid."

Mac flushed, but Steele could see that he was bursting with pride.

"Besides," Fidus interjected, "if it hadn't been for you, I might not have found the children in time to save them from the worms."

"What did I do?" asked Mac.

"You told me how to solve the maze," answered Fidus. "I left my corporeal body in the care of Steele and Maddie Fey and, in my spirit form, I travelled up to where I could look down into the maze."

"I did help, didn't I," said Mac. "You really needed me after all."

Maddie Fey smiled. "Yes, Mac. We owe you a great debt."

Next, she turned her attention to Riley.

"I didn't do anything," said Riley miserably. "Except cry a lot."

"No, Riley," said Maddie Fey. "You also proved that friendship is more powerful than all of the dark forces combined. At times, you were even more afraid than Mac. Still, you followed Steele and made him strong by being there. You were a friend to Sydney when she needed a friend. And you are intelligent and brave."

No one was surprised when Riley burst into happy tears.

Finally Maddie Fey turned to Steele. "I know that you want me to tell you that all of this is a dream, that you are not a Mage, that you will wake up and everything will be the way it was. But I can't do that. I can only say that I am proud to know you, Steele Miller."

"And I," said the old man, "am absolutely delighted that you are a fellow Mage. Welcome to our order, Steele." He reached out and clasped Steele's hand warmly.

Steele bowed his head, his face burning. He didn't know what to say because his thoughts were in turmoil. Maddie Fey was right, though. He *didn't* want to be a Mage. He wanted things to go back to the way they were before she came to his school. The knowledge of what was waiting for him in the underground chamber GM had knit preyed on his mind. And if he had to choose between Dirk and the

Jerks and the Fire Demons, he'd gladly take Dirk and the Jerks any day.

Then he saw the small boxes that Maddie Fey had placed in front of them. Filled with guilt, Steele opened his. Inside was a multipurpose pocketknife made of a silvery metal and studded with precious gems in the design of a dragon.

Steele's breath caught. "It is not a weapon," said Maddie Fey. "But it may help you out of a tight spot."

Mac and Riley opened their boxes to find similar gifts.

"It's beautiful," whispered Riley, examining the gem-encrusted handle of hers. "Thank you."

"Cool," exclaimed Mac. He opened the blade and ran his thumb along the sharp edge. Then he closed it and shoved it hastily in his pocket, almost as if he were afraid Maddie Fey would take it away from him.

Steele wracked his brain for something profound to say to Maddie Fey, but in the end, he looked at her and said simply, "Thank you."

"Now then," said the old Mage. "Let us get down to business. We have won a small battle, but we have yet to fight the war."

"I know," sighed Steele. "We found over a hundred kids. According to Sydney there are still more than a hundred of them out there somewhere, including Ryan Massey and Dirk the Jer—. We destroyed five Fire Demons, but there are still lots of them left."

"Several thousand," said Fidus brightly.

"No way!" cried Mac. "If there are that many, what's stopping them from attacking all at once?"

The old man thought for a moment. "We believe it has

something to do with the children's memories. Let me put it this way. Think of the Fire Demons as motor vehicles, and the children's memories as gasoline. They might have gathered enough memories for four or five Demons to escape at the same time, but not for two thousand."

"If that's true," said Riley, "then a lot more kids are going to disappear."

Maddie Fey and Fidus nodded.

"And nobody's heard a peep from the wardens yet?" groaned Mac.

"I'm afraid not, Mac," said Maddie Fey.

"What happens now?" asked Steele.

"Besides finding the stolen memories," answered Fidus without hesitation, "we must stop the Demons and the worms from snatching more children, and we must locate the wardens and the other missing children."

Disheartened at the enormity of what lay before them, Steele took a deep breath and stared at the log burning in the huge fireplace. How were they going to accomplish all of those things?

"Mr. Fidus," said Riley, a puzzled expression on her face. "You said that the memories are like fuel for a car. Well, wouldn't they get used up, just like gas? Then they wouldn't exist anymore and we wouldn't be able to find them."

Fidus smiled. "Excellent thinking, Riley. But tell me, have you ever used up a good memory? Have you ever thought about something over and over again until it disappeared?"

"No," admitted Riley. Then her eyes lit up. "I get it. The Fire Demons can reuse the memories."

"So I believe," said Fidus.

Steele looked from the fireplace to the old man. "Why do the Fire Demons want to kill me? You and Maddie Fey are very powerful—why don't they go after you?"

"I could probably fight five or six of them at a time," answered the old man. "And Maddie Fey proved that she can handle two or three, or even more. But, Steele, you have the power to destroy all of them."

"How do you know that?" pressed Steele.

"We don't really know anything," admitted Fidus. "What we know is that your mother was carrying something to Earth to stop the Fire Demons if something ever happened to the wardens. And we know that when your mother left for Earth, the only thing she was carrying was you."

"But we don't know how you are supposed to stop the Demons," added Maddie Fey.

Steele placed his elbows on the table and dropped his head into his hands. He wondered if he should tell them that he knew how he was supposed to stop them. Should he tell them what he had seen in GM's knitting? Tell them how he was supposed to absorb the Fire Demons' heat into himself, until he exploded? It was certainly tempting. If he told them, he wouldn't feel so alone. He stole a quick glance at Maddie Fey, thinking as he did so that she was going to be awfully disappointed when she discovered that he was a coward. *I might be a Mage*, he thought, *but I can't do what they want. I won't stop the Fire Demons.*

"By the way," said Fidus, "how is your grandmother, Steele?"

Steele couldn't hide his surprise. "You know GM?"

The old man chuckled softly. "We were friends once," he

said. "On Arjella. Before she came to your world." His blue eyes twinkled at Steele. "I am looking forward to seeing her again and talking over old times."

"My grandmother stopped speaking eight years ago," Steele said matter-of-factly. "All she does now is knit."

"I am sorry," said Fidus. "But I would still like to see her. When Maddie Fey told me that she was to travel here to find you and discover what had happened to the wardens, it was decided that I would accompany her."

"It was Fidus who found you, Steele," said Maddie Fey. "Since then, he's been keeping an eye on you."

"In Toronto, in the park that evening—it was you, wasn't it?" asked Steele.

"Yes, my friend, I was there," replied the old Mage.

"The voice that scared Dirk the Jer— I mean Dirk . . . was that you?"

Fidus nodded. "But it wasn't my voice that frightened the boy, Steele. It was something he saw."

"What?" asked Steele.

The old man's eyes glinted mischievously. "He saw his baseball bat turn into a serpent."

Steele grinned. "You made that happen. You used magic. But what were you doing there in the first place?"

"Exactly what Maddie Fey said I was doing—keeping an eye on you," he answered. "The Fire Demons were there, Steele. There were three of them in the park that evening. I had to get those other boys safely out of there."

The news astounded Steele. "Fire Demons in Wychwood Park. I don't think—"

The old man cut him off. "They were there, in human shapes."

"But how did you know they were Fire Demons?" asked Steele. "Maddie Fey didn't know when one of them came right into her house."

"Maddie Fey had no reason to be suspicious," he said. "But I, on the other hand, am a suspicious old man. I sent my power through the park, searching for live humans. Except for you and those boys, and of course myself, it found none."

Steele shivered. Fire Demons lurking in the park so close to his house was too terrible for words.

"Where are they? How come I didn't see them?"

"Only you know the answer to that," said Fidus. "But they were there."

"What happened to them? What if they're still there?"

"They were there for one purpose only—to find you and kill you. Now that you are no longer there, there is no reason for them to remain."

"But they got Dirk," said Steele. "They must have followed him home."

Fidus placed his hands flat on the table and studied them for a moment. "I know the Demons didn't follow the boy home, because *I* followed him." He hesitated. "There is something about this Dirk business that I do not understand . . . yet."

"If you knew those Fire things were in the park, why didn't you blast them away?" asked Mac.

"Well, Mac," said Fidus. "I could not risk 'blasting them away' for two reasons. One, they would shed their human forms and become creatures of fire that would endanger the neighbourhood. Two, I did not wish to reveal my true identity. They thought I was just another homeless person, and so were not suspicious when they noticed me hanging about

Steele's area." He turned back to Steele. "Tell me about the Prince of Darkness."

Steele explained about the voice he had heard in Wych-wood Park and about the horrible face he and his friends had seen in the grate. "And then Sydney said there was this crea-ture in the tunnels under New York who called himself the Prince of Darkness. I think it's the same creature I heard in Toronto."

"What happened in the tunnel when you heard his voice?" prodded the old Mage.

"I don't really know," said Steele. And then he told the oth-ers about the sounds he had heard and how he could follow them. "I was just thinking that I might be able to find the missing kids by following sounds . . . when I heard the Prince of Darkness. It freaked me out because I thought he was actu-ally right beside me, speaking in my ear."

The old man slapped his hand against the surface of the table. "Amazing!" He looked at Maddie Fey. "And he's had no training."

Maddie Fey nodded. "I have studied for many years and I do not have the power to project my hearing."

Steele resented the way they were talking about him as if he weren't there. "If you think I did it on purpose, you're wrong," he said. "It just happened. I probably couldn't do it again if I tried for a hundred years."

Fidus gazed at him for such a long time that Steele began to squirm.

Finally the old man leaned toward him. "Is there some-thing you have not told us? Perhaps something Ees showed you?"

Steele paled. "No!" he responded quickly, wondering what made the old Mage ask such a question. *Did he know?* He felt the others staring at him as if they didn't believe him.

Mac rolled his eyes toward the ceiling. "I haven't got a clue what you're talking about," he said. "But I want to know two things. Why did Steele's eyes turn silver when he went into that trance and heard those voices? And . . . just what sort of animal is *that?*" He pointed at Wish.

When Maddie Fey laughed, Steele felt as if a heavy weight had been lifted off his chest. He found himself grinning at Mac's questions.

"Silver is a Mage colour," said Maddie Fey. "Sometimes our eyes turn silver when we perform magic. But sometimes they change for no reason at all."

"Can you *make* them change colour?" asked Riley.

"I do not know," answered Maddie Fey, "because I have never tried."

"Be quiet, Riley," said Mac. "She still hasn't answered my second question."

Maddie Fey reached out and brushed her hand against Wish's head. "Wish is an Arjellan Great Hound. He is very intelligent, and loyal. He chose to give me his loyalty when he was just a pup. That was a long time ago and we have been friends ever since."

A momentary silence settled over the room as all eyes rested on Maddie Fey's silver hound.

Then Mac asked another question. "Is it a Mage thing? Does Steele get to have a hound?"

"No, Mac," said Maddie Fey. "It is not 'a Mage thing.'"

Fidus pushed back his chair and stood. "Now, my young

friends. It is time to plot our future course. Mac and Riley, you may return to your homes and that will be the end of it for you."

"No!" cried Mac and Riley at once.

"It's not fair to send us away now," added Riley.

"We're going with Steele," said Mac.

The old man sighed, but he didn't look displeased. "I was afraid you'd feel that way."

"Can we go home for just a little while?" asked Riley.

Maddie Fey shook her head. "I can't stop you from going home. But I strongly advise against it, especially for Steele. He'd only be placing himself and his father and grandmother in danger."

"GM's a Mage. You said so. Surely there's nothing to fear if she's there."

"I do not know your grandmother. I do not know if she still has the use of magic after relinquishing it."

"Well then, can we at least call home?" asked Riley. "My parents are probably both dead of heart attacks by now."

Maddie Fey laughed softly and turned to Fidus. "Do you think it is safe?"

The old man nodded several times.

"All right!" cried Mac. "Where's the phone?"

"There are no phones here," said Maddie Fey. "But Nilats will show you the way outside."

"Come on, guys," said Mac. "Let's go."

The red rat led them to a doorway. They stepped out onto the street, and gasped. It was clear as day that they were no longer in New York, or even Toronto. But where were they?

//Λ\\

Deep in his underground palace, the Prince of Darkness gazed into a black globe and watched Steele and his two companions looking about his kingdom in wonder. He rubbed his hands together, his shoulders shaking with silent laughter. *Come into my parlour, little flies.*

Find out what happens next in the exciting follow-up book

The Black Pyramid
The Mole Wars, Book Two
by J. FitzGerald McCurdy

Coming May 2006

Turn the page for an excerpt . . .

Distracted

Steele sighed heavily and let his squinted gaze travel along the broad street. *Where are we?* he wondered. *We were just in New York.* Or at least Steele *thought* they had been in New York. But when they had stepped out of the limousine, anxious to call their parents in Toronto, they found themselves on a bridge in an unfamiliar city, turning blue with cold.

At some point over the past week, Steele had figured out that the doors of Maddie Fey's limousine were portals to other cities or worlds, but that didn't lessen the shock of suddenly finding himself in a strange city. He didn't understand how Maddie Fey's house could be somewhere—in some sort of netherworld—on the other side of those doors. It boggled his mind.

As he stared at the monstrous vehicle, he noticed the giant red rat leaning against the front fender on the driver's side, casually brushing something from the shoulders of its chauffeur's uniform. But Steele noticed that the creature's gleaming yellow eyes were watchful, belying its casual pose. Steele snorted rudely. The human clothes might disguise the rodent's form, but nothing could hide its slimy red tail that was lashing from side to side impatiently. As if it felt Steele's eyes physically touch it, the rat glared at him and bared its sharp teeth in what could have been a snarl or a twisted grin. Steele looked away quickly, frowning with loathing and disgust.

"I hate that rat," he muttered through clenched teeth.

Riley tugged on his arm again. "Forget about Nilats. Come on."

"Wait," cautioned Steele, nervously scanning the bridge in both directions. "We don't even know where we are."

"We're still on Earth," chirped Mac cheerfully, waving his arm in a wide arc that encompassed streetlights, signs, and buildings. "I doubt another planet's cities would look exactly like ours."

"But where is everyone?" asked Riley, moving closer to her friends.

Steele hadn't noticed the absence of people and traffic until now. Nothing moved on the bridge or the narrow river or the broad street stretching ahead of them. It was as if the great city and everything in it had been abandoned. And, except for the wind whining about the girders, the city was as silent as death.

Where were all the people, the automobiles, the busses? The river on either side of them, the lights on the bridge and along the empty street, the stars in the silver sky above, all hung in the emptiness as if nothing else existed at all.

What on earth had happened here? Had the people run away or were they dead? Had the Fire Demons already been here? Steele shook his head. No. There'd be signs—ashes and burning, and a really horrible smell. Gazing at the pale, glowing buildings, Steele experienced a crawly feeling. It was as if he were standing before a vast one-way glass window and something or someone he couldn't see was watching him from the other side of the glass—its intent dark and hostile.

"There's no one there," he chided. But he couldn't rid himself of the feeling that unseen eyes were following his every move.

Mac shoved his hands into his jacket pockets and hunched his shoulders. "I don't like this," he muttered. "No people. No traffic. It's creepy, man. Maybe we should go back to the limo and try a different door."

"Come on, guys," pressed Riley. "Since we're already here, wherever *here* is, let's call home and get it over with." She pointed at a brilliantly flood-lit building on the opposite side of the street at the end of the bridge. "There! There's sure to be phones in the lobby."

"Last one there has to eat a worm," challenged Mac, breaking into a run. "Get it? A big New York WORM!"

"Shut up, you idiot," Riley muttered under her breath. "I hate idiots."

The anger in her voice shocked Steele. Usually Riley couldn't resist a challenge from Mac. Their constant bickering and baiting used to drive Steele out of his mind, but they had always been quick to laugh and make up.

Everything's changed, thought Steele with a twinge of regret. *Riley's changed. I've changed. What's going to happen to us?*

"You guys are no fun," shouted Mac, stopping and waiting for them to catch up to him.

Steele shook his head. Mac was the only one who appeared untouched by the horrors they had seen. "Or perhaps he's just better at hiding it than Riley and me," he said.

Riley went ahead, ignoring Mac, and marched purposefully across the deserted street towards the white building. Mac shrugged at Steele as if to ask, "What's eating her?" When Steele didn't react, he took off after Riley.

Steele followed slowly, glancing about. A flash of blue caught his eye. He glanced to the right side of the bridge at a row of giant blue letters and read them aloud, "The Chicago Tribune." He had solved the mystery. "Hey!" he called to his friends. "We're in Chicago."

But Mac and Riley were too far ahead to hear him. He broke into a run, squinting up at the building they were heading towards. As he got closer, he realized that there were really two buildings, connected at some time in the past. On the front of the nearer structure, a tower the height of the building jutted into the sky. Halfway up the tower was an enormous clock, the hands pointing to a quarter past eight. Lit up like a billboard, the structure was such a dazzling white that it looked as if it were made of electric icing sugar.

It also looked familiar.

"Where have I seen that building before?" Steele wondered aloud, a frown darkening his face. He had never visited Chicago in his life, so how could he possibly recognize the building? It was certainly puzzling. Then, like a brick falling on his head, he knew. He picked up his pace, suddenly uneasy.

"Stop," he shouted through the wind. "Don't go in there."